Savage Risk

Jane Blythe

Bear Spots Publications
Melbourne Australia

Paperback
ISBN-13: 978-0-6456432-5-1

Cover designed by RBA Designs

CHAPTER ONE

November 30th
7:19 P.M.

She was so damn beautiful.

As he watched through the window, hidden in the shadows, the woman glided around the room with a fluid grace that was impossible not to appreciate.

Skye Xenos was petite, with delicate features, jet black hair that tumbled down her back like an inky waterfall, and large brown eyes flecked with gold. Despite her beauty, there was an untouchable quality about her.

He had been watching her for days, and saw the way she was with people. Reserved but not standoffish, compassionate, and yet not intimate. She obviously kept everyone at a distance, not allowing them to get too close. Not allowing them to glimpse the real Skye, the one she hid behind a mask of professionalism.

Except now.

Unaware she was being watched she had lowered her guard. Her eyes were bright, a small smile curled her plump lips up at the corners, and even through the glass, he could hear her crooning to one of her animals.

Even as he enjoyed seeing her like this, part of him wanted to turn her over his knee for paying so little attention to her surroundings. Just because there were four walls encompassing her didn't mean she was safe, especially in this part of the city.

Had she even bothered to check the door was locked when she said goodbye to her colleagues twenty minutes ago?

He'd been in his car then, not wanting to be spotted until he

1

was ready to make his move, but as soon as he'd known she was alone he hadn't been able to stay away. Although he hadn't been close enough to see, he could guess she hadn't thought to check the lock, her attention instead on the animals under her care.

Crazy woman had always connected with animals better than she did people.

It was one of the things he found the most endearing about her.

She was like an animal whisperer. There wasn't a single animal that didn't seem to gravitate toward her. From pets to wild animals, he'd seen her talk down a fox stuck in a wire fence, murmuring soothingly and keeping it calm as she freed it, and he'd seen her calm horses no one thought could be tamed.

Skye had a gift, and she'd chosen to channel it into becoming a vet.

He knew more about her than he should.

More about her than was likely appropriate, but it was impossible to stay away from the beautiful, quiet woman.

Lifting a hand, he touched it to the window aching to touch her. It had been so long, he'd dreamed about her more nights than he could count. It was because of her and the memories he had of the time they'd shared that had gotten him through the worst moments of his life.

He cared about her more than she would ever know.

Although if anyone were to tell her that she would laugh in their face, scoffing that there was no possible way that could be true.

But it was.

One mistake had cost him his chance with her, and he wanted another.

Was here for another.

At least that was all she would ever know.

If she knew the truth it would ruin any chance he might have of getting her back. She would be lost to him forever, and he couldn't stomach that thought.

Whatever it took, he had to make her believe he cared about her. That what had happened in the past was a mistake, one he would regret every day for the rest of his life. And he had to do it all without exposing the real reason he was back.

Inside the back room of her practice, two of the eight cages were occupied with animals recovering from surgery or injury. Skye moved to one of the cages, pausing to stroke a silky-looking smoky gray cat. After checking it over and showing it a little love, she moved on to the other cage. The golden retriever gave her a thump of its tail, and when she opened the door, its ears perked up and it lifted its head, indicating it wanted pets. He could see her lips moving, and the dog watched her intently as though understanding what she was saying.

When she leaned in and touched a kiss to the top of the dog's head, he groaned. "Lucky dog," he muttered, wishing her soft lips were touching him.

Once she'd closed the dog's cage, she moved around the room, collecting her things, turning off lights, and as she moved closer to where he was, he could hear her singing.

She had the voice of an angel.

Memories of when she used to sing for him flashed through his mind, pain stabbing through him with each one. He'd had a chance with this woman and he'd thrown it away.

The only thing he could say in his defense was that he'd been young and stupid. Hadn't realized what he'd had until it was gone.

Until it was too late.

Over the years, he'd tried reaching out to her, but every attempt was ignored. As much as he hated that he was here with ulterior motives, he was selfish enough to use this opening to his advantage.

If that made him the scum of the earth, then so be it.

Knowing he should head back to his car and approach her in a more appropriate manner, he didn't move as she slipped on her coat. It was a warm golden brown and brought out the flecks in her eyes making them look like two glowing orbs. They were the kind of eyes you could get lost staring into.

How had he not realized how beautiful they were?

How had he been so blind?

Being young wasn't really any excuse, especially not for how badly he knew he'd hurt her. It was stupid, and he was ashamed of the things that he'd done. What if there was no way to make up for the pain he'd caused?

Were those wounds irreparable?

Was he fighting a losing battle here?

It killed him to know that he might be. Especially since he was here for a job and not just to try to make things right with Skye.

As much as he hated that he was going to deceive her, use her, and take advantage of the fact they'd had a prior relationship, there was no way he could have turned down this opportunity. When he'd first been asked to do it, the punch to the gut and overwhelming guilt almost had him saying no.

Never before had he told his boss no, but he'd come dangerously close this time.

If it wasn't for the fact that other people were counting on him, he might very well have gone with his gut reaction. Instead, he'd agreed. The only alternative to him coming here and getting close to Skye was for someone else to take the job.

The idea of another man playing games with her, getting close to gather intel, and using whatever means necessary to gain that information was too much for him. He was a master of interrogation. There wasn't anything he couldn't get out of someone. It wasn't something he was proud of, but he'd used sexual intimacy to get intel from women and every torture technique he knew to get intel from men.

Marks on his soul.

One for every person he'd used.

One for every person he'd inflicted pain on.

The biggest mark of all was for what he'd done to Skye.

It was crazy to think there was any way he could make things up to her. Yet it didn't mean the hope inside flickered out.

That hope was there. It grew as he watched Skye scoop up her purse, wrap a scarf around her neck, and head toward the door. It kept his feet rooted to the spot as she stepped out into the cold evening, rubbing her hands up and down her arms a couple of times before locking the door behind her.

Instead of slipping further back into the shadows as he knew he should do so if she turned, she wouldn't see him lurking there, he couldn't move. If she saw someone hiding outside her practice, obviously watching her through the windows, she'd be afraid.

Rightfully so since his motives for lingering here weren't pure.

Tomorrow, he'd approach her the right way. The normal way, through the front door of her practice, not hiding in the small parking lot out the back. Not acting like he was some creepy stalker.

Right now, he was balancing precariously close to the creepy stalker category.

Caleb "Brick" Quinn sighed and rubbed his temples, he hated that he'd hurt Skye worse than any stalker ever could, and by the time this was over he'd likely wind up hurting her even more.

Life sucked sometimes.

* * * * *

November 30th
7:34 P.M.

Skye hummed to herself as she hurried across the parking lot to her car.

These few minutes alone at her practice at the end of each day were her downtime. Her staff all left at seven, and without them there, she could let down her guard and just be herself.

The Skye it had taken her a long time to find.

One who wasn't pushed around.

Who didn't let anyone control her.

Who allowed no one to get too close.

Letting people in only gave them an opportunity to use that opening as a weapon to hurt her, and she had vowed fifteen years ago that she would never again be that stupid.

She had no complaints about her life. She was happy, and between her work and volunteering, her best friend and fellow vet, plus caring for her own pets, there was no time to be lonely. Everyone who knew her thought she was a little odd, preferring animals to people as she did, and they definitely thought she was standoffish. If they couldn't see firsthand her love for the animals who crossed her path they would likely think her cold as well.

Not that she cared.

Caring about what others thought only led to pain and she had no intention of ever suffering more pain again.

When she reached her car, Skye shoved her hand into her purse, scrounging around to try to find her keys.

And came up empty.

Again.

This was the second time this week she'd left the darn things behind on her desk. It was because she always popped out to buy her lunch—if she had time to take a lunch break—then rushed back in to deal with something and threw them on her desk instead of back in her bag.

"Ugh," she groaned, leaning down to lightly bump her forehead against the side of the car. Darn her forgetful little brain. Give her information on an animal's anatomy and it superglued itself inside her head, but anything else and … she was embarrassingly forgetful, especially for someone with an IQ as high as hers.

Annoyed with herself, not just for forgetting but because she knew once she got back inside, she was going to be there for at least another fifteen minutes, unable to resist one more pet of her overnight guests, Skye turned around.

And promptly froze.

She wasn't alone.

Someone was standing over by the window.

Horror hit hard.

Had the person been watching her?

Indecision rendered her frozen for several long seconds. She didn't have the keys to her car so she couldn't get in and drive away. Should she just turn, run, find somewhere safe, and call the cops? Or should she try to get back inside, hoping she could make it before the person did ... whatever they were here for?

Likely to steal drugs.

Wouldn't be the first time a druggie had broken into her practice to steal drugs. In the three years since she'd opened her own vet clinic with her best friend, they'd had half a dozen break ins. As much as it made her angry, and as much as she'd like to rail at this person that her animals needed those drugs, she wasn't stupid.

Run it was.

Trying to keep the car between her and the druggie, who she could have sworn was just standing there staring at her, Skye edged toward the street, almost afraid that any sudden movements would startle him out of his apparent reverie.

A horrible thought occurred to her.

What if he wasn't a druggie?

Or a dealer?

What if he was here for entirely different motives?

Feeling sick to her stomach, Skye gave up on her moving slow plan and took off toward the street, cursing this tiny parking lot hidden around the back.

Footsteps pounded the concrete behind her.

He was coming.

It was like he had superhuman speed because even though he'd been yards away she could hear him closing the distance way too quickly. Was he high? Best case scenario he was, and he just wanted to rob her, then she could offer to open the doors, let him inside, let him take whatever he wanted when he finally caught her.

And he would catch her.

A split-second later arms closed around her chest, pinning her arms to her sides.

Skye had taken a lot of self-defense classes, and she immediately stowed her fear and did what she had trained to do.

But each move she made was blocked like the man expected them.

Just who was he?

He didn't seem like a druggie, which meant he was here for her.

There was no way she was going down without a fight.

No way.

Never again was she going to be a victim.

It had taken a lot of hits, a lot of getting knocked down, and believing she could never get back up and carry on with her life, for her to finally realize that nobody could ever love and respect her if she didn't love and respect herself.

Did she particularly want anyone to get close enough to love her?

No.

Not really.

She was content alone, happy with her life, and she finally had respect for herself, which meant more than she'd realized. She had done nothing wrong, she hadn't deserved to be treated the way the people in her life had treated her, and she didn't deserve whatever this druggie or pervert or whoever he was had planned.

"Calm down, little wildcat. I'm not going to hurt you."

Skye froze.

She knew that voice.

She cursed the way it washed over her like a warm blanket, cocooning her in the same bubble of safety it used to, but then came the memories of how badly he'd hurt her.

The way he had cut her out of his life like she was nothing. Leaving her alone with no safety net when she endured the hell she kept secret from the rest of the world.

Without that safety net, she'd very nearly drowned.

But she hadn't.

She'd clawed her way up and out of that deep hole all by herself.

Now she had no use for Caleb Quinn and no desire to see him or talk to him.

"Get your hands off me, Caleb," she growled.

While he released her, his hands lingered on her arms, and even through the layers of her sweater, her scrubs, and her coat, they seared her in a branding touch she hated. She didn't want anything to do with him and had no idea why he was there.

"Don't touch me," she hissed, taking a step back. In her haste to put distance between them, she stumbled, too shocked to be steady on her feet right now and windmilled her arms so she didn't land flat on her backside on the cold ground.

Turns out she needn't have worried.

Caleb reached out with lightning-fast reflexes and curled his hands around her biceps, steadying her and keeping her standing.

His hands were so large, she could feel their strength, and yet his touch was gentle enough that it made tears burn her eyes. It reminded her of the boy she used to know, the one who was the only light in her life, who was her everything from the first time she laid eyes on him, no matter that they were only four years old.

Those memories were bittersweet because even though he had been everything to her then, he'd cut her out of his life with a ruthlessness that made her feel like everything had been a lie.

On the heels of the pain was a weariness she felt down to her bones. Caleb would never know just how badly he'd hurt her or how hard it had been clawing her way out of a pit of depression that had almost pushed her to end her life.

Stepping back, more carefully this time, she looked at the man who had crushed her like a bug. The years had been kind to him. He was taller than she remembered, his dark hair still thick and he wore a beard, his dark eyes which had always been so expressive were now empty, almost carefully so, and his sweater molded to his cut chest.

Of course, he looked like delicious perfection.

Fate would love that.

"Why are you here, lurking outside my clinic?" Skye asked.

Tenderness touched his features, and she would have believed he actually cared about her if she hadn't known better. Caleb didn't now and never had cared about her at all. If he had, he never would have treated her the callous way he had. It was thanks to Caleb that she no longer trusted anything anyone said to her. She took nothing at face value, suspicion saved her a lot of trouble in the long run.

"I wasn't *lurking*," he said, his mouth quirking into that smile she remembered so well, the one that always felt like a beam of sunshine warming her from the inside out.

Now it just made her feel cold.

"I'm tired, I have nothing to say to you, and I'm not in the mood for your games. Leave me alone, Caleb."

Brushing past him, Skye headed back toward her practice to get her car keys. It had been a long day and she just wanted to get home to her babies. Her two dogs and cat would be waiting for her with all the unconditional love she could ever need and after this run-in with her past, she needed their love more than ever tonight.

"I can't leave, Skye. I'm here for you, and I'm not going anywhere until I earn your forgiveness."

CHAPTER TWO

November 30th
7:40 P.M.

The expression on Skye's face clearly communicated how badly he was going to fail on all his objectives without her having to say a word.

In that moment, Brick knew there was little to no chance he was going to be able to get close enough to her to learn anything about her father. Surprisingly, he cared less about that—which was the very reason why he was here in Virginia—than he did the fact that this beautiful, strong woman who he had carelessly tossed aside could never forgive him.

Weariness filled her eyes, and she dropped her gaze to the ground before resolutely raising it again to meet his. "Go away, Caleb."

When she moved to go around him, it was instinct that had him reaching out to grasp her elbow, keeping her nearby. Over the years he'd sent emails, text messages, voicemails, even letters, expressing his regret and sorrow about how he'd ended their friendship.

Each one of them had gone unanswered.

Now he was here, and she was here, and it was like a piece of himself that had been restless had finally quietened.

Found peace.

It made him selfish, but he didn't know how he could let her go again.

Once had almost killed him, even though in his young, stupid mind he'd thought it would be easy. Now thirty-two, older, wiser, with years serving as a Navy SEAL under his belt, along with his years working for the world-renowned Prey Security as part of Alpha Team, he recognized what he'd thrown away, he just didn't know how to get it back.

"Don't touch me like that," Skye said, and he realized that his thumb was brushing across the inside of her elbow. A lover's touch and they were anything but.

"Skye, you can't know how much I regret ..."

"No!" Her outburst was sudden and unexpected. The girl he had known had been sweetness personified. She cared about everyone. She shone light into the world of every person she met.

At least she used to.

Now her spark was gone.

Was that his fault?

Had he done that to her with his carelessness and selfishness?

"You do not get to come here and tell me you "regret""—she used air quotes and then fisted her hands at her sides—"ending our friendship in the way you did. You weren't just nasty you were cold and callous. Cut me out of your life as effectively as any pair of scissors could do. Some things can't be stuck back together. You have *no* idea what you did to me when you decided I wasn't pretty enough and cool enough to be in your life anymore. *None.* Now go and leave me alone!" The last was yelled almost at the top of her lungs as she stormed past him and back inside her clinic.

If possible, the knot of regret he'd carried around in his gut for the last fifteen years grew bigger.

Brick had been a stupid seventeen-year-old kid back then. His head cheerleader girlfriend had been jealous of his friendship with Skye, and when she'd demanded he stop spending time with her, he'd been stupid enough to agree. Back then, he'd thought he was going to marry Mirabella. She was gorgeous and sexy, with big breasts, and willing to have sex with him.

Wasn't until he decided that he wasn't going to follow his

father into politics but join the military that he realized she wasn't who he'd thought she was.

Still, he'd fought for the relationship, believing she was what he wanted.

Until he returned from his first deployment to find she'd moved out of their apartment and was involved with some guy who'd also gone to their elite private school and had plans to go into politics and work his way up to President.

He'd thrown away something real with Skye, a friendship he believed could have grown into so much more, for hot high school sex and the prestige of being the star quarterback dating the head cheerleader.

Stupid.

As he looked over his shoulder at Skye's clinic, he could see her standing in the window, palms pressed against the glass, staring at him.

Her shoulders heaved, and he knew she was crying.

Pain unlike anything he had experienced before almost knocked him to his knees.

What had she meant when she'd said he had no idea what he'd done when he'd ended their friendship?

Even as an idiot teenager, he'd felt shame for going along with what Mirabella demanded. He'd hated giving up his friendship with the quirky, intelligent, funny Skye. The hours after school they'd spent together doing their homework had been some of the highlights of his life.

Now, knowing there might have been more damage he'd caused ate at him.

There was no way he could leave until he'd made things right.

Because he knew she wasn't going to come back out until he was gone, Brick shoved his hands into his pockets, bowed his head, and headed for his vehicle.

Once inside, he turned on the engine, drove around the corner, then pulled over to wait. Skye didn't know it, but her father was involved in a dangerous plot to take over the government. As the last man standing, Hemmingway Xenos had everything to gain and everything to lose, and Brick was worried there might be blowback on Skye.

No way was he going to let that happen.

As he waited for her, his cell phone buzzed and he pulled it out, noting his boss' name on the screen. Prey was run by six siblings, founder and CEO Eagle Oswald was the head top dog.

"Hey," he said when he answered.

"Any progress?" Eagle asked.

"I made contact today." Not the way he'd wanted, but Skye had turned and spotted him, been afraid, and he'd had no choice but to let her know she wasn't in any danger.

"And?"

"And I don't think this is going to work. I told you our relationship is complicated and that it wasn't likely I'd be able to make enough of a good impression with her to get anywhere close to her father."

"Right now, you're all we've got so don't give up."

Brick sighed and massaged his temples, trying to alleviate a stress headache. "She doesn't deserve to be played like this. She hasn't done anything wrong, and I've hurt her enough."

"She doesn't," Eagle agreed softly, and from the tone of his boss' voice he knew the man didn't like using Skye any more than he did, but they were desperate.

What had started as a plot from a survivalist with plans to usher in his own utopia had grown to include a family law firm used as a front to raise finances, a former Prey operative turned rogue weapons dealer, and a Russian Bratva family. With everyone else eliminated, all they needed was proof that Skye's father was the man Kristoff Mikhailov had chosen to be the next President. A puppet for the head of the Bratva family to use while he ran the country from behind the scenes.

Without proof, nothing was stopping Hemmingway Xenos

from getting himself elected and carrying out whatever plans he'd made with the Bratva. Since they knew those plans had included an eventual overthrow of the government, Hemmingway was dangerous, and with no one to censure him could make his own power grab now.

He had to be stopped. Brick acknowledged that. He just hated using Skye to do it.

She'd suffered enough.

More than he had obviously realized.

"If you really can't handle it, I'll send in someone else," Eagle offered. An offer he'd made before, one Brick had almost taken.

If he could stomach the idea of another man getting close to Skye he'd say yes.

It was definitely inappropriate, but he was damn possessive of his Skye.

"I can do it. If anyone is going to break her heart it may as well be someone she already hates."

"Hang in there and keep me updated," Eagle said.

Just as he'd ended the call, Brick saw Skye's car drive past, and he pulled out behind it, intending to make sure she got home safe, and then sit outside her house to watch over her.

He had to find a way to show her how sorry he was for hurting her by making her believe she meant nothing to him. Brick was filled with an all-consuming need to know what she'd meant when she told him he didn't understand how much damage he'd done to her, and how he could fix it.

If it was fixable.

What was he going to do if it wasn't?

As much as he wanted to finally wrap up this mission and eliminate the threat to the country he had served almost half his life, he wanted to fix what he'd broken between him and Skye more.

Without her in his life, there was a gaping hole nothing else could fill.

* * * * *

December 1st
12:56 A.M.

Something ripped her from sleep.

Skye wasn't sure what.

Her bedroom was quiet, dark, and the warm weight of Foggy her cat was pressed against her legs.

There was no noise from her two poodles, asleep in their crates downstairs in the living room.

Same as always.

Maybe it was just because she was restless and unsettled over the sudden reappearance of Caleb Quinn in her life.

She didn't want him back, didn't want anything to do with him, she had moved on with her life as best as she could and his coming back dredged up all those dark memories she had worked so hard to bury.

No, she *had* buried them.

And buried things didn't need to be dug up.

There was no way she was allowing Caleb to do that to her.

Maybe it was unfair to blame him, he wasn't responsible for other people's actions—Skye knew and accepted that—but his cold rejection had been the straw that broke the camel's back. He had snatched away the only ray of sunlight she'd had in her world, leaving her alone and cold.

So very alone.

And scared.

Hopeless.

With an irritated sigh that all of this *was* in fact being dragged back up despite her determination not to let it, Skye carefully rolled over.

As sweet as her kitty could be, she could also be a little

monster when her sleep was disturbed, and Skye didn't fancy sporting a couple of new scratches. Cuts and bites were a given when you tended to animals when they were hurt, sick, and scared. Even with her ability to soothe them, she still went home more days than not with her arms littered with marks.

Meow.

Skye smiled at Foggy's protest and murmured, "Sorry, little princess, go back to sleep."

She cracked an eye as she reached down to pet Foggy, soothing her so she'd go back to sleep quickly and not decide it was time to run zoomies around the bedroom.

That saved her life.

There was a figure dressed all in black slinking through the bedroom.

Big, hulking, at least twice her size.

Yet moving like a shadow, not making a single noise.

Even though she couldn't see his eyes through the dark mask he wore, she knew they'd connected with hers.

Felt energy sizzle through the room between them.

A knowledge that she was going to fight with everything she had but would wind up losing anyway.

He lunged toward the bed just as Skye scrambled backward, managing to evade the knife he'd swung down toward her.

Foggy, who hadn't alerted her to the presence in the room, now proved her worth when she meowed loudly and sprung at the intruder.

For the second time, her cat saved her life.

Distracted by the clawing, scratching, biting menace locked onto his arm, the man swore and tried to shake Foggy off.

Good luck.

Skye knew from experience that when a cat was determined it was harder than it looked to get them to disengage those claws of theirs, she had the scars to prove it.

Edging around the room, staying as far away from the intruder as she could as she made her way toward the door, she saw him lift his knife.

Light seemed to glint off it, although where the light would come from she had no idea. Maybe it was just her imagination playing tricks on her.

"No!" she screamed as he swung it toward her sweet kitty.

Taking that as her cue, Foggy leaped off the man and careened out the bedroom door.

Hot on the animal's heels, Skye followed.

She had to get out of here. She had been marked for death, Skye knew that without a doubt.

Unless she could get away from the intruder, he'd take her life.

In her panic, she couldn't remember where her cell phone was, not that it mattered.

The man was coming after her, she'd never have time to stop and make a call anyway.

There were no locks on any doors in her house.

The bathroom lock had broken some time last year and she'd never got around to fixing it. Living alone, she hadn't really thought it mattered. Who was going to barge in on her while she was doing her business or taking a shower?

No one.

Until now anyway.

Her only hope was to get out the front door and scream her lungs out, hoping someone heard and called 911, and that her attacker got spooked and decided she was too much trouble and bolted before he could be caught.

Of course, nothing in her life went that simply.

She was at the top of the stairs when he caught her.

A large hand wrapped around her ponytail, yanked her back and up against a chest that may as well have been carved from marble.

"He said I could have some fun with you before I kill you," his voice whispered in her ear, making her shudder in repulsion.

Yeah, no thanks.

Using every bit of strength she possessed, Skye flung back her elbow, catching him squarely in the stomach.

He grunted, swore at her, and his grip loosened.

Taking advantage, she propelled her body weight forward.

It wasn't enough to get away.

His hand was still tangled in her hair.

But her move overbalanced them and the next thing she knew they were falling.

Bumping their way down the stairs, pain exploded throughout her body with each hit that it took until they landed together in a heap on the floor in her front hall.

Although her dogs hadn't alerted her to the intruder—they were too sweet and trusting to worry about strangers—the commotion of the tumble down the stairs had both of them barking and bouncing in their crates, anxious now to get out and help their owner.

By some stroke of luck, the man had cushioned her fall, landing beneath her.

The door was just a few feet away.

Could she make it?

Slamming her knee up into his groin she was rewarded with a howl of pain, but the hand still tangled in her long, dark hair prevented her from getting away.

No.

She couldn't die this close to freedom.

With more strength than she could ever hope to possess, he flipped her onto her back so he was above her, his big body crushing her into the floorboards.

"I'm going to do you as you're bleeding out all over the floor," the man snarled, then threw in a long string of colorful curses some of which she'd actually never even heard before.

He lifted the knife.

Held it high above her.

The hand that clutched her hair tilted her head back so her neck was exposed.

Skye had been through some horrendous things in her life, but never had she felt as vulnerable as she did in this moment.

Desperately, she clutched at his wrist, trying to stop the knife from making contact with her skin, ripping open her neck and having her bleed out probably before he was even finished.

Try as she did the knife moved closer, just inches separating her from certain death.

Her entire focus was on trying to buck the mountain of a man off her body and stopping the knife from slitting her neck, so she barely registered the sound of her front door being broken down.

More men?

Had he not come alone?

There was no way she could fight off a whole army of men, she couldn't even fight off this one.

Then all of a sudden he was gone.

Poof.

Just like that.

Like her fairy godmother had arrived and cast a spell to make him vanish because surely that could be the only reason she wasn't already lying in a pool of her own blood.

Sounds of a struggle drew her attention to the living room to her left where she could see two dark shadows fighting.

Had she not just imagined her door being broken down?

Was someone really here?

A savior?

Weak, shaky, pain pounding through her from the top of her head to the tips of her toes, Skye dragged herself backward until she touched the wall, then used it to help her maneuver into a sitting position.

Who had broken in here?

A neighbor?

Had someone heard the scuffle and her dogs going crazy and

decided to come and investigate?

Whoever this person was, she would forever owe them a debt of gratitude she could never hope to repay. They had literally saved her life, and from the looks of the fight going on in the other room, they were risking theirs in the process.

She had to help.

There had to be something she could do.

With two against one, the intruder had no hopes of coming out on top.

Again, Skye had to use the wall to help get onto her feet, but once she was up, she scanned the room looking for something she could use to subdue her attacker.

Hell, she didn't want him subdued, she wanted him dead.

Her gaze fell on the knife he must have dropped when her savior came barreling into her home.

Skye didn't hesitate.

She snatched it up and stumbled across the room.

Neither of the men paid her any notice. They didn't even seem to know she was there.

She knew which was the man who had broken into her home because he was dressed all in black with his face covered while her savior was wearing a white shirt.

The irony of the black bad guy and white good guy wasn't lost on her as she shoved the knife blade into her attacker's back.

It wasn't her blood staining her floors tonight but the man who had intended to kill her.

Her savior took the guy down with a couple of quick blows and then turned toward her, and she froze.

Caleb.

The man who had saved her life was the one who had so effectively destroyed it fifteen long years ago.

Skye's mind spun.

Shock, terror, pain, and confusion swirled in a messy mass inside her head.

She swayed.

And then it was lights out for her as she collapsed.

CHAPTER THREE

December 1st
1:03 A.M.

Brick sprung at Skye when her legs buckled, and her eyes rolled back in her head.

He caught her before she hit the ground.

Swinging her up into his arms, he stepped over the body of the man bleeding out all over her living room floor and set her down on the couch.

Immediately, he picked up her wrist and checked her pulse. It was a little erratic but given the shock she'd just been through it was no wonder. She was dressed in nothing but an oversized sleep tee, and he got a glimpse of her long pale legs. Despite the fact she was short, topping out at not quite five foot one, her legs seemed to go on for miles. It made him a pig to notice while she'd just fought for her life, killed a man to save him, but he couldn't shut down his attraction to her if he tired.

And he'd tried a lot over the last fifteen years.

"Come on, honey, wake up for me," he urged, kneeling beside the couch and stroking her hair back from her face.

She looked so peaceful lying there like she was just asleep, but he could see red marks on her skin that would soon turn to bruises. It looked like she and her attacker had taken a tumble down the stairs. He needed to know how badly she was hurt, and if the man had assaulted her before he'd gotten to her.

When he'd seen movement through her windows, he'd about had a heart attack. Then when he'd approached and heard her dogs going crazy fear like nothing else had coursed through his veins. Brick would be eternally relieved he'd decided to spend the night in his car watching over Skye's home.

If he hadn't ...

She could be dead right now.

"Baby, I need you to wake up for me." Palming Skye's cheek he let his fingers caress the soft skin he could only ever dream about. Other than a chaste kiss they'd shared back in seventh grade, he and Skye had just been friends. They'd teased each other, laughed together, played together when they were young, and she'd tutored him as they got older, but they'd never had an intimate relationship.

He'd wanted one, but he'd sensed she wasn't ready, and then he'd started dating Mirabella and thought he'd found what he wanted.

How very wrong he'd been.

This was what he wanted.

This strong, beautiful woman who he'd been unable to get out of his mind since the moment he tossed her away like she didn't matter to him.

Skye's thick, dark lashes fluttered on her cheeks, and he slightly increased the pressure as he continued to sweep his fingertips across her face. "Come on, honey, there you go. Wake up for me."

A small groan escaped, and he felt her body tense.

"You with me, honey? It's Caleb, you're safe now." He refrained from mentioning the attacker was dead since she had been the one to deliver the death blow. The man had been highly trained, likely former special forces, and while Brick was confident he could have taken him, the fact that Skye had stabbed him had given him the upper hand, and he'd knocked the guy out, but the stab wound had been fatal.

His girl had guts.

Well, Skye wasn't his ... yet ... but he'd always known that she should be, and if there was any chance he could earn her forgiveness for the pain he'd caused he would spend the rest of his life making up for it.

"Caleb?"

Damn, he loved the sound of his name on her lips. Had missed it something crazy. "Yeah, baby, right here."

"Don't call me baby," she muttered, opening her eyes and spearing him with a glare that went a long way to calming his racing heart.

If his girl was feeling well enough to give him sass, she was going to be all right.

Easing back a little but not moving from his spot at her side, Brick curled his hands into fists on his thighs so he didn't reach for her. He'd called his team leader Luca "Bear" Jackson while grabbing his weapon and crossing the street to Skye's house the second he realized she was in trouble. That meant cops would be here soon, but before they arrived, he needed to know what had happened.

If this could be related to her father.

"Can you tell me what happened?" Brick asked.

Glancing over his shoulder, he could tell Skye's gaze fell on her attacker because she shuddered. "Is he dead?"

"Yeah, he's dead. Can't hurt you again."

"Did you …? Or did …?" When she shifted her gaze to meet his, he could see the warring emotions battling in her eyes. Relief the man was dead, revulsion that she might have taken a life.

Wanting to give her acceptance that she had done the right thing, he broke his own rule and reached out to take her cold hands, rubbing them between his to warm them. "The wound you inflicted was fatal. You did the right thing, Skye. Absolutely. No questions asked. All right?"

She gave a shaky nod and didn't make a move to pull her hands from his grasp, so he continued to hold them between his.

"Can you let my dogs out of their crates?" she asked, looking over her shoulder where both poodles were watching her, whining softly.

"Sorry, honey, your house is a crime scene, better leave them there so they don't mess with the evidence."

Skye didn't complain or beg and plead. Brick almost wished that she would then he wouldn't feel so bad about refusing her the comfort she obviously needed.

"Can you tell me what happened?"

Skye gave another nod, but it took her a moment to start talking.

He gave her that time, knowing she needed to pull herself together and accept that she was safe now.

"Something woke me up, but I didn't know what it was. I thought it was because I was all worked up about ..."

"Me?" he supplied when she didn't continue, pleased that she was as tied in knots about him as he was about her.

"Yeah, you. Anyway, I was worried about disturbing Foggy because sometimes once she wakes up she likes to play and I have to be up early for work, so I rolled over carefully but disturbed her anyway. She meowed, I went to pet her to calm her down, and that's when I saw him."

Fine tremors wracked her delicate body, and he ached to pull her into his arms and hold her until her fear receded. "What happened next, honey?"

Her eyes narrowed at the endearment, and a little of the fear appeared to be chased away. "We looked at each other. I tried to get out of bed, would have gotten stabbed if Foggy hadn't launched herself at him. I got to the bedroom door, he was going to stab my cat, I screamed, Foggy let go, I ran, and he followed. I got to the stairs then he caught me. I fought, we fell, he was about to stab me when you came in."

For a moment he could hardly draw enough air into his lungs.

Imagining Skye fighting for her life against a man more than double her size filled him with a sick kind of terror he didn't think would ever completely fade.

"You did amazing, you know that, right, Skye? You didn't give up, you fought, and that's why you're alive."

Sinking further into the couch cushions her eyes took on a haunted bruised look. "Wouldn't have done any good. If you hadn't come in when you did, he was going to slit my throat then rape me while I bled out."

Anger punched him in the gut. "He told you that?" he growled.

Skye nodded, hiccupped, then her face crumpled, and he couldn't hold back any longer. Gathering her close he pulled her to his chest, rocking her gently, one hand cradling the back of her head.

"I won't let anyone hurt you, honey," he promised. A vow he intended to keep. Skye was his no matter that he'd messed up so many years ago letting her slip through his fingers.

"You won't be here, Caleb," she said, her voice muffled against his chest.

"Like hell I won't. You're in danger. That's just another reason for me to stick around."

"I don't want you to," she muttered, but there was no heat to her words, and she didn't pull out of his hold.

This couldn't be a coincidence.

He'd shown up in Virginia a couple of days ago ready to connect with Skye for both professional and personal reasons, and the same night they made contact she was attacked in her home.

Someone had to be watching her.

They knew he was here, knew he was with Prey, and had to assume that it had something to do with Kristoff Mikhailov's plot.

A plot her father was almost definitely involved in.

Had her father ordered a hit on her?

No way was he going anywhere while she was in danger.

"Too bad," he said firmly.

Skye pulled back, her eyes wide as saucers. "Did you just say too bad?"

"There's my spunky, sassy little sun, moon, and stars."

Her face paled further. "Don't call me that, Caleb. You lost that right when you threw me away like I was worth nothing."

"You're worth everything," he said as he reached out to brush his knuckles across her wet cheek. "Everything."

Skye's brow furrowed in confusion, but the spark of annoyance was back in her eyes, and he much preferred it to the naked fear that had been there moments ago. His girl was a fighter, whatever was going on she'd get through it, with him at her back, and his team at his, whoever was out to get her didn't stand a chance.

All of a sudden, the remaining color in her face drained away. "Caleb, I just remembered."

"What, baby?"

"The man, before we fell down the stairs, he said something to me, he said, "He said I could have some fun with you before I kill you." Someone sent him here. This wasn't random. Someone sent that man here to kill me."

* * * * *

December 1st
1:16 P.M.

"What is with you today?"

Skye startled at the sound of the voice and turned around from the window so fast she swayed a little.

The lightheadedness had absolutely nothing to do with the fact that Caleb's arms had been around her just twelve hours ago, doing crazy things to her body.

Definitely nothing.

It was just the break in.

That was more than enough to have her out of sorts.

She'd come so close to being murdered.

Murdered in her own home.

A place that should be safe.

A place she knew often wasn't.

But that was the past, and this was now. She'd bought her little house and spent months renovating it, doing almost all of the work herself. Skye had loved every second of it. Working with her hands, building something that was all hers. Building not just a house to live in, but a place that really was safe and secure. Every color, every furnishing, every piece of furniture, it had all been chosen with such care and precision.

For two years, that place had been her own little sanctuary, and now that was ruined.

Snatched away from her in one single night.

Fingers snapped in front of her face, and she startled all over again, this time a strangled shriek flew past her lips.

Embarrassed, a hand flew to cover her mouth, wincing at the protests her bruised body gave. There were bruises on her arms, hips, back, legs, and chest, plus one on her right cheek from her tumble down the stairs with the intruder. Thankfully it was almost winter, the weather already cold, and she could cover them with her clothes. The one on her face had been trickier, but she applied makeup, and all anyone would see was a faint shadow.

Not faint enough given the looks she'd been getting from her colleagues and patients' families, but better than nothing.

"Skye."

The exasperated voice drew her attention, and she blinked and saw her very best friend in the whole entire world standing before her.

Ashleigh Christou was just a year older than Skye, and they'd met while studying veterinary science in college. After graduating, they'd both gone to different cities to work, but four years ago they'd met by chance and decided to open a practice together. Sharing the costs, they'd managed to scrounge up enough cash to get it up and running and over the last few years it had grown to be one of the best and most respected clinics in the area.

"Yeah?"

"You have been a mess all day," Ashleigh said. There was no annoyance in her tone, just concern.

"Have I?"

"You know you have."

Instead of answering, Skye turned to look out the window again. Was it really only last night that she'd found Caleb in her parking lot?

It felt like a lifetime ago.

Then she'd thought dealing with his unexpected—and unwanted—reappearance in her life was going to be her biggest problem. Little did she know.

Now she wished that was all she had to deal with.

As awful as seeing him again was, it was preferable to knowing that someone had sent a man to her house to kill her.

"Any plans to explain the bruises?" Ashleigh pushed. Her friend was mom to two adorable little kids, and there wasn't any information she couldn't weasel out of someone.

Skye sighed and wrapped her arms around her middle as she walked away from the window. "I was attacked last night."

Ashleigh gasped. "You were what now?"

"Someone broke into my house. Foggy distracted him, and I almost got away, but he caught me at the top of the stairs. We took a tumble." Although she delivered the words calmly, like she was reciting events that had happened to someone else, her insides were a swirling mess of terror.

Not only had she come way too close to being killed, but she'd come just as close to being raped as well.

If Caleb hadn't been there, or if he'd been just a couple of minutes slower, she would have spent her last moments alive being violated.

"Oh, Skye." Ashleigh looked positively horrified, and she

reached out and gave her a very gentle hug. "Why didn't you call me?"

"Didn't want to wake the kids. Plus, I knew your husband was on night shift last night. If I'd called you would have wanted to come, would have tried to find a sitter to stay with the kids. I didn't want to be a bother."

Ashleigh's eyes narrowed. "Trying really hard not to be offended here. If you didn't look so haunted I'd tell you exactly how stupid you sound. You shouldn't have been alone after going through something like that."

"I ... uh ... wasn't."

This time Ashleigh's brows about flew off the top of her head. "What?" she squealed. Actually, squealed like they were back in middle school. "Does this have something to do with the man I saw sitting in his car across the street from the practice?"

Caleb was still out there?

After she'd dropped her revelation that her attack wasn't random, the cops had shown up, paramedics too. She'd given her statement, allowed the medics to check her over, and been assured that it was self-defense and neither she nor Caleb would face any charges. Once they were all done, it was basically time to get ready and come to work.

Of course, bossy Caleb hadn't wanted her to go to work, but what else was she going to do today? Sit around her house and replay what had happened on a loop until she drove herself crazy?

No, work was where she had to be right now.

Where she *needed* to be.

"Who is he?" Ashleigh asked, her brown eyes full of curiosity.

"Someone I used to know," she answered vaguely. Now was definitely not the time to get into a dark conversation. Skye had never told anyone about Caleb and how badly he'd hurt her. Hadn't ever intended to either. He was a part of her past that she had escaped and she didn't intend to get dragged back down into that hellhole.

"Skye, is it possible that he …?" Ashleigh trailed off, but she didn't need to finish the sentence.

Skye had thought of little else.

Was it a coincidence that Caleb randomly showed back up in her life and that very same night she was attacked in her home?

The intruder's words played in a loop in her mind.

He said I could have some fun with you before I kill you.

Thanks to a near photographic memory the words would never leave her mind. Neither would the fear, the feel of the man's hands on her, each painful blow as her body collided with the stairs, trying to hold back his arm holding the knife, and knowing it was a battle she couldn't win.

All of that was etched into the recesses of her brain and would never leave.

Was Caleb the *he* the man had been talking about?

Caleb had been adamant that she was in danger and should go with him, and he would protect her. Although she knew he had served in the military and now worked for some security firm, the truth was she didn't trust him.

Skye was grateful for his timing, but she couldn't help but be suspicious as well.

Had he sent the man after her and then had second thoughts? He had obviously been outside her house because it was the only way he could have known that something was going on.

The problem was, she couldn't figure out if her distrust of Caleb was because he had shown up the same day she was attacked or because of what had happened between them in the past. He had already shown her that he wasn't someone she could trust and so now she would see everything he did as suspicious.

Confused, unsettled, hurting, and tired, Skye rubbed at her temples where a stress headache pounded.

All she wanted was to quietly live her life, care for animals, and find happiness wherever she could. Why did that seem so unattainable?

An only child, her father had been furious when she refused to follow him into politics. Skye hated that lifestyle, hated what it had done to her family, hated the lies and secrecy, the game playing, and the power grabs. It wasn't for her or who she was. So as soon as she was old enough, she got out of that lifestyle and never looked back.

Now her perfect little bubble of an existence was being threatened.

By Caleb?

Someone else?

The problem was, she didn't know and didn't know how she was going to figure it out.

Meeting her best friend's gaze, Skye slowly shook her head. "I don't know if he's involved or not. All I know is that the man who attacked me said that someone had sent him to me. I'm scared, Ashleigh," she admitted, hating the tremble in her voice.

Hating that once again she felt lost and alone, swaying in a sea of violence with no idea how to escape.

Or if escape was even possible.

CHAPTER FOUR

December 1st
6:58 P.M.

"Tell me we know something," Brick growled into his cell phone. He'd been calling his team leader religiously throughout the day, desperate for an update on the case.

"Got an ID on the body," Bear said, and Brick sighed in relief.

"Finally."

"He's a merc, wanted in connection with a couple of other rapes and murders. Suspected of being for hire, the kind of man you call when you need something taken care of and have the money to make it happen."

Brick hadn't needed the cops to tell him the guy was a mercenary, he'd had the word all but tattooed on his forehead. "What else?"

"Former special forces. *Russian* special forces," Bear added.

"So chances are he's somehow connected to Kristoff Mikhailov and Zara Duffy. This has to be her father." Xenos was wealthy enough to pay the mercenary's asking fee and would already have connections to him through his partners in crime.

"Not disagreeing, but we need proof," Bear said.

Proof.

He was beginning to hate that word.

Agreeing to come to Virginia to find proof that Hemmingway Xenos was involved in this crazy plot was going to cost him any chance of ever winning Skye's trust back.

"You doing okay?" Bear asked quietly.

Brick was getting damn tired of being asked that question.

"No. Not even close. You didn't see how close he came to killing her last night. He intended to slit her throat then rape her while she bled out."

"I know, man. I get it. Trust me."

Brick knew that his team leader did in fact understand what it was like to see the woman you loved in danger. Bear had met the woman he was now married to, the mother of his son, when Mackenzie was abducted by her insane brother. Back then, they'd thought that Storm Gallagher was the man behind a plot to overthrow the government, using military vets to do it. Then they'd learned the plot went so much deeper and that Storm was nothing but a smokescreen, used and manipulated by people with much more evil motives.

That was over a year ago, and over that year each of his teammates had fallen one by one.

Asher "Mouse" Whitman had fallen for the woman who saved his daughter from being kidnapped. Phoebe had been on the run from an abusive ex and wary of trusting another man, but now the two were happily married and expecting a baby.

Then Antonio "Arrow" Eden had made his move on Prey's psychiatrist, a woman he'd been interested in since he met her. Piper was being stalked at the time and had reservations about dating a patient, but the two planned to get married at the beginning of the year.

Next had been Dominick "Domino" Tanner who had fallen hard and fast for a gorgeous investigative journalist they'd met in Somalia. Somehow Julia had managed to soften the edges of the hard man, and the two were engaged.

And last was Christian "Surf" Bailey who had just recently fallen in love with a former child star. Lila had barely survived a horrific ordeal in Switzerland and was scheduled for surgery as soon as she was strong enough.

That only left him.

Alone.

And pining after a woman who hated him and didn't trust him as far as she could throw him.

"She thinks I might be the one who sent that man in to kill her," he admitted. "I messed up badly enough, hurt her so much, that she actually thinks I might have someone try to murder her." There were no words to describe what that felt like.

"I'm sorry, man. But I promise you we're doing everything on our end to get proof that her father is involved so you don't have to use her."

"I know, and I appreciate it. More than anything I want her to be safe." Brick paused and frowned when he saw Skye come out from the side of her building on foot and not in her car. "I got to go."

"Check in when you can."

Brick barely managed to throw out an agreement before he was out of the car and jogging across the street.

When Skye saw him, she froze for a second, then turned and hurried down the sidewalk.

He easily caught up to her and moved so he was blocking her path. There was a small flare of panic in her wide brown eyes, and he hated that she was afraid of him on top of being angry with him. The last thing he wanted was to intimidate her or make this worse when she was already scared, but he wasn't letting her go until he knew why she wasn't in her car.

"Why are you walking?" he demanded.

"One of my tires was flat. I wasn't in the mood to deal with it and wait for someone to come and change it. I'll deal with it tomorrow," she replied.

Accident or deliberate?

Getting Skye to walk home rather than driving made her a whole lot more vulnerable.

"Want me to change the tire for you?" he offered. Call him desperate, but he was prepared to take whatever time with Skye he could get.

"No. Thank you. It's fine. As I said, I'll deal with it tomorrow." The skin beneath her eyes was dark giving her a haunted look, and he could see the bruises she'd tried hard to cover with makeup.

Nodding, Brick stepped in beside her, and her head tilted up to look at him in confusion.

"What are you doing?"

"Walking you home."

"That's really not necessary."

"Necessary or not that's what I'm doing. Unless you want a ride?" He gestured over his shoulder at his vehicle. Brick would much prefer to get her out of the cold and off her feet. She looked exhausted, and he was consumed with a need to take care of her, but he suspected she wouldn't agree.

"No way am I getting in a car with you."

"Walk it is then."

"You don't need to walk with me," she said as she started off in the direction of her home.

"I know I don't. I want to."

"Because I'm in danger?" Skye looked nervously around like she expected the bogeyman to jump out at her at any second.

"Because I want to spend time with you."

"That's ridiculous. It's been fifteen years since you told me I wasn't good enough for you," she scoffed, but he could hear the pain laced into every word.

"I'm so sorry for hurting you. So very sorry," he whispered.

Skye stumbled but jerked away before he could reach out and steady her. Brick could tell his apology had surprised her. Yesterday he'd told her he wanted her forgiveness and regretted hurting her, but he hadn't outright said the words he knew she needed to hear.

The words he owed her.

"You'll never know how much I hate that I hurt you. My beautiful, sweet sun, moon, and stars. I threw away what we had.

What we could have had," he added, acknowledging that his thoughtlessness hadn't just cost them their friendship but their future. "Tell me what to do, baby, please. Whatever it takes to get you to forgive me I will do in a heartbeat."

"There's nothing you can do," Skye said sadly.

"Anything," he repeated brokenly. Whatever she needed he'd do. Throw himself off a cliff, walk through hell, get down on his hands and knees here in the street.

Pleading for forgiveness on his knees had worked for Arrow when he'd messed up with Piper, and ended things with her after he'd tried to kill her while stuck in a nightmare despite her plea they talk things through. And it had worked with Surf when he broke up with Lila to keep her safe because Kristoff Mikhailov's Dark Beauty had vowed vengeance on their entire team.

Could it work with Skye?

He was willing to try anything.

Grabbing her hands, Brick knelt before her.

"What are you doing? Get up. People are looking, and you'll catch your death of cold kneeling on the frozen sidewalk, there are snowflakes in the air."

"I don't care who's watching, baby, and I don't care if it's blowing up a blizzard. I'm so sorry I chose her over you, that I ended our beautiful friendship for some mediocre sex. She was never right for me, I know that now. It was you. It was always you."

Even on his knees, he was tall enough that his head was almost level with hers and he swept his fingers across her skin before taking her chin between his thumb and forefinger.

"I made the biggest mistake of my life that day. And every day since I have hated myself for hurting you. You are without a doubt the most beautiful, intelligent, sweet, and strong woman I have ever met. I want a chance with you, Skye. You're the sun, moon, and stars of my world and it's been so damn dark without you in my life. I will always regret hurting you, and no words I can give you will ever adequately express how sorry I am, but I'm not giving up on you, honey. On us. Not ever. Not for anything."

* * * * *

December 2nd
12:32 P.M.

He was getting what he wanted.

In a way, Skye was irritated that Caleb's impassioned pleas were getting to her.

The cruel words he'd flung at her, and the way he had cut her so completely out of his life, leaving her in a stormy ocean with no life ring, made him deserving of her anger. He didn't deserve to be forgiven, and yet ...

Did she want to be the kind of person who held onto a grudge when the person apologizing seemed sincere?

No.

She didn't.

Skye acknowledged that.

Forgiving him if he was truly repentant was the right thing to do. The only problem was, she didn't know if he really was truly repentant.

She felt so confused when it came to Caleb Quinn.

They'd grown up in the same world. Wealthy, parents in politics, private school, and anything money could buy, but despite that, both of them were honest people. They didn't play games, weren't cut out for the world of politics, at least that's what she'd always thought, but it was painfully apparent she hadn't known the real Caleb.

Was he playing her now like he'd played her back then?

Was he responsible for the attack?

Was he telling her what he thought she wanted to hear to get her to lower her guard?

"You're thinking really hard over there."

The voice startled her out of her thoughts, and Skye was annoyed that Caleb had messed with her head so much these last two days that he was all she could think about.

"What are you doing here?" she asked. Okay, she sounded rude and a little snarky, but her nerves were completely strung out. Dealing with Caleb popping back up in her life would have been bad enough, but then add in the attack and the fact she knew it wasn't random, and it was just too much.

Apparently, not put off by her hostility, Caleb held up a brown paper bag. "I brought lunch."

It was on the tip of her tongue to tell him she wasn't hungry, but her traitorous stomach chose that moment to remind her she had been running late this morning and had skipped breakfast.

The grumble it gave was loud enough she could never hope that Caleb hadn't heard it, and from his chuckle, she knew he had and intended to use it to his advantage.

"Looks like I got here just in time." His grin was smooth and easy, but in his dark eyes there was a hint of insecurity.

It about knocked her to her knees.

Never in all the years that she'd known him had Caleb ever been anything other than utterly and completely confident in himself and his abilities. He moved with a confidence not many men possessed, but it wasn't a smarmy, arrogant one. He just believed he had the skills and capability to take on any situation he might find himself in.

Why was he insecure now, here with her?

Was it because of her?

Could he really have meant everything he'd said to her last night?

Again, he didn't seem put out by the fact she was standing staring at him, her mouth hanging open in shock. Nudging her out of the way, he opened the bag and pulled out a sandwich, setting it down on her desk.

"I asked them to lightly toast the bread, just enough to give it a little color, and the avocado doesn't have any dressing on it. Oh, and I asked them to cut off the crusts," he added with a charming smile. Yeah, there was a little smugness to it as well because he knew he had gotten it just the way she used to like it as a kid.

The way she still liked it now.

He'd remembered something that small?

Skye narrowed her eyes. "This is from the bakery down the street. They won't toast the bread for me, I know, I've asked. How did you get them to do that?" Of course, she had never asked them to cut the crusts off. She was a grown-up and adults were supposed to eat their crusts, but she'd tried a few times to get them to toast the bread for her. Apparently, since it wasn't on the menu they weren't allowed.

"Might have used all the charm in my arsenal," he said, his eyes sparkling with mischief.

It was that same sparkle that had gotten them into a whole lot of trouble when they were kids. She would have followed him anywhere, tagged along after him even knowing she would be punished when they were caught.

As though his own thoughts had taken that same turn, he inclined his head at her desk chair and made himself comfortable in the chair from Ashleigh's desk, picking up his own lunch.

"Eat," he said when she didn't move to sit down. "You look pale, and I'd bet anything you barely ate after I walked you home last night."

He'd be right.

Edgy and unsettled after his heartfelt declaration, she'd been unable to settle. Remembering and replaying the assault every time she glanced at the stairs didn't help. In the end, she'd eaten a cup of soup and then fallen asleep on the couch with both dogs and the cat keeping her company.

Refusing would be petty so Skye dropped into her chair and picked up the sandwich. She took a bite, and it was every bit as delicious as it looked. He'd obviously told them how much to toast the bread because it was exactly the way she liked it. It stirred her heart in an almost painful way to think that he'd remembered something so small and insignificant about her after all these years. "Thank you."

The way he beamed at her praise made her feel weird. Things were so awkward between them, and she didn't know if she wanted to change that.

It was safer to keep him at a distance.

Yet words to ease the tense atmosphere came out of her mouth anyway. "Tuna?"

"Yep. Still love fish," Caleb said. "Remember the time we filled your swimming pool with fish we sneaked out of your dad's aquarium because no one would take us fishing so we decided to make our own lake?"

A reluctant smile tugged at her lips. "I remember. I don't think we actually managed to catch any of the fish."

"Probably because they died in the chlorine." Caleb winced. He'd felt bad that they'd killed the fish even though it hadn't been their intention. They'd been eight and hadn't realized that chlorinated water would kill the fish. They'd just thought that water was water.

"The gardener found us pretty quickly and got most of the fish out, I think only a couple didn't make it," she reminded him, for some reason wanting to soothe him.

"Watching you try to throw the line and getting it tangled in your hair was pretty funny." Caleb snickered, and another small smile curled her lips up.

"I don't remember you being much better. You're the one who threw your fishing rod too hard and sent it sailing through the air and into the gardener." Despite their mishaps, it had been a fun afternoon, worth the beating she'd taken later for daring to touch her father's precious aquarium. "You were always getting me into trouble."

Since he didn't know about her home life and thought she just meant the scrapes they got themselves into, Caleb grinned. That same smile led her to follow after him time and time again, even knowing the price she would have to pay.

"Hey, I seem to remember you getting me into trouble just as much as I got you into trouble," he teased. "Like the time you found that mouse in your house and were so worried the housekeeper would call in an exterminator. You thought sneaking the mouse with us to school, then ditching school to let it go in the park was a good idea."

Skye smiled at the memory. Her heart had always hurt at the thought of any animal suffering, and it had led her to do some silly things she knew would enrage her father. But life for her as a child had been all about weighing the benefits with the risks. The risk of anything she did was enraging her father. It wasn't hard to do, and anything from a less-than-perfect grade to simple childish play could be the trigger.

In the end, she'd always chosen to enjoy that moment of joy because they were things she could hold onto in those moments when her father took great pleasure in inflicting pain on his only child.

"You always had the biggest heart." Caleb moved his hand so it rested on the desk, just beside hers, close enough that their fingers brushed. "Always worrying about everyone else, caring about everybody else, but who is worrying about you? Who's caring about you? Who's taking care of your heart?"

Caleb hooked his pinkie finger over hers, and Skye felt the connection deep down into her soul.

The problem was, he'd already shattered her heart once, and his sudden reappearance in her life coinciding with her attack made her extra wary of him.

She'd be an idiot to put her heart in his hands again.

CHAPTER FIVE

December 2nd
7:03 P.M.

Slow and steady wins the race.

Brick had to keep reminding himself of that.

The alpha in him wanted to grab Skye, drag her into his arms, demand that she forgive him for hurting her, and kiss her until she gave in and surrendered her body and heart to him.

It seemed only fair since she owned his.

The calmer, more rational side of his mind kept telling him that it was going to take time. That he'd hurt her badly, ruined something special, and that if he wanted to build something lasting with her, he had to make sure he'd created a solid foundation for what he hoped was going to be a relationship that lasted a lifetime.

They had already wasted so many years apart, which was completely his fault, but he didn't want to waste any more time.

As he watched, the front door to Skye's clinic opened, and she stood there talking to a family with a dog. The same dog he'd seen in a cage the night she'd caught him watching her. Looked like the pup had been released and was heading home with its very excited family. A little boy was bouncing from foot to foot, and a little girl threw her arms around Skye when she said something to her. The woman was smiling at Skye, and the husband had his arm around his wife's shoulders and looked so grateful as his gaze kept bouncing from the dog to his family and then to Skye.

Did she realize what a difference she made in people's lives?

Or did she think that what she did was nothing special?

Knowing his girl, she downplayed the impact caring for people's pets had on the community. Skye had never been one to seek out praise. Although she'd been brilliant in school, she was a little quirky and didn't have a lot of friends, mostly because she rebuffed attention whenever possible. But he didn't know of anyone who hadn't liked her, she just had this way of shining light everywhere she went, and that light was infectious.

Until he'd been sent on this mission, he hadn't admitted to himself just how badly he wanted to get Skye back.

Life on Prey's Alpha Team was a busy one. Between working mission after mission with little downtime and the mess of the last year as they worked to unravel the conspiracy and eliminate each threat, it had been easy to bury himself in work. But watching his teammates fall one by one, and then the revelation of this link to Skye's father, an opportunity to spend time with her, and the surge of emotion the first time he touched her, he couldn't avoid his feelings any longer.

He wanted her.

Badly.

Skye's colleagues began to spill out of the building, and Brick climbed out of his car and crossed the street.

The other vet who worked here, Ashleigh Christou, gave him a suspicious frown when she caught sight of him. It was clear the woman was protective of her friend, but he wasn't sure if she was suspicious of him because she knew about his past with Skye or because his arrival timed with Skye being attacked and she was feeding off Skye's suspicions.

He knew she didn't completely trust him, but whether she realized it or not, deep down Skye knew he would never harm her physically because if she didn't, she would have turned him in to the cops.

Brick was already around in the parking lot behind her practice by the time she came out the back door. When she caught sight of him, she froze, but he could have sworn he saw a moment of relief at seeing him before her walls came up and she guarded her expression.

Wishful thinking?

"You again," she said, but there was no heat in her tone.

Was she softening toward him?

Brick, who was usually an expert at reading people, honestly couldn't tell. This new Skye held her cards very close to her chest, so very different from the girl he used to know.

"I'm not hiding in the shadows this time," he joked and was rewarded by a tiny smile. He wanted one of her big, bright ones, wanted her to beam joy at him, but for now, he would take what he could get.

"No, you're not," she agreed, "so at least I don't have to worry about being attacked by a druggie."

His body grew cold. "You been attacked before?" If she'd encountered druggies outside her clinic before she should be taking her safety more seriously. Alone out here in the dark, with a clinic full of drugs behind her, she was a much too easy target.

Skye shrugged like it was no big deal. "Nothing serious."

When he growled, a low rumbling sound, her eyes widened in surprise. "You being attacked is not nothing serious."

"Okay, okay," she soothed, reaching out to touch her palm to his forearm. The touch—though simple—seared him like a brand and he had to wonder how he had survived a decade and a half without her.

Taking advantage of the fact she had reached out to him, Brick grabbed her hand and tightened his hold when she tried to pull it free. "You organize getting your car fixed?"

She groaned. "No, I completely forgot. Although I blame you. It was a busy day. Normally I would have done that in my lunch break, but you showed up and took up all my time."

No way was he complaining about getting to spend a little extra time with her rather than following her back to her place in his car. "I'll have it fixed tomorrow."

"That's okay, I can do it myself," she said stubbornly as he led her down the driveway and out onto the sidewalk.

"I don't mind."

"It's my responsibility."

"And I'm happy to help out."

"It's not necessary."

"I'm aware."

Skye stopped walking. "Caleb, *I'm* not your responsibility."

Stopping, he tugged on her hand, moving her so she was facing him, then he bent his knees until they were eye to eye. "That's where you're wrong, honey. You are my responsibility because you're mine."

She spluttered and stammered, seemingly unable to come up with a response to his bold statement. "Caleb, you're being ridiculous."

"I'm being honest." Reaching out, he brushed his fingertips across the soft skin of her cheek before dragging his thumb across her bottom lip.

Heat flared in her eyes, but he knew it was an instinctual reaction. Desire still bubbled between them just like it had when they were teens, old enough to start noticing the opposite sex. Back then, he hadn't wanted to explore it because he had been scared of ruining their friendship, so he'd turned to other girls, ones his father would approve of.

Damn his father for always making his approval conditional on the choices Brick made.

Without that pressure, he might have succumbed to the temptation to make Skye his.

Instead, he'd gone along with dating Mirabella. It wasn't until Skye was out of his life that he realized how empty the future his father wanted for him was. He had zero desire to go into politics. At first, the military was a way to escape. Escape his father's strangling hold on Brick's life, escape Mirabella and a relationship he knew by then he wasn't really committed to, and escape the hole left behind by the loss of Skye.

Straightening, he resumed walking, taking Skye with him. If he didn't get her home and away from him, he was going to do something stupid like shove her up against the wall and kiss her senseless. As badly as he wanted to do just that, Brick also knew the timing wasn't right.

She didn't trust him.

To her, it would be just sex and he wanted more.

He wanted it all.

"So you had a busy day?" he asked, returning the conversation to more neutral ground.

Apparently happy enough to talk about something she was comfortable with, Skye talked about her day for the remainder of the walk to her place. He asked a few questions, and it wasn't until they were standing outside her house that things got awkward again.

Brick wanted to order her to go and stay in a hotel until she was safe, or better yet, go back to New York with him, but she'd been adamant that she wasn't going to be pushed out of her home. The cops were doing regular drivebys, and he would be sleeping in his car again, but he wanted her somewhere he could guarantee her safety.

No one was going to take her away from him.

"Umm, thanks for walking me home," Skye said nervously, chewing on her bottom lip.

His body instantly responded. He wanted nothing more than to kiss those delectable lips, taste her sweet mouth then explore every inch of her body.

"Babe, don't do that," he ordered gently.

"Do what?" Her brow furrowed.

"That." He touched his thumb to her lip. "Unless you want me to kiss you out here where your neighbors would get a clear view of the show."

Her eyes went almost impossibly wide. "Oh … umm … yeah

… no … that's not what I want."

Liar.

From the heat burning in her eyes and the way her body swayed almost imperceptibly toward his, he knew she wanted exactly that. But she was scared and wary, and that was all on him.

"Go on inside." Brick took a deliberate step back, needing a little distance between them if he was going to be able to think clearly.

Skye didn't move.

"It's cold, honey, and you're exhausted. Go take a bath and get some sleep. Sweet dreams."

Because he was a weak man, and one completely in love with the woman standing before him, he crowded against her, noting that she didn't back away.

"One taste. Just one," he murmured as he dipped his head and feathered his lips across hers.

Then because he knew if he didn't go now he wouldn't go at all, he turned and walked back down the street to get his car, well aware of the fact that Skye's gaze followed him.

* * * * *

December 3rd
2:46 A.M.

Something was buzzing.

The cat?

Dogs?

Stuck half in sleep, Skye couldn't quite figure out what it was.

"Go away," she mumbled to the sound. She'd finally fallen asleep and was having the most wonderful dreams. Caleb was there, they were surrounded by candles and rose petals, he was seducing her slowly, and her body was throbbing with an intense need unlike anything else she had ever experienced.

The last thing she wanted to do was wake up before he satisfied the need he created in her.

Skye groaned when the buzzing continued.

Blinking, she sat up, drawing the covers with her to ward off the sudden chill. She'd decided to tackle sleeping in her bed last night. There was no way she was going to be scared out of the home she'd built for herself, and the last thing she wanted was to develop a phobia about using her bedroom, so she'd made herself do it. Because she needed a little support, she'd brought the dogs with her, and they were both thrilled to be sleeping on the bed.

A glance at the clock showed her it was nearing three in the morning. Although she'd gone to bed early it had taken her hours to fall asleep. As much as she would like to blame it on nerves and the fear of being back in the room where she'd first seen the intruder, it was only partly that.

The other part was all Caleb.

Why did he have to do crazy things to her hormones?

It wasn't just that though, it was that apology he'd given her. On his knees, on the sidewalk, out in public. Uncaring that anyone might see him or overhear his words because his priority had been her.

When had she ever been someone else's priority?

Never.

The buzzing had stopped, and she wondered if it had just been part of the dream. Skye was about to settle back down, hoping she wasn't too awake to slide smoothly back into sleep when it started up again.

More awake this time, she quickly realized it was her cell phone.

A call at two in the morning was never a good thing.

A knot of dread formed in her stomach as she reached for her cell on the nightstand. The number was unknown, and she wanted to ignore it, pretending it was nothing but a wrong number, but something inside her told her she had to answer.

"Hello?" she said shakily.

"Ms. Xenos?" an unfamiliar male voice said.

"Y-yes. Who is this?"

"I'm Detective Harding. I'm afraid I have bad news for you, ma'am."

Her parents?

Was he calling because something had happened to them?

She had little to nothing to do with them. They didn't catch up for holidays or family events, they didn't talk on the phone or send texts about their day, and she hadn't even seen them since graduating college. However, she did know her father had decided to run for President. As a senator and a presidential candidate, he'd have a whole security team protecting him and her mother. Surely someone couldn't have gotten through them and hurt her parents.

Skye might not love them—they'd done nothing to deserve her love or respect—but she didn't want them to be horribly murdered.

"Bad news?"

"It's your practice, ma'am. There's a fire."

Panic hit her hard. "My practice? A fire?"

"I'm sorry, ma'am."

"I'll be right there," she said, already throwing the covers back and scrambling out of bed.

Both dogs whined at the interruption to their slumber, but she ignored them. She had no idea what clothes she put on, for all she knew she'd mismatched sweatpants and a blouse, she just grabbed the first things her hands landed on when she opened her closet.

Dressed, she shoved her feet into a pair of shoes, grabbed her cell and purse, and ignored her hair. She didn't care if it was a mess when the clinic she had invested so much time and money in was burning, and ran down the stairs. The dogs had followed her, and she quickly popped them into their crates before hurrying out the door.

Her car was still at the clinic, possibly on fire as well, so she'd have to walk.

Normally there would have been a bit of trepidation in walking alone in the middle of the night, but now all she cared about was getting to her practice as quickly as possible.

Skye was just on the sidewalk when a figure came running toward her.

Any fear she might have felt was quickly abated when the shadowy figure spoke.

"Skye? What's wrong?"

"Caleb? What are you doing here?" He'd been here the other night as well. Her gaze fell on a large, black SUV across the street, the front door standing open. Had he been sleeping in his car outside her house?

Why would he do that?

She could see he might have been tonight, watching over her because she'd been attacked. But why had he been there that first night before he knew someone wanted her dead?

There was no time to figure it out now, she had bigger things to worry about.

"I-I got a c-call, it's my practice, it's on f-fire," she told him, her voice shaking. Body too. Tremors rippled through her that had nothing to do with the cold.

Caleb swore then dragged her into his arms. His body was throwing off heat like a furnace, and she wrapped her arms around him and held on.

For just one moment she'd let him hold her up, let herself borrow a little of his strength and a whole lot of his heat.

"Come on, let's get you over there."

When he led her toward his vehicle she didn't protest, allowing him to bundle her into the passenger seat. Once he was in he turned the engine on, aimed the vents in her direction, and cranked the heat up high.

She was pretty sure he ignored every road law that existed on the journey there, but there was virtually no traffic, and she wanted to get there as quickly as she could, so she didn't complain.

Maybe two minutes later they were pulling up outside her clinic.

Or what used to be her clinic.

There were two fire trucks parked in the street, and a couple of cop cars as well. There was a lot of smoke, and she could see a couple of fiery flames lighting up the night, but all in all, it didn't look as bad as she had been expecting.

Caleb was at her back as she clambered from the car and ran toward her practice.

Someone stepped up, blocking her path, and she felt Caleb move closer, protective vibes emanating off him in steady waves.

"Ms. Xenos?" the man asked.

"Detective Harding?"

"Yes, ma'am. And you are?"

"A friend," Caleb answered vaguely. "What happened?"

Even in the dark, she could see the cop eye her as though uncertain whether or not she could handle it.

He had no idea what she could handle.

No one did.

Straightening her spine, she tightened her muscles to still the tremors and looked the detective directly in the eyes. "What happened?"

Nodding as though approving of her spunk, the man replied, "Looks like it might have been deliberately set. When we learned who the place belonged to and that you had another incident the other night, we have to wonder if the two were related."

Were they?

Whoever had sent that man to kill her had to know that she wasn't going to be inside the clinic at three in the morning, so why set fire to it? Was it just because he harbored some hatred toward her, or was it because he wanted to break her, make her vulnerable before he came after her again?

Despite her determination to stand strong and show no fear, another shudder about took her to her knees.

Arms wrapped around her from behind and she was pulled back to rest against Caleb's sturdy chest.

She was … glad … he was here.

Being here alone would have been so much worse.

"I have to call Ashleigh," she murmured. "And my insurance company. All the employees. At least … at least there were no animals in there tonight." Horror had bile burning her throat. "Oh, Caleb, what if there had been someone's pet in there when they set the fire?"

The thought of some sweet, innocent animals in there suffering the horrific death of being burned alive just because someone hated her was too much.

Tears flooded down her cheeks, and she swallowed down a sob.

So much for pretending she had it all together.

Caleb swore again then turned her so her face was pressed against his hard chest. His arms around her were like bands of steel, and his warmth enveloped her in a little tiny bubble of protection.

As long as he was here whoever was after her wouldn't get to her.

Skye felt that deep down inside.

This man might have shattered her young heart and done damage not even her father could inflict. His reappearance in her life was suspect, and yet, her very soul seemed to understand that he would never hurt her like that.

Never try to kill her.

Never burn her business to the ground.

Snuggling closer, needing more of him, Skye curled her fingers into his sweater and held on.

Letting him be here to support her was a bad idea in so many ways.

While Caleb might not be a physical threat to her safety, he could take the tattered remains of her heart and utterly obliterate them.

Still, she didn't let go.

CHAPTER SIX

December 3rd
10:27 A.M.

"Something has to give," Brick growled into his phone. "We can't keep going on like this."

"We're doing everything we can," Bear assured him.

He wished that was enough.

But it wasn't.

He couldn't get out of his mind the devastation in Skye's eyes last night when she'd stood outside her burning clinic. Everything she had worked so hard to build had been destroyed.

The damage to the clinic was severe. Between what the fire had done, then the smoke, and the water, there wasn't much that could be salvaged. As Skye herself had said, things could have been worse. One of the animals under her care could have been inside when someone set the fire, he wasn't sure that was something Skye could have survived, she would have taken that loss and internalized it, blaming herself.

"That's not good enough, I need this over. Now. I need her safe." Brick had never felt this helpless. Skye was in danger, it was his job to keep her safe, and yet his presence here was likely what had put her in the crosshairs of her father.

It was no coincidence that he turned up and within days Skye was attacked in her home and almost raped and murdered, then her clinic was targeted and burned basically to the ground.

This was on him.

Her father would know that Prey was hunting him. Seeing him show up in Skye's life likely made the man believe that his daughter was working with them to bring him down.

Now he wanted to get his daughter out of the picture.

Permanently it seemed.

What kind of man would try to eliminate his own child?

Surely it would make more sense for Hemmingway Xenos to go after him. *He* was the one working for Prey, trying to find proof of the man's involvement in the conspiracy to overthrow the government. Yet there had been no attempts on his life, no one had made a move to come after him. Xenos must have had someone watching Skye, it was the only way he could know she was in contact with him.

Was it just the betrayal of blood turning on him?

Brick's gut said it was more.

That there was an important piece of the puzzle he was yet to uncover.

"I don't think we should have tried to use her. I don't believe she knows anything. If she was aware her father was neck deep in a terrorist plot, she would have said something since she knows the attack on her was ordered by someone else," he said, pinching the bridge of his nose. Using Skye had always made him uneasy, but now it made him downright terrified.

This was his fault.

He'd brought this down on her.

Put her in danger and cost her everything she loved.

Brick knew he should back off and ask Eagle to send someone else to be with Skye. There was no way he could be objective here. He was going to miss important information because he was all tied up in Skye and her pain.

What he wanted to do was soothe her and take away her fear. There wasn't a chance in the world he could be pumping her for information, subtly interrogating her with every conversation they had.

He didn't want that between them.

Didn't want to betray her all over again.

"There is zero evidence that she has any meaningful relationship with her father," Mouse said.

"From what we can figure, she doesn't see or speak to him or her mother," Arrow added.

"I don't think she's close enough to him to have any information we can use," Surf said.

"Then this mission has changed. It's not about me using Skye to try to get intel on her father, it's about keeping her alive." He needed someone to absolve him of the burden he was carrying knowing he was going to destroy his sun, moon, and stars by breaking her heart all over again.

A betrayal he knew she wouldn't recover from.

There would be no coming back from this.

"I'll speak with Eagle," Bear assured him.

"I'm not coming back unless Skye's with me," he warned. "We did this. I did. I put her in danger. If I hadn't come here, her father wouldn't have had any reason to take out a hit on her." Knowing he was the cause of her suffering gutted him. Even if he did win her back, and she never found out why he'd really come back into her life, it would always be between them.

A silent ghost judging him.

Was it something he could overcome?

Could he deal with keeping this secret from Skye even if her knowing would do no good for anyone?

"That's what we should be focusing on," Domino said, and Brick was glad no one argued with his need to stay here and protect what was his.

Neither did they offer him absolution.

His team might not know the details of his past with Skye, but they knew something had happened between them. Something that had led Brick to build a wall between himself and the rest of the world, not allowing anyone in. They knew Skye was important to him, and he had wrestled with the job of using her for intel.

Skye deserved better.

Better than how he'd treated her.

Better than them.

And if he was a better man, he would walk away and hand her protection over to someone who wasn't emotionally invested.

But he couldn't do that.

"Focusing on the attacks on Skye could lead us to what we wanted in a roundabout way," Bear agreed.

"If he is behind the attacks, and it makes sense that he is, then we need to prove it," Mouse said.

"We'll keep digging into it. There has to be a way to link the dead Russian who broke into Skye's home with Xenos. You keep your focus on Skye's protection," Bear said. "And, Brick, if you need back up, you let us know and we'll be out there immediately."

Having his team's support meant everything to him.

They were the family he'd always wished his own had been.

There was unconditional love and support between them, unlike his own family, where love was doled out only as a reward for compliance.

Remove the compliance and the love disappeared.

He knew that because it was what had happened when he'd bucked against his father's wishes and joined the military.

A decision he didn't regret. Would never regret because in life you had to blaze your own trail. It was the only way to find contentment.

True contentment for him was all tied up in the gorgeous woman currently standing outside her burned vet clinic. Skye had her arms wrapped around her middle, offering herself the comfort he so badly wanted to be the one to give her.

She'd been happy to have him there last night, he knew that she had, but once the sun rose, she'd put the barriers between them back up. He'd hovered nearby while she gave statements to the cops and spoke with the firefighters about the extent of the damage. When he'd said he should take her back home so she could get some rest, she had flatly refused and then politely asked him to give her a little space.

Reluctantly, he had given her what she asked for, retreating to his vehicle where he could watch over her but also give her space and check in with his team. What he wanted was for her to drop the politeness. She'd given him a little taste of the anger and hurt she harbored, and the only way for them to move forward was to clear the air. The only way to do that was for her to let everything out.

The more she held in her feelings, the more they festered.

Given everything she was dealing with, Brick was loathed to push for a confrontation. He was going to have to remain patient, be there to offer her support, watch her back, keep her safe and alive, and then when they had her father in custody, he would do whatever it took to get her to forgive him.

He deserved her anger and so much more and would gladly take that burden from her so she could be free.

Was it possible to soothe the hurts you had caused?

"We've all been there, man, right where you are right now," Surf said. "We know how much it hurts to know the woman you love is in danger, to know all it takes is for one tiny thing to go wrong and you could lose her. We know what it's like to fear not just for her safety but that something you did will cost you her love. It gets better, you have to believe that."

"I'm trying to," he admitted softly. Letting people in wasn't easy for him. Wasn't something he enjoyed doing. Letting anyone get too close only reminded him of how he'd had the most special connection he'd ever experienced to the perfect woman and yet thrown it away.

How could he ever deserve to have a connection when he'd had one and so carelessly discarded it?

"Not sure I deserve her forgiveness," he said.

"You're a good man, Brick. Human," Bear said. "We all have doubts, all have insecurities even if that's not a word men like us want to use in conjunction with ourselves. We have to believe in our strengths to do what we do, but we make mistakes. You made one with Skye, you're truly repentant about it, she'll see that. Just give her time."

Brick wanted to believe that time was all it would take.

But at the back of his mind, there was that fear that refused to be abated, that mocked him with constant reminders that time didn't heal all wounds.

* * * * *

December 3rd
1:19 P.M.

"Skye!"

At the sound of her name, she turned to see Ashleigh running toward her.

A sob caught in her throat as her friend collided with her, and they clung to each other. Skye had been doing her best not to fall apart. She hadn't been able to leave. Caleb had tried several times to convince her to go home, reminding her there was nothing she could do here, but she just couldn't make herself leave.

This was the culmination of all her dreams.

Freedom to break out from her father's thumb by being able to support herself without having to rely on her trust fund meant he had no say in her life and the choices she made. She'd worked three jobs to put herself through college, worked hard to save enough to open this clinic, and now it was lying in tatters before her.

"I'm so sorry," she whispered. "This is all my fault."

Ashleigh pulled back. "Don't say that."

"It's true. Someone tried to kill me and then our clinic gets burned down, no way that's not related. That means that this was because of me. I'm so sorry. This is our livelihood and you have kids to support, I've cost you your ability to do that. Oh, Ashleigh, I'm so sorry, how can you ever forgive me."

Pain splintered through her body leaving her feeling raw.

How would she ever look her friend in the eye again?

"Skye, listen to me." Ashleigh was using her don't argue with me mom voice, and like magnets her eyes were drawn to her friend's. "I don't *ever* want to hear you say that again. Do you hear me? If someone is trying to hurt you that is *not* your fault. Not at all. I don't blame you, not even a little bit, and with insurance, we'll rebuild. It will be okay."

"How can you be so nice to me?"

"Because you're my friend and I love you."

"I don't deserve you."

"Oh, sweetie, yes you do. Come here." Ashleigh pulled her in for another hug and even though she tried, Skye couldn't hold in another round of tears.

"Everything okay?" Caleb asked from behind them. There was a protectiveness to his tone that said if Ashleigh had made her cry she would have to deal with him.

That only made her cry harder, and when she heard Caleb make a distressed sound another sob broke through.

Why was he still here?

She didn't understand what was going on and it was only making things worse.

Didn't he know how badly he affected her?

"Shh, sweetie, it's going to be okay," Ashleigh murmured. "We're fine, just giving my girl here a few home truths," she said, obviously to Caleb.

When she didn't hear his receding footsteps, Skye drew in a breath, knowing she couldn't hide from this, her past, or her future forever, and lifted her head.

"I'm okay," she told Caleb, sensing he needed to hear it from her.

His stance relaxed slightly. His eyes gave her an assessing once over, and it was clear from his expression he didn't like what he saw. "You should go home. Rest. You've been through hell these last few days."

"He's right, sweetie. Let me drive you?" Ashleigh asked.

Possessiveness radiated off Caleb, but he didn't say anything, and since she was exhausted, and there wasn't anything she could do here, Skye gave a defeated nod.

"I'll talk to you later," Caleb said. Tugging her gently from her friend's grasp his large hands covered her shoulders, kneading gently. His eyes said there were a million things he wanted to say to her, but instead of saying anything at all, he leaned down, touched his lips to her forehead, holding them there for a long moment. Then he straightened and walked back to his vehicle.

Ashleigh led her to her car, and neither of them spoke on the short ride to her place. Inside, Skye cranked the heat up high hoping it could ward off the chill settled inside her, then headed to the kitchen, letting the dogs inside first.

"Tea?" she asked, after she'd petted both her dogs and given them a little love.

"Yes please."

"I think there are a few gingerbread men left in the cookie jar, I made them last week," she said. Last week, before her life had fallen apart. It felt like a lifetime ago.

"Yum," Ashleigh said, opening the cookie jar. "The kids loved the ones you made for them."

"Maybe next year they can help me bake some." Skye loved Ashleigh's kids as though they were her own, and she always had fun when she babysat them.

"They would love that. They love you, Skye, me too. I hope you know you're not alone."

Her friend's words had more tears burning the backs of her eyes. She would have thought she was all cried out by now.

Once she'd made a pot of tea, she carried two mugs over to the table and dropped down into one of the kitchen chairs, suddenly drained and bone weary.

"I see the guard dog hasn't backed off," Ashleigh said, curiosity in her tone.

"You mean Caleb?"

"Unless you got another gorgeous hunk of a man all protective and fierce following you around."

That got a half smile out of her. "Trust me, one is more than enough."

"You ready to tell me why Mr. Hunky is suddenly in your life, following you everywhere you go, and why you never told me about him."

"It's complicated."

"So, let's work on uncomplicating it."

Skye sighed. Was she ready to get into this?

Wasn't like she could avoid it forever. She got the vibe that Caleb wasn't going anywhere anytime soon.

"I ... didn't have the best home life," she admitted.

Ashleigh frowned. "Can I take that to mean you were abused?"

"Yeah."

"Isn't your dad Hemmingway Xenos?"

"He is."

"The mega-popular senator. Kids think he's cool, women think he's hot, and guys relate to him."

"Yeah, he's good at putting on a show," she said bitterly. Too bad none of it was real.

"He's running for President, isn't he?"

"Apparently."

"A man who beats on a defenseless little girl shouldn't run a country," Ashleigh said fiercely, and Skye offered her a sad smile.

"Appearances are everything."

"If he's elected, won't you have to have secret service protection?"

"No, I'd refuse and not cooperate. He's nothing to me. I haven't seen him since just after I graduated when he tried to intimidate me into going back to school and following him into politics. I'm not part of his life and anyone who tried to use me as leverage against him would be sorely disappointed. Safe to say, my father doesn't care if I live or die, and he'd only care about me being hurt in the sense that he didn't get to be the one to inflict that pain."

"How does the hunky guard dog play into all of this?"

"Caleb's father is also in politics. His family moved in next door to mine when we were four. I swear, Ash, it was love at first sight for me. I didn't even know what love was, but I saw him and I just knew. He was mine."

"He didn't feel the same way?"

"I think in a way he did. We were the best of friends. I was a quirky kid, super smart, a little awkward, and more interested in animals than people. No one ever bullied me or anything, I think the other kids all liked me, but I was hiding a huge secret about my home life, and it was hard for me to let people in."

"Not Caleb though."

"Not Caleb," she agreed. "I couldn't keep him out if I tried. We were inseparable, did everything together, he was the only good thing in my life until he wasn't."

"He hurt you."

"Oh yeah. Destroyed me. Once we hit puberty our friendship began to change slightly. We were still close but now there was an attraction there too. At least I thought there was. Then he started dating the head cheerleader. She was everything I wasn't. Tall, blonde, gorgeous, big breasts, willing to give him sex. Caleb was the star quarterback, the most popular guy in school, all the girls wanted to date him, and all the guys wanted to be friends with him. Even after he started dating Mirabella, Caleb and I were still close, I just thought he needed time to realize what we had."

"But he didn't."

"Nope. Mirabella was jealous of our friendship, she ordered Caleb to cut me out of his life. Completely."

"Oh, sweetie, he did that?"

"Yep. He told me I wasn't popular enough or pretty enough to be friends with anymore, and that he didn't want to spend time with me. He might as well have reached inside my chest and carved my heart from my body. At first, I thought he couldn't really mean it but he did. He didn't come around to my house anymore. Didn't call or text. If he saw me at school he completely ignored me, wouldn't even look at me. He was the only good thing I had in my life and then he was gone."

"I really want to rip Mr. Hunky to pieces right now," Ashleigh growled.

That surprised a laugh out of her. "Get in line. That was our senior year, I didn't do anything that year but go to class and go home and study. The next year I left for college. My father was furious I wanted to become a vet, but anyone who knew me knew it was what I was born to do. About three years later I heard from Caleb. Over the years he's called and texted, sent emails and letters, but when he showed up outside the clinic a few days ago it was the first time I'd seen him in person since high school."

"What did he want when he contacted you?"

"He was apologizing."

"And?"

"And I never replied. I wasn't ready to deal with his betrayal."

"And now?"

"Now he's here and he's apologized several times, told me that he regrets it, knows it was a mistake, and hates that he hurt me. He says he should have chosen me, that he wants me now. But how can I ever trust him again, Ash? I loved him, I would have coped if he hadn't felt the same way, but he was so cold and callous and just cut me out of his life like I meant nothing."

"He was the only person you felt you ever mattered to."

"He *was* the only person I ever mattered to. Only maybe I never did. Maybe he never felt what I felt."

"No," Ashleigh said firmly. "I've seen the way he looks at

you."

"How?" she asked desperately. "How does he look at me because I don't trust myself when it comes to him anymore."

"He looks at you like you're everything to him. The sun, moon, and stars of his universe."

Skye gasped.

"What?"

"That's what he always called me, even when we were little. Because my name was Skye and he said I always brightened the world of anyone I came into contact with, no matter how dark their life was."

Reaching over, Ashleigh grasped her hands. "I think he is truly remorseful for what he did. As badly as it hurt, and as angry as I am for him hurting my girl, he was a kid back then. A stupid kid. He made a mistake that cut you deeply, but maybe it's time to forgive him and move on."

Could she do that?

Was she strong enough to let go of the pain Caleb had inflicted?

CHAPTER SEVEN

December 3rd
4:38 P.M.

"Well?" Hemmingway Xenos growled at the man who walked into his study.

"She's got protection," Grigoriy Golubev said. The man had been a friend of Kristoff Mikhailov, who had approached him almost three years ago with a plan.

Okay, that wasn't quite the way the head of the Mikhailov Bratva had broached the topic.

Kristoff had come at him with blackmail.

Proof that Hemmingway had abused his daughter.

Somehow, Kristoff had gotten his hands on medical records showing the number of times his "clumsy" daughter had been in and out of the hospital.

Not irrefutable proof, but in the world in which he lived it was more than enough to ruin him. If word got out then reporters would track down his daughter, and knowing Skye, she might actually be stupid enough to admit that he used to beat her.

It was a risk he couldn't take, and Kristoff knew that.

The plot was simple. Gaining the compliance and finances of a number of wealthy and influential Hollywood stars by threatening them with the loss of their children, they would use that to influence the public. With a crazy survivalist who believed in regressing society back to an age where people lived off the land without all the benefits of modern technology, they would destabilize the government.

With bombs going off across the nation, people would become

unhappy with what the government was doing to keep them safe and protected.

Enter him.

He knew how to play to any audience, read them and tell them what they wanted to hear.

Already an up-and-coming politician with a stellar reputation as a senator, he was the perfect candidate. Kristoff would fund his presidential campaign so long as Hemmingway agreed to follow his instructions once he was elected.

As if.

He'd never had any intention of following through on that. Once he was elected, he'd planned to have the Bratva family raided by the cops, then no one would believe Kristoff's claims he was abusive to his daughter, it would sound like revenge.

Fate had a way of working things out and he hadn't even had to do anything to get rid of Kristoff Mikhailov, or the man's crazy lover Zara Duffy. Ironically, it had been Prey Security's Alpha Team who had done that for him.

Only now they were after him.

He didn't know what Zara had told them about him, but whatever it was they were now working with his own daughter to take him down.

They were crazy if they thought that was happening.

Hemmingway was more than prepared to sacrifice his daughter to earn his position as the leader of the greatest country in the world.

Nothing was going to stop him, and certainly not his stupid daughter.

Skye had been a disappointment from the day she was born. He'd wanted a son, but got a daughter. He'd wanted a strong child he could mold into his image. He'd gotten a weak one who thought playing with animals was a worthwhile legacy to leave.

Ridiculous girl.

Traitorous girl.

Working against her own father was a step too far. He'd been willing to ignore her, pretend she didn't exist, and let her live her own life because he had more important things to worry about. But he would not allow her to destroy everything he had worked so hard to build.

"I don't care if she has protection, I want her eliminated," Hemmingway growled as he stormed across the room to pour himself a drink.

"It's not that easy. Not if you want it done right. I told you hiring Dimitri was a bad idea. The man likes to play with his victims before he kills them. That leaves room for error. If you hadn't been rash and panicked because you saw the Prey man hanging around your daughter, I could have given you the name of someone who would have done the job properly."

"Time was of the essence," he gritted out between clenched teeth. He hated that this man wasn't afraid of him. Grigoriy was wealthy and powerful, the diplomat had immunity so he never worried about dabbling in the illegal. The former Russian had fled the country as a young man and moved to a castle in Romania.

"No, you only thought that because you panicked. Making informed and intelligent decisions is of the essence. Another day wouldn't have changed anything, now you're floundering, lashing out, making it more than obvious that the woman is in danger."

Hemmingway huffed but knew he couldn't argue.

Because the man he had hired had failed, the cops now knew that Skye was in danger and that it wasn't a random break in. His contact at the police department said his daughter had told the cops that her attacker had told her he was sent to her, now they were searching for who was after her.

"Having her clinic burned down was childish," Grigoriy rebuked as though Hemmingway was just a recalcitrant child.

"The girl betrayed me. Me. Her own father. She deserved to be punished."

"Perhaps. Disloyalty is punishable by death in my world, but

73

that move will only serve to prove to the cops that she is in great danger, making it harder to get to her. Plus, Prey Security is a formidable opponent. Eagle Oswald is a brave man, brave and honorable. He will not take kindly to an innocent young woman being in danger. He could very well send in the rest of Alpha Team to guard her. How will you get through six highly trained and dedicated special forces operatives?"

"I'll find someone who can take her out. Take them all out if I have to, but no one is going to destroy everything I have built," he screamed.

Grigoriy tutted. "It will not be as easy as you seem to think it will be. If you take out an entire Prey team you will have Eagle Oswald on your back for the rest of your life. The man is very wealthy and very powerful. He has contacts everywhere. He will make it his mission to prove your involvement in Kristoff's plot, and sooner or later he will find proof."

"There is no proof," he said confidently.

"There is *always* proof," Grigoriy contradicted. "You are not wise if you do not acknowledge that. Nothing in life is certain. All you can do is mitigate the possibility for things to go wrong."

"I am not going to let anyone ruin this for me," Hemmingway hissed. Not after so many years of hard work, not after the sacrifices he had made.

"And I am not saying that you should. But if you go after the woman again so soon you only give the cops more to work with. Pause, take a step back, draw a deep breath, and then go at the problem again by another angle. There are other ways to make a person disappear without killing them."

"You making a suggestion?" He had zero emotional attachments to the girl. He didn't care what came of her so long as she couldn't work against him. There shouldn't be anything other than the fact he had abused her that she could tell either the cops or Prey. She hadn't been part of his life for many years, and she knew nothing of his plans. Still, if she did—or already had—told

Prey he used to beat her then they could still use that to bring him down.

"She is a beautiful woman, and I have been looking for a gift for my son, I could perhaps purchase her from you."

An interesting proposition.

One he would consider.

Would serve his disobedient daughter right to wind up as a sex slave to a reportedly very violent and ruthless young man.

"I would be prepared to do that," Hemmingway agreed.

"Perfect. I'm sure my son will be very pleased. But you need to be patient, Xenos. Do not be rash. The foolish rush in without proper forethought, the wise analyze every angle before making one move. You have already failed once so now you lack the element of surprise. Don't make another mistake."

With that, Grigoriy stood and sauntered out of the office, leaving Hemmingway fuming, he detested being dismissed like that.

What was supposed to be an easy in-and-done murder of his traitorous daughter, a random and very tragically senseless death, had now grown into something that required more thought and attention than he cared to give it.

He just wanted her out of the way.

Working alongside Prey Security, they just might be able to bring him down. There was no way he could let that happen. Not when he was so close to having all the power and control he could ever want.

The entire world would be at his fingertips.

No stupid girl was going to change that.

Skye was going to be taught a lesson. Never mess with the man who gave you life. He had created her, and she was his to do with as he chose. If the attempted murder and the burning down of her clinic weren't enough to have her running far and fast from Caleb Quinn, then he would sell her off to Grigoriy Golubev.

Hemmingway had always believed Caleb was trouble. The

number of times the boy had led his daughter astray was more than he could count. Really, it was Caleb's fault that Hemmingway had been forced to take such a heavy hand with Skye, therefore the reason anyone had a chance to gather blackmail on him.

Perhaps he should take both of them out of the equation.

Getting rid of his daughter and her lovesick puppy would bring him immense satisfaction.

CHAPTER EIGHT

December 3rd
6:15 P.M.

Was Skye okay?

Brick wanted to head inside and check on her, but he was trying to be respectful and give her some space to process what she'd been through.

Her friend had left about an hour ago. Ashleigh Christou had paused before getting into her car, stared across the street, and looked at him with a contemplative expression. There was no hostility in her face now, no suspicion either, and he wondered what had changed.

If the friend had left then that meant Skye was okay.

It had to.

But what if it didn't?

What if she'd just been pretending she was okay so her friend didn't worry? What if she was in there, in the place she'd already almost lost her life in such a traumatic manner, scared, upset, and crying?

Alone.

He had to curl his fingers into fists so he didn't reach for the door handle. He just needed to see her. Even for a second. Just so he knew she was okay. A glimpse through the window would suffice, anything so his racing heart could finally calm.

Then as though he'd conjured her right out of his mind, the front door to her home opened and she stepped out. She was still dressed in the sweatpants and hoodie she'd thrown on last night, her feet were bare, but she didn't seem to notice it as she wrapped her arms around herself and walked down the path that led from the porch to the sidewalk.

Brick didn't think.

He was out of the car and moving toward her before he even realized it.

Was she okay?

Did she need him?

"Honey, you okay?" he asked when he reached her. She was pale, her face free of makeup making the bruises and marks of exhaustion under her eyes look so much darker. Without thinking, he reached up and smoothed a finger under one eye, wishing he could wipe away her fear.

"Hanging in there. I was just …"

"Just what, sweetheart?"

"Coming to see if you were still out here."

"Nowhere else I'm going to be. You're in danger and I won't let anyone hurt you."

Something flitted through her eyes, and she chewed on her bottom lip again causing his hormones to go crazy. Brick reined them in though because this wasn't about sex, it was about rebuilding the connection he had severed with his selfish thoughtlessness.

"Because you feel bad and guilty about what you did?" she asked.

"No, my beautiful sun, moon, and stars. Because I love you and I won't let anyone hurt what's mine."

Her expression settled and she looked over her shoulder at her open door. "Did you want to come in for dinner?"

His heart stuttered in his chest.

She'd come out here specifically for him. To invite him to come in and have dinner with her. Relief hit him hard and something warm and soft unfurled inside him.

Maybe this wasn't hopeless.

Maybe all wasn't lost.

"Honey, nothing would make me happier than to spend some time with you. I'd love to have dinner with you."

"Okay. Come on in then."

Although she was clearly nervous, Skye didn't back peddle as she led him inside her home and closed the door behind them. Immediately, her two poodles ambled over, sniffing at the hand he extended. Once he'd given them pets they lost interest and wandered off to flop down onto their beds.

Even though he'd been in here the night he saved her from certain death this was the first time he'd really had a chance to look around. The house was beautiful. Wooden floorboard that had been stained a dark brown, and a beautiful fireplace with a marble mantle. The walls were wallpapered at the top with white wainscoting at the bottom. Each room had different wallpaper, but they were all floral.

Skye led him through the living room, dining room, and into the kitchen at the back. "Dinner is nothing fancy," she told him, "just pasta in a plain tomato sauce. I wasn't in the mood to cook much."

"Pasta is perfect," he assured her. Better than the takeout he had planned to order later and have delivered to Skye's place where he would have met the delivery driver in the front yard to pay for it.

"There's soda, and juice in the fridge if you're thirsty. Milk too," she added with a small smile. As a kid he had been obsessed with milk, and one summer they'd made milkshakes every day, experimenting with flavors. Some had been delicious, others disastrous as they combined unusual pairings just for fun.

"Sit, I got it." Brick nudged her out of the way when she went to dish them both up bowls.

"Thanks." Skye sunk wearily into a chair at the table while he bustled about her kitchen, filling the bowls she had on the counter, getting cutlery, finding glasses, and pouring them both glasses of sparkling apple juice.

When he joined her at the table, he found she was watching him with a funny expression on her face. "What?"

"I've been thinking about what you said to me the other night, and Ashleigh and I talked about it. About everything, our friendship, and how it ended, and that you've tried reaching out to me a few times over the years before you showed up here a few days ago. I'm sorry I never replied to any of those attempts, I don't think I was ready then."

Brick froze.

Did she mean what he thought she meant?

"And now?" he asked.

"Now I realize that even though you hurt me very badly, you have apologized, and I believe that you mean it."

"I do, honey. I mean it more than anything," he assured her. "Hurting you like that will always be the biggest regret of my life. I wish I could take it back, but I can't, it's out there, and I hate that no matter what it will always be between us. All I can do is tell you once again how very sorry I am and how much your forgiveness would mean to me."

"You have it."

He hardly dared to believe she was actually saying this. "I have it?"

"My forgiveness."

Dropping his fork, he scrambled to close the small distance between them and dropped to his knees beside her chair, taking her small hands in his much larger ones. "Say it, baby, please. I need to hear you say that *you* forgive *me*."

"I forgive you, Caleb."

Dragging her against him, Caleb was aware he was probably holding her too tightly, but he couldn't seem to loosen his grip.

The relief was overwhelming.

Never had he thought this day would come.

"Thank you, Skye. You will never know what that means to me. I don't deserve your forgiveness but I'm going to take it."

Tilting her head back she smiled at him. It was a little strained, but they were making progress. Baby step by baby step they were getting closer to where he wanted to be.

Releasing her slowly, he set her back in her chair and returned to his. "You're amazing, do you know that?"

"Caleb," she said slowly, and a little of the relief he'd been feeling faded away.

"What?"

"I forgive you, I truly do, and I mean it from the very bottom of my heart. I don't want to hold a grudge any longer, it's hurting me and it's hurting you, but being around you is still painful."

He winced at her words, and she looked upset.

Brick understood she wasn't doing this to hurt him, but it did.

Forgiveness was one thing, but he wanted more.

He wanted her.

All of her.

"I want you to leave. If you think I'm in danger then I'll talk to the cops and get a recommendation for someone I can hire to watch over me. It will be tight swinging the cost, but I don't want to die a horrible death alone in my home, so I'll find a way to make it work."

Despite her desire to push him away, Brick smiled. His sweet, stubborn girl hadn't changed. He would bet his entire life savings that she hadn't spent a single cent of the money in her trust fund. She wanted to prove that she could make it on her own and not just because she got a leg up from her rich senator father.

"Oh, honey, you don't get it yet, do you?"

"Get what?" she asked, brows furrowed.

"How much I love you. I don't just regret that I hurt you, Skye, I regret that I lost you. I want you back."

"Caleb—"

Reaching across the table, he touched a finger to her lips. "I don't want to cause you more pain, honey, believe me, that is the absolute last thing in the world I want to do, but I'm not going to just walk away. I won't give up on you. If it takes me the rest of my life, I *will* win back your heart and your trust. Earning your forgiveness was the first step, but I want more. I want it all. There should have never been any doubt in my mind that you were the woman I should have chosen, but make no mistake about it, it has always been you. You are the only woman in the world that I want. The only one I need."

Locking his gaze onto hers, Brick stood slowly, and once again moved so he was beside Skye, who had to tilt her head up to maintain eye contact.

Like she was in a trance it seemed she couldn't look away either.

Very slowly he lowered himself until he was kneeling beside her.

"I'm going to kiss you now, honey," he whispered, giving her time to pull away if this wasn't what she wanted. Just because he wasn't going to walk away didn't mean he would force himself on her.

When she didn't move, he leaned in and captured her lips in a kiss that had been a lifetime in the making.

* * * * *

December 3rd
6:36 P.M.

She had waited a lifetime for this kiss.

It was worth it.

As a content sigh rolled through her, Skye knew it was *more* than worth it.

It was everything.

Caleb's hands framed her face, tilting it so he could get a better angle, and when his tongue touched her lips, seeking entrance to her mouth, she happily obliged.

Was this what heaven felt like?

Skye had to believe that it did. What could be better than this warm, soft feeling that enveloped her, transporting her to a plane of existence she hadn't realized existed?

When he drew back, she mewed a small sound of protest.

"Is this okay?" Caleb asked. His dark eyes were so serious, so uncertain, so unlike the man she had always known.

It was weird seeing Caleb like this. Not because she wanted him to suffer, she wasn't that petty, just because he'd hurt her didn't mean she wanted him to hurt in return. Keeping her distance and ignoring him these last fifteen years had been about protecting herself not about punishing him.

Now that she'd let go of the pain he'd caused her she felt free.

Up until a few seconds ago, she had been so sure she couldn't maintain any sort of relationship with Caleb because all she had to offer him was forgiveness.

But now …

In this moment …

Skye felt like she could give him everything.

"More than okay," she whispered.

His entire being seemed to relax and there was a light in his eyes that she remembered from their childhood.

Responding to that light, her soul seemed to brighten and this time she was the one to lean in and start the kiss.

Caleb's long fingers tangled in her hair, his palms warm against her skin. Not content just to kiss him, Skye placed her hands on his chest and began to explore his amazing physique.

Since she hadn't seen him since they were kids, all of this was new to her. Back then, he'd had a teen's body, tall and lanky, his muscles just beginning to develop. Now he'd filled out into a man.

A very big man.

She had never seen a man like this, certainly never been touched by one. And Caleb wasn't just touching her he was consuming her.

"More," the word fell from her lips with no conscious thought. Skye wasn't thinking right now, she was just feeling.

And her body was telling her that a kiss wasn't enough.

"Not yet, baby," Caleb said, his breath warm against her lips. "You don't trust me yet."

Those words touched her heart. If you'd asked her just a week ago if there was anything Caleb could say to her to get her to forgive him, she would have answered with an emphatic no. Yet those heartfelt words he'd given her the other day were real. She could tell that they were. He wasn't just telling her what he knew she wanted to hear, he was truly sorry that he had hurt her so deeply.

That mattered.

It changed everything.

Desire flooded her system, making her almost delirious with need. She didn't want to wait. She'd already waited much too long to have this man.

"Now, please," she begged. Skye had never begged for a man before. The few times she'd been intimate it was while she was in a relationship, sex had just been a given once they were both ready to take that step. Both her previous boyfriends, the one she'd dated in college, and one she'd broken up with just before starting her practice, had been nice guys but there hadn't been this spark.

They weren't Caleb.

Even while she hated him for hurting her, there was part of her soul that recognized him.

Soul mates.

There was no other way to describe their relationship. From the moment they had first met, Skye had known Caleb was special. She'd believed he would never hurt her like her father did. Never stand by while someone inflicted pain on her like her mother did. Never pretend everything was okay when they knew it wasn't like the staff who worked at their home.

But he had hurt her.

Because he was human and he'd made mistakes.

Skye certainly wasn't perfect, she'd made her own share of mistakes, starting with never telling anyone what happened inside her home. If he'd known, she knew deep in her heart that Caleb would have claimed her so much sooner. He would never have stood by and let her father beat her.

"Skye ..."

Not going to be deterred, she shoved his sweater up and touched his bare skin. Hard muscles, and smooth skin, Skye traced his six-pack, marveling at his exquisite physique. The indentations of his six-pack were a thing of magic and when her greedy hands delved lower, heading determinedly toward the tent in his jeans, she felt those muscles flex beneath her touch.

"Skye," Caleb started again.

"I need you," she said softly as she unzipped his jeans. "I feel like a part of me has been missing all my life. Please, Caleb. Give me that piece of myself. Don't deny me that. Please."

When she slipped her hand inside his pants and cupped his impressive length through his boxers he growled and stood, sweeping her up into his arms in one smooth move.

"Not taking you in the kitchen like a sex-starved animal," he said as he headed for the stairs.

Skye didn't care where they were so long as he was with her.

Touching her.

Bringing her a pleasure she hadn't been able to find with another man.

She'd had orgasms before, but never during sex, always on her own with a toy. Was it because she just wasn't with the right man or because there was something wrong with her?

In her bedroom, Caleb set her on her feet, and when she went to pull off her clothes—or rip them off in a frenzy—he stopped her.

"Let me, honey."

Feeling a little awkward, Skye let her hands drop to her sides, standing there not quite sure what to do. She'd never been seduced like this. Sex had always just been in bed before they went to sleep, fast, unfulfilling, knowing that her partner didn't care enough to make sure it was good for her and that part of it was her fault for keeping a wall between them.

Gripping the hem of her hoodie, Caleb lifted it slowly, letting the pads of his thumbs brush across her stomach. There were callouses, reminding her of what he did for a living, he was a protector, a hero. He put his life on the line to make the world a safer place.

He was putting his life on the line now for her.

She wasn't wearing a bra because she was still wearing the same clothes she'd thrown on last night when she got the call about her clinic. As his thumbs traced between her breasts, his knuckles grazed her already pebbled nipples and a shiver rocked through her, heat pooled between her legs.

Even though she wanted to hurry him up, get him touching her where she wept for him, she was enjoying this.

Pulling the hoodie over her head and down her arms, he let it fall discarded on the floor but kept his hold on her hands. He stroked each finger, then brought her hand to his lips and touched soft kisses to the tip of each of her fingers.

"These hands are so small, so delicate, fragile, yet so strong. You hold life and death in these fingers," he marveled as he kissed her palms. "And these are perfection." Releasing her hands, he claimed her breasts. He cupped them and his rough palms caused the most delightful friction against her hard nipples.

Losing her mind as sensations she'd only read about assaulted her body, Skye moaned, and thrust her chest out seeking more.

Needing more.

His eyes were bright, alive, and brimming with desire.

For her.

This gorgeous hunk of a man thought she was attractive, and when he looked at her like that she felt attractive. She felt beautiful.

Scooping her up, he cupped her backside, his fingers kneading, so close to where she wanted him that she mindlessly ground her throbbing center against his hard ridge.

"Mmm, that feels amazing, baby. Does it feel good for you?" Caleb asked as the tip of his tongue darted out to touch one of her nipples, then blew on it, causing her brain to go haywire.

"Feels so good, too good," she murmured.

"I'm going to make you feel a whole lot better, baby. Hold on."

When she had her hands braced against his shoulders, he took one of her breasts into his mouth. His tongue did amazing things to her, swirling across her nipples, then suckling hard, making her back arch as she sought more of his heat.

More of his anything.

As he tended to first one breast and then the other, Skye rocked her hips against his length. It throbbed, it twitched, it pulsed, it was like the appendage had a mind of its own and it wanted to bury itself inside her.

Carrying her toward the bed, he dropped them down in one smooth movement, careful to keep his weight from crushing her.

"You're wearing too many clothes," she complained, trying to shove away his shirt. "Need to get them off."

"Later." His hand circled her wrist tugging it away, and then he was shoving her sweatpants down her legs. "Need to get inside you soon or I'm going to embarrass myself and come like a teenager."

Beneath her pants she was bare, and he groaned as he slid a finger along her center, collecting her juices. He swirled them around her needy bud before a finger prodded at her entrance.

"Tell me what you like, baby," he urged as one thick finger slid inside her.

"I … I like that," she said breathily.

The smile he gave her was pure sex. "Then you're going to love this."

Another finger filled her, and his thumb found her bundle of nerves, working with expert precision.

"Like that," she said as her breathing grew ragged.

Feelings were building inside her and she didn't know whether to embrace them or run from them.

They were too much.

Too good to be true.

But Caleb didn't stop his delicious assault, his lips found hers as his fingers thrust into her, grazing a spot inside her she'd read about but doubted existed. His thumb never left her bud, and she was powerless to stop the crescendoing pleasure.

It built until nothing else existed.

Until it consumed her.

"Caleb!" she screamed as it hit a peak and her entire world dissolved into fiery stardust.

"Beautiful, baby." He was looking at her almost in wonder as he climbed off the bed and shoved his jeans off. Then he froze. "Don't have protection, honey. I didn't come here for sex, I came to win your trust back."

"I'm clean and on birth control," Skye said.

His entire body seemed to turn to stone. "Are you sure? I've never done it without a condom. I'm clean too though."

"I'm sure." All she wanted was Caleb's body joined to hers. It wouldn't fix everything, wouldn't magically rebuild the bridge between them that had been broken fifteen years ago, but it was a good first step.

Cupping her cheek, he leaned down and touched soft kisses to her forehead, her cheeks, her lips. "Thank you, for trusting me with this."

When his boxers came off, Skye's mouth dropped open. He was so big. Was he even going to fit inside her?

"Relax, honey," he said as though reading her mind, and stretched his larger body out over hers. "That's why I wanted to get you off first, need you to be ready for me. But you'll come again before I do."

"Don't think I can come again."

"Oh, baby, you can."

His confidence was sexy and when she felt his length at her entrance, she lifted her hips off the bed and took him inside her.

"Easy, honey," he said as he moved slowly, filling her bit by bit until he was buried completely inside.

Then he began to move.

Pulling out then thrusting back in.

His pace was lazy at first, and Skye didn't really expect to come again. She'd come once already and she'd never come just from penetration alone.

But then she felt a tingle low in her belly.

"Come, Skye. I want to see that wonder fill your eyes again."

"Can't, I … can't."

"You will."

Caleb increased his pace, his gaze never left hers, and something passed between them. A connection forged that she didn't think could ever be broken. Then he reached between them, touched her where their bodies joined, claiming her already overly sensitive bud and rolling it between his thumb and forefinger.

The touch made her fall apart all over again.

She cried out as her release overwhelmed her, consumed her, reached out its tendrils through every part of her body.

Vaguely she was aware of Caleb finding his own pleasure high, emptying himself inside her, claiming her in a different way.

When the haze of ecstasy cleared, she found him watching her with a tender smile.

Without a word, he kissed her forehead, then eased out of her. He entered her bathroom, returning a moment later with a warm washcloth that he used to clean between her legs. Once he'd returned it to the bathroom he joined her on the bed, lifting her enough so they could get under the covers, then tucked them both in.

Caleb spooned his large body against her smaller one, covering her in a blanket of safety she'd dreamed of all of her life.

"Sleep now, honey. I have you. I'll always have you."

With his promise ringing in her ears, Skye let her mind drift toward sleep, praying he never betrayed her again.

There would be no coming back from that.

CHAPTER NINE

December 4th
7:20 A.M.

Skye was so soft in his arms.

So small and fragile.

Only Brick knew that his girl was a whole lot tougher than her small stature and delicate features suggested.

In just the last few days, she'd faced him barging back into her life, being attacked and almost raped and murdered, and having her clinic burn down. Not only was she still standing through that tornado of upheaval, but somehow, she had found the strength to offer him forgiveness he wasn't sure he deserved.

Tough as any SEAL he'd ever worked with.

After sex last night, she'd crashed and crashed hard, had barely stirred throughout the night, just snuggled in his arms and gotten the rest she so badly needed. They'd never gone down to actually eat the dinner she'd offered as a peace offering, and he really should wake her and get some food into her. The threat to her was only going to grow and she needed to keep her strength up, plus he wanted to take care of her.

For as long as he could remember, Skye had been going it alone. Now he suspected there was more going on in her life than he'd realized, but even back then as kids he'd known she didn't have much of a relationship with her parents.

Now she had him, and he intended to make sure she never lacked for anything, especially love.

Brick wasn't even going to pretend that he wasn't madly in love with Skye.

Always had been.

Might have taken him a while to figure out it was more than just friendship, but he'd known that for more than a decade now. Part of him had always recognized that she was his, but he'd been young and stupid and a little slow to get with the program.

He knew the exact second Skye woke.

Her body immediately stiffened, and he could already feel her emotional withdrawal even if she was plastered against him.

Guess things looked different in the cold light of day.

"Caleb," his name fell from her lips with a tinge of regret, and something inside him went cold.

Did she regret what they'd done?

They shouldn't have had sex. He knew that, had known it last night as well. Now not only was he the man who had betrayed her, but he also the one who had taken advantage of her while she was vulnerable and dealing with a lot. But he'd been weak, given in to temptation. Was he now going to pay the price for that?

Needing to know just how much he'd set back the tentative trust they were painstakingly rebuilding, he hauled her over so she was lying across his front, and hooked a finger under her chin.

"Do you regret last night?" he asked. They were both adults, there was no point in beating around the bush. If he now had another hurdle to overcome, he wanted to know it up front.

Skye's expression softened. "No. No, Caleb. I don't regret it, I'm just not sure it was the best idea."

The cold knot inside him thawed a little. "Why? What's worrying you the most right now?"

She hesitated, and he wanted to soothe all her fears away.

Wanted her to trust him completely even as he knew that was hypocritical given he was still keeping major secrets from her.

Secrets he had to pray never came out.

Because if Skye knew he wasn't being one hundred percent honest with her then any hope he had at strengthening this little tendril of a bond would be gone.

Forever.

"I know we grew up together, but we don't really know each other anymore."

"Ask me anything," Brick said immediately.

There was still hesitation in her eyes, and he wondered if she was going to throw that up as a barrier between them. Use it as an excuse to keep her distance. He couldn't blame her, it would take time for her to learn to trust him again. Forgiving him was one thing but trusting him not to hurt her again was quite another.

But he wanted her trust.

So very badly.

Would do anything to get it back.

Undo what he'd done.

"Can you tell me about your job?" Skye eventually asked. "I know you were in the military and that you now work for Prey Security, but I don't know any details."

"I was a SEAL," he told her.

"Wow, that's amazing. I mean, I could guess that you were special forces because your body is ..." Skye trailed off and her cheeks turned the most adorable shade of red.

"You think I'm hot, baby?" he asked, lifting his head to nip at her bottom lip.

She rolled her eyes and huffed a laugh. "You know you're hot, you don't need me to stroke your ego."

"Maybe I do," he said, allowing a hint of vulnerability to seep into his tone. Sure, Brick knew he was a good-looking man, women ogled him regularly, but those women meant nothing to him. He wanted to know that his woman was attracted to him, not just to his body but to all of him.

Skye's eyes narrowed as though she wasn't sure if he was playing her, but whatever she saw in his eyes made her soften again and she touched a kiss to the tip of his nose. "You're hands down the best-looking man I've ever seen. I thought you were hot when we were kids, and you've certainly filled out since then."

"You are the single most beautiful thing I've ever laid eyes on," he told her.

"Caleb, you don't have to …"

Hating that she didn't know how gorgeous she was, he cut her off with a kiss. Never again would his girl doubt anything about herself, especially how much he was attracted to her.

"The most beautiful," he whispered against her lips.

When she lifted her head, she had a worried look on her face. "I have another question."

"Nothing you can't ask me."

"You and … Mirabella … were you the one who ended things or was she?"

The naked vulnerability in her face gutted him.

And knowing he wouldn't give her the answer she wanted hurt so much worse.

"She left me while I was on my first deployment."

Skye flinched as though he'd inflicted a physical blow.

If he could rewrite history, he would go back and do what he should have done and asked Skye out before any other girl came along. Or he would have ended things with Mirabella long before she'd left him, he'd already known that he didn't love her.

When Skye tried to move, he locked an arm around her waist, holding her against him. "If she didn't, I would have broken up with her anyway."

"You don't have to say that." Her tone was so very defeated, and it tore at his insides.

"I'm not lying to you, honey. I was young, stupid, and desperately wanted my father's approval. He wanted me to date Mirabella, thought she was a good match for me, for what he wanted for my future. After I lost you, things started to change. I started to realize no matter what I did it would never be good enough for my father, he was always going to want more, always find fault, and always withhold his love because he didn't really love me."

Someone who could use love as a weapon clearly didn't know what it was.

Once he'd accepted that, it had given him the strength he needed to break free and live his own life.

"I prioritized myself back then. What I wanted, or at least what I thought I wanted. But once I lost your love, I realized I was alone in the world. My parents wanted to use me, so did Mirabella, and I wanted to be in charge of me. That's why I enlisted. I wanted my life to mean something, I wanted to be a man who was worthy of you. By the time I deployed, I already knew I didn't love Mirabella or see a future with her. It was *you* I thought about when I was going through the hell of Hell week. It was *you* I thought of every time my team went on a mission and I knew I might not make it home. Ah, baby, I wish I could go back and make it so I never hurt you. Never destroyed what we shared."

His voice was ragged, and there were tears on Skye's cheeks. The emotion in the room was palpable, but he could feel their bond growing, strengthening. Giving Skye the honesty she deserved was helping her to trust him again.

"I've had a taste of you now, Skye. I know what you feel like when I'm buried inside you, I know what you sound like when you let go, I know how amazingly strong you are in forgiving me. I'm hooked on you, Skye, and I'm not walking away, not giving up. I'm going to spend the rest of my life loving and protecting you."

* * * * *

December 4th
11:43 A.M.

"Oh, my goodness. You slept with him!"

Ashleigh's squealed exclamation had Skye's head jerking up in surprise.

"How could you possible know that?" she asked.

"I can tell just by looking at you. You did, right? You slept with the guard dog guy."

Was it really written all over her face?

Skye would be more embarrassed, but she was here at the clinic, seeing what could be salvaged, and she'd told the rest of her employees there was no need for them to come in so she was here alone. No one else to see that she'd had wild passionate sex last night.

Okay, so it wasn't really wild, but it had been passionate. Hands down the best she had ever had. Better than all the girlish dreams she'd had of her and Caleb making love. Better than she could ever have imagined.

But she didn't want everyone who saw her knowing, that was mortifying.

"Yeah, Caleb and I slept together," she admitted, dropping her head into her hands.

"And you're not happy about it?" Ashleigh asked.

Happy about it?

Yes and no.

Problem was, she didn't know which one was going to win out.

"Talk to me, Skye, we can work this out."

Slowly, she lifted her head. She *did* need to talk about it. It was just that she wasn't used to talking things through with anyone. Ashleigh was her very best friend in the whole world, and they talked about everything, everything except her and her feelings. Because opening up and letting anyone in was hard for her. To say she had trust issues would be a major understatement.

Trusting for her was almost impossible.

But Ashleigh was standing there looking at her with such empathy and she found that for once she *did* want to talk things out.

Wasn't like it could make things worse.

"I don't know if I made a *huge* mistake," Skye admitted.

"You can't forgive him?"

"No, that's not it. I can. I have. I'm ready to move on and knowing that he really feels bad about it helped a lot."

"So, what's the problem?"

"I don't trust myself when it comes to Caleb."

"Because of what he said to you?"

"I don't want to make it seem like my forgiveness isn't genuine, because I wouldn't have slept with him if I hadn't forgiven him, but at the back of my mind I keep wondering if this thing between us is real."

"You want it to be real though?"

"I think I do, and that scares me."

"What specifically scares you?"

"Caleb is saying *all* the right things, he's sincere, and sweet, and …"

"Hot," Ashleigh added with a grin.

Skye huffed a chuckle. "Yeah, he's hot. The thing is he's perfect, and he hasn't said a single wrong thing. But fifteen years ago, I never could have suspected that he would hurt me like he did. It came completely out of the blue. I wasn't expecting it, didn't ever think anything could make Caleb cut me out of his life like that. What if I let him back in and he does it again?"

"Oh, Skye." Ashleigh pulled her in for a hug. "I can see why that would scare you, but Caleb isn't a stupid kid anymore, he's a man now. I don't think he'd play games like that anymore. Not that being a kid was an excuse, he made the choice to hurt you and he's owned up to that. Why would he come back into your life, fight to get you to forgive him, and then hurt you again?"

"I don't know." Just because she didn't have a reason didn't mean it wasn't so.

"Okay, let's talk that through then. Here, let's sit." Ashleigh guided her over to the couple of folding chairs Caleb had found somewhere and brought in so she could sit while she sifted through what was left of the clinic she'd been so proud to start and build into something successful.

Caleb was being so thoughtful. Attending to things she hadn't even thought of, and it only made her that much more confused.

"What's your biggest hold up?"

"The timing. I still can't figure out why Caleb was watching my house that first night. He came running in right in time to save me and the only way he could have done that was if he was already outside and saw that I was being attacked. Why was he there? How did he know I was going to be in trouble? I get why he's watching over me now that we know someone sent someone to kill me. But how did he know before it happened?"

"I can't answer those questions for you. Only one person can. Have you asked Caleb?"

Twisting her hands in her lap, Skye dropped her gaze to the floor. "No."

"Why?"

"I'm afraid of what his answer will be. Right now, he's everything that I always dreamed he would be. He's being sweet, and attentive, and he says everything I want to hear, it's almost *too* perfect. What if it's all another game? What if he was the one who sent that man after me and that's how he knew? What if it was a ploy to get me to trust him? I'm already invested in Caleb. I always have been. I've loved him since I was four. I don't want to learn that he's playing with my heart all over again. I don't think I could survive that, Ash."

"Oh, honey. You have to talk to him. The sooner the better. You need to clear the air and find out the truth. Have you heard from the cops?"

"They identified the man, he's some Russian born mercenary. They don't know who sent him after me and I had nothing useful to offer. Who would want me dead? I'm just a local vet. Sure we have some families who lash out when we're unable to save their beloved pet, but none of them would go so far as to hire someone to break into my home and kill me. I honestly have no idea who it is, so I haven't been much—probably no—help to their investigation."

It probably wasn't smart of her, but Skye was more concerned about Caleb and if she could believe what he was offering her was real than she was about knowing someone wanted her dead. And not just dead but wanted her to suffer first.

Caleb had been her whole world, the only good thing she had, until he wasn't.

The fear he would hurt her again was near paralyzing.

"I have one question for you." Ashleigh's hands covered hers and squeezed lightly. "Do you regret sleeping with Caleb?"

It would be so much easier if she did.

Then she could walk away with a clear conscience.

"No."

"Then I think you already know if you made a mistake or not."

"He said he loves me, Ashleigh. He said he's had a taste of me now and he won't walk away, won't give up, that he's hooked. I want to believe him so badly. Even when I hated him I loved him. But I won't let him hurt me again. I can't be stupid and just take everything he says at face value. I have to protect myself. Protect my heart." Skye wasn't trying to be dramatic she just knew that her poor heart couldn't take being betrayed by Caleb again.

"I think you're overthinking things, sweetie. I get not wanting to be hurt again, and you have valid reasons for not wanting to offer this man blind trust. I don't want to diminish how badly he hurt you, and the two of you definitely need to sit down and talk. You have to ask him why he was there that night, voice your fears, don't let them fester, because if you do then they're going to get in the way of what could be an amazing relationship. But for now, just take a step back, let go, and see where things wind up. Maybe they won't go anywhere, but maybe they will."

"I think that maybe I could do that." At least she could give it a try. Putting all this pressure on herself, on Caleb, on trying to figure things out right away, it was too much. If she kept this up, she was going to give herself a break down.

"I'm here for you, Skye. If you and Caleb work out, I'll be your biggest supporter and I'll be so happy for you. And if it doesn't work out and he hurts you again then I'll kick his smoking hot butt for you."

Skye laughed, glad she had someone in her corner.

Once upon a time Caleb had been the person she'd thought was in her corner. The one person who would never cause her pain.

Life wasn't always fair, and even those you trusted the most could cause wounds that never healed.

They caused the worse kind of pain because you loved them.

She was hopelessly in love with Caleb, and she prayed that he would never hurt her again.

CHAPTER TEN

December 4th
5:39 P.M.

"Okay, honey, that's enough for today."

Skye looked up from her sorting as he walked inside her partially burned down clinic. Since he'd dropped her off here this morning after they'd gotten clearance that the remains were stable, she'd been going through the space, recovering anything salvageable. He'd brought her some lunch a couple of hours ago, but other than that he'd given her some space.

As much as he wanted to wrap his arms around her and keep her tied to his side, he knew she was processing a lot and she needed some space to get her thoughts in order.

Brick couldn't stay away any longer though.

"I'm almost done, just another hour or so," Skye protested.

"No," he said firmly. "Enough for today. We'll come back tomorrow morning to finish off."

After being stuck inside her ruined practice all day, surrounded by the stench of smoke and the lingering damp from the water, she needed to get out, get some fresh air, and let go of the stress he knew being in here for so many hours must have stirred up. His job was to take care of her and that was exactly what he intended to do.

Skye opened her mouth, and he was sure a disagreement was about to come firing out, but then she closed it, dropped her head, and her shoulders sagged like all the fight had drained right out of her. "Okay, I don't like it but you're right. I'm done in for today."

Taking her home, feeding her and getting her into bed at a decent hour was the smart move.

The best move for her.

But he hadn't had her in his life for fifteen very long years and he wanted to soak up as much time with her as possible.

Needed to.

His declaration that he loved her and wasn't going anywhere had carved some inroads, and Skye had told him she didn't regret sleeping with him, but he could see she still had doubts.

Doubts he was determined to erase.

"Can I take you out for dinner, Skye?" Brick felt as nervous as an adolescent asking a girl out on his first ever date.

Skye's head darted up, and she studied him. There was something in her expression, and he wondered if it had to do with her talk with her friend earlier.

Had Ashleigh's guidance been helpful or harmful to his cause?

"A date or as friends?"

It was probably smart to tell her just as friends, that was more likely to get her to agree. But that would be a lie and he couldn't keep heaping lie on top of lie if he wanted any chance at a future with her.

"A date."

She dragged in a long breath and Brick fought the urge to hold his own as he waited for her answer.

An answer that felt way too important.

Like if she said yes it wasn't just to dinner but to giving him a real chance at earning her trust back and making this thing between them work.

"Okay. But I'm not really dressed for dinner, and I smell like smoke."

"We can go back to your place, and you can shower and change." No way was he letting her say yes but then pack peddle and wiggle out of it.

"Sounds like a plan."

Ushering her out to his car—since hers had been at the clinic when the fire was set it had been damaged as well—Brick drove her home, waiting downstairs while she went up to ready herself for their date.

A date he was determined to make use of in winning his girl's heart all over again.

To know he'd had her heart, held its delicate beauty in his hands and thrown it away, left a pain in his own heart he knew would never completely fade. Making things right was as much for his sake as it was for hers. He needed this woman in his life.

Thirty minutes later, he looked up as he heard footsteps on the stairs, and the breath was knocked right out of his lungs.

"You look … stunning … that's not even a strong enough word for how utterly gorgeous you are," Brick stumbled over his words like a tongue-tied teen.

A blush stained Skye's cheeks a pretty shade of red that matched the dress she'd chosen. It was a deep, dark red, was loose enough fitting not to give everything away, but clung to her small but perfectly formed breasts. She'd paired the dress with black knee-high boots, her hair hung in soft waves down her back, and the little mascara she'd added made her long lashes appear endless as they framed her big, brown eyes.

"You look pretty good yourself," she said as she descended the rest of the stairs.

While Skye had been showering and getting ready, he'd changed into a pair of black jeans, a white shirt, and gray sweater. "No one is going to be throwing me a second glance when they get a look at you."

Skye laughed. "Sure. Because women don't drool all over you everywhere you go. You forget how much time we spent together when we were younger. Even as a kid, girls were always falling all over themselves to get your attention."

Reaching out to tuck a lock of hair behind her ear, Brick let his fingertips linger on her skin. "You know there was only one girl who got my attention back then." Only one girl who had held his heart all these years and hadn't even known it.

"You're a smooth talker you are," Skye said with another laugh, this one a little breathy as her gaze dropped to his lips.

If he kissed her now, they'd spend the evening in bed, and while his body ached to make love to her again, first he was going to take her out.

"Come on, let's go. I have reservations for seven at a cute little Italian restaurant if that sounds good?" he asked as he helped her into her coat and led her outside to his truck.

"I love Italian," Skye said.

He knew that. With a Greek father and Italian mother, she'd enjoyed both her cultures, especially the food, and he knew that she had been close with her maternal grandmother before the woman had passed away when Skye was eight.

There were so many things he knew about her, and yet he felt like there was one big piece of the puzzle that he was missing. The reason why it had hurt her so deeply when he'd cut her out of his life. Not that what he'd done wasn't mean, but she'd hinted that he didn't yet grasp why it had cut so deeply.

The ride into town was a quiet one, but not uncomfortable. And when he parked and helped Skye out of the car, he was beyond pleased that when he took her hand in his she didn't pull away.

"I love all the lights at Christmastime," Skye said with a delighted sigh as they walked down the street. All the shop windows were dressed for Christmas, there were lights on all the trees, wreaths hung from the lampposts, and there were a few snowflakes swirling in the air. He couldn't have picked a better night to take her on their first date.

"I remember how disappointed you used to get each holiday season when your parents hired a firm to decorate your house instead of letting you do it."

"They didn't get it. They thought it was about having the best

Christmas decorations money could buy, but I wanted to just enjoy the process. I wanted to talk and laugh, be like a normal family, make traditions and memories that would last me a lifetime. Instead, a whole team of people would come in while I was at school and I'd come home and the house would look like a Christmas wonderland. If only it had *felt* like one."

There was sadness in her tone he ached to take away. "Remember that year we decided to decorate your house together before your parents got it done?"

She huffed a small chuckle. "I remember. You fell off the roof while we were trying to string up lights and broke your arm and your leg. I was so scared when you fell and I couldn't get you to wake up."

"Ah, my first concussion," he joked, but instead of laughing, or even smiling, Skye's smile faded, and dark shadows lurked in her eyes.

Before he could comment on them, she wiped them away and pasted on a smile anyone with eyes could see was fake. "I'm starving, I think I'm going to have lasagna. It's been way too long since I've had any, especially one that didn't just come out of a box."

If his beautiful Skye thought she was going to get away with hiding her pain from him she was sorely mistaken. He'd let it pass for now, enjoy a nice dinner, but he was determined to find out what she'd meant when she'd told him he had no idea how badly he'd hurt her.

The only way to pave the road to the future he wanted was for there to be no more secrets between them.

Which meant sooner rather than later he had to tell her why he had reappeared in her life and pray she wouldn't hold it against him.

* * * * *

December 4th
9:42 P.M.

Skye tossed her head back and laughed.

It felt so good.

Freeing.

When was the last time she'd laughed like this, with such joy and peace in her heart?

It was awful that she couldn't even remember. It wasn't like she hadn't been happy in the years since Caleb broke her heart, she had. She'd had fun at college, finally away from her father and his violence, she'd gone on dates, had some friends, and was proud of her accomplishments.

But there had always been this rock sitting on her chest.

A rock of pain and uncertainty.

Why had Caleb broken her heart?

Why had he been so cruel?

Why had he extinguished the only light she had in her life?

Without him, a part of herself had been missing, but his return had given it back, and slowly his steady presence was healing those old wounds, loosening the constricting band of fear any time she had to put her trust in someone.

"I couldn't believe you went along with that one," Caleb said as he took the key from her hand and unlocked her front door.

"I always went along with your crazy schemes," she reminded him. Those stolen moments of joy were all that got her through the dark times. They were something to hold onto, and honestly, her father was going to beat her no matter what she did, he would always find an excuse to justify it, so she may as well have her fun when she could.

"I know, but this one was crazy *and* dangerous."

"Only because you thought you were way smarter than you were," she teased as she walked through the house to let the dogs inside.

"Hey, figuring out if you could add confetti to fireworks was *your* idea."

"Right, but you were the one that actually wanted to try to make it happen, my wondering was more hypothetical." Skye flopped down onto the couch and after locking the door, Caleb joined her, gently guiding the dogs onto the floor so he could sit beside her and slinging an arm across her shoulders, tucking her close against his side.

"Do I need to remind you we were following *your* plans."

"I was fourteen. What did I really know about creating your own fireworks let alone adding confetti to it?" Playfully she punched at his broad shoulder.

"Well, your internet search skills didn't help us any, we blew up your whole garage, nearly set fire to your house."

"The fireworks *did* go off, and we *did* get confetti everywhere," she said, remembering the loud bang as their homemade fireworks went off before it was supposed to.

"We were lucky we didn't kill ourselves."

They were.

If only Caleb knew just how close she had come to dying because of those fireworks.

Her father had been absolutely livid that they'd destroyed the garage and his favorite vintage car. It was the angriest she'd ever seen him, and she had been convinced he was going to kill her in his rage.

Skye sighed as her joy and peace seeped away.

Caleb being back in her life had helped old wounds to heal, but she suspected that until she was completely honest they would just continue to scab over then be ripped raw all over again.

It was time.

Time to tell him everything.

Shifting so she was facing him, Skye edged backward a little, needing to put a bit of space between them so she could get these words out. Caleb would be only the second person she'd ever told, and she hadn't gone into any details with Ashleigh.

"We need to talk," she announced. Sensing her distress both her dogs moved closer, sitting so they pressed against her legs.

"You ready to tell me what you meant when you said that I had no idea just how badly I'd hurt you?"

Skye gave a shaky nod.

Reaching out, Caleb gave her hands a quick squeeze before withdrawing his, obviously respecting her need to put a little space between them. "You can tell me anything, Skye. I hope you know that. Anything at all."

She gave another nod. Her trust in Caleb was still tentative, repairing but growing, and she knew he would listen and not judge her.

Problem was she judged herself.

"My home life was … bad," she admitted, finally saying the words she should have said to him so many years ago. "Really bad."

"Your dad hit you?" Caleb's entire body was tense, brittle, like one small hit would shatter him.

She was about to deliver that hit.

"He didn't just hit me, Caleb. He was sadistic, took pleasure in causing me pain. It wasn't always physical. There was this box in the attic, a metal box, sometimes he would take me up there, lock me inside it and leave me there overnight. It was small, especially as I started getting bigger, and so dark inside. It was also hot. One summer night when he'd put me in it there was a storm, the power went out, and there was no air conditioning. What little cool air it generated up in the attic was gone, and it was so hot locked inside that box. I remember being so thirsty, drenched in sweat, crying and begging to be let out but nobody came. If anyone else knew I was up there they didn't care enough to check on me. By the time the sun rose, and he came for me I was severely dehydrated."

"Baby," Caleb groaned painfully. "I'm so sorry. I didn't know."

"I didn't want you to know, Caleb." Absently her fingers stroked her dogs' soft fur, taking comfort in their steady presence and complete lack of judgment. "I didn't want anyone to know. I was ashamed and embarrassed, and so terrified of what my father would do if I told. He was wealthy and powerful, I was scared he would be able to pay people off and no one would believe me, no one would help me, and I'd be trapped in that house with him forever."

"I would have believed you, honey." This time when Caleb reached for her hands he didn't pull away and neither did she, now desperately needing this connection.

"He liked to use his fists, always on my back or front, never arms or legs where it might be seen, and definitely not my face. Sometimes he'd fill the bath with freezing water, sometimes hot, and shove me in it, pushing me under and holding me there. When he was really angry, he would pick me up and throw me across the room, he broke bones a few times doing that. There were days he wouldn't let me eat anything, and days where he'd take my clothes and make me walk around the house naked. No one ever did anything. They never *did* anything," she repeated on a sob.

"Oh, baby, come here. Come here," he murmured as he scooped her up and set her on his lap, rocking her as the dam burst and tears broke free in a messy outburst.

Skye lost track of how long they sat like that, her curled up in Caleb's lap, face pressed against his neck as he rocked her and stroked the length of her spine with his hand, rubbed circles on her back, and whispered soothingly in her ear. His words didn't register but the soft sound of his voice warmed her, reassured her that she wasn't alone. Her dogs too offered their own comfort, she could feel their wet noses pressed against her legs and hear their soft whines.

"You got punished after you followed me into one of our crazy schemes, didn't you?" he asked brokenly.

"I knew the risks, Caleb, and chose to follow you. I couldn't control what my father was doing but I could find joy where I could. You brought me joy. You were everything to me, my lifeline, the light in my dark world."

"Then I carelessly extinguished that light."

Even though she knew it would gut him, Skye nodded. "After you were gone, I thought about ending things. One night I climbed up onto the roof. I was going to jump but I couldn't make myself do it."

Horror marred Caleb's handsome features. "Oh, baby, I am so sorry. So very sorry. I know no apology can fix what I broke, and if you had of died because of me I would never have forgiven myself. But you have to know how much I regret what I did, even more so knowing how brave you were, how strong, how much you were enduring. I was a stupid, selfish kid, who was so desperate for my father's love I would date the girl he wanted me to, convince myself I was in love with her and had to do what she wanted. In being selfish I hurt the best thing in the world, my sun, moon, and stars. I hate myself a little right now."

Lifting her head, she took his face between her hands, not letting him look away. "I didn't tell you to make you feel worse, Caleb, I swear I didn't."

"I know that, honey." Framing her face with his hands just as she was holding his, he pulled her closer so he could touch his lips to her forehead.

"I just wanted you to understand, no more secrets between us. If we're going to build something here, have a relationship, become a couple, then I want to do it the right way. I should have told you back then, I know I should, but I won't ever keep things from you again, I promise. Nothing is more important to me than being honest with you so we can do this right."

Skye would have sworn she saw a flare of guilt in Caleb's dark eyes, but then he was crushing his mouth to hers.

"I love you, Skye. Always have, always will."

"I love you too, Caleb. From the first time I laid eyes on you until I take my final breath. Let's not mess this up again."

CHAPTER ELEVEN

December 4th
10:09 P.M.

Let's not mess this up again.

Skye's words ran through his head leaving shame and guilt in their wake.

Brick knew he *was* going to mess this up again if he didn't tell her the whole truth about why he was here. That it was true he wanted her back in his life, but that he'd also come to see if he could get information from her about her father.

If she ever found out he'd lied to her, even if it was only a partial lie since he had been wanting to get her back for over a decade, she would never forgive him.

Nor would he deserve her forgiveness.

Telling her now was the right thing to do.

But then Skye reached out and touched the bulge in his pants and he sucked in a breath as his body instantly responded.

Grasping her wrist, he gently tugged her hand away. Her gaze turned desolate when she lifted it to meet his.

"You don't want to?" Skye asked. "Did what I tell you change things between us? Did it change how you see me?"

There was so much vulnerability in her voice, and he could see she was placing some amount of blame on herself for what her father had done to her. Brick hated that but he understood it was a manifestation of her guilt for not telling anyone what was happening to her. He also understood why she hadn't. Her father was a wealthy and powerful man and could have paid people off to paint Skye as a liar, or as an emotionally unstable self-harmer out for attention.

If he'd had any doubt about her father's guilt and involvement in Kristoff Mikhailov's plot, he didn't anymore. A man who would abuse his own child was capable of anything.

Right now though, his focus was Skye and soothing her fears.

Crushing his mouth to hers, he wrapped his arms tightly around her, fearing if he let her go he would lose her. Not just would she scramble to put physical distance between them, but emotional distance as well.

Their fledgling relationship was still so small, fragile, that he was afraid one little thing could destroy it.

"Baby, the only thing it changes is that now I think you're even stronger than I did before. I wish you'd told me back then because I would have backed you up, done whatever it took to make sure you were safe, and it makes me regret even more that I chose wrong, but none of that is on you." The jagged scar across his heart from the pain he'd caused Skye had deepened, it was a wound he would have to learn to live with. "You are so brave, so beautiful, and so very strong to have survived that hell."

"So you are still attracted to me?"

Brick hated that there was uncertainty in her tone and was determined to do whatever it took to wipe it away and make sure it never came back.

Shifting her so she was straddling his thighs, he took her hand again and once he'd unzipped, he rested it on his thick, hard length.

"Honey, there is *never* a time where I am *not* wildly, insanely attracted to you. When we were kids I thought you were pretty. When I realized I never should have ended our friendship and tracked you down, I thought you were the most gorgeous thing I had ever laid eyes on. It's always been you, Skye. Always will be. Don't ever doubt that all I have to do is think about you and I get hard."

"Really?"

Nodding at his erection, "You really have to ask?"

"I … I'm already … wet for you," Skye said shyly.

He'd noticed last night that she wasn't altogether confident in her sexuality. She was no virgin—a thought he didn't care to entertain, nor was it fair to since neither was he—but she had seemed surprised to find how easy it was for her to orgasm.

Obviously, her previous lovers hadn't helped her learn what she liked, nor was she confident enough to ask for it.

Brick was determined to help her find that confidence.

"What do you want, baby?" he asked.

Skye's eyes widened in surprise as though she hadn't even thought about it, then her gaze dropped to his lap. "I want to … touch," she said softly as she traced a fingertip from his base to his tip.

"Touch all you want, babe." To show her that this was her show, Brick rested back against the couch and spread his arms.

Pushing down his boxers, she watched as his length sprung free, and then with tentative fingers began to explore. Her touch was soft and gentle, but the more she stroked him the firmer it got as her confidence grew.

With each stroke of her fingertips, sensations began to build, but he didn't want to come until he was buried in her sweet heat, so he gritted his teeth and refused to let himself have any release.

Not yet.

"Strip, babe, let me see every inch of you."

Her gaze darted up, desire making her brown eyes two big glowing orbs. Slowly she stood, her fingers shaking slightly as she stooped to grasp the hem of her dress, pulling it up and over her head.

The most perfect pair of breasts he'd ever seen were covered with red lace and he groaned as his length seemed to sit up and take notice.

Skye grinned, a sexy little smile that made him want to drag her down onto his lap right this second, take her here and now. "You like the bra?"

"Love it, babe."

"I thought of you when I was putting it on."

"Yeah? What were you thinking?"

"Of you undoing the clasp, and … my breasts spilling free into your hands."

"What did I do with them?" he asked, voice husky.

"You … touched them … rolled my nipples between your fingers, then …"

"Then what, baby?"

"You put your … lips on them. Your mouth was so hot, and wet." She shivered, and he didn't think she'd noticed it, but one of her hands had lifted to cover one of her breasts.

"Step out of your boots, Skye," he ordered.

Bending over, she unzipped and removed first one boot and then the other, leaving her in just her lacy bra and stockings.

"Is that matching panties?" he asked on a groan as he caught sight of more red lace.

"I like buying bra and panty sets."

"Babe," he groaned, now all he could picture was Skye parading before him in nothing but bras and panties in every color of the rainbow.

The smile she gave him was everything.

Pressure built in his chest that had nothing to do with sex and how badly he wanted to take her. His love for her was growing with each second they spent together.

"Stockings off."

Skye didn't hesitate to comply, and then she was all creamy white skin and red lace, utterly delectable, the most delicious treat.

And she was all his.

"Come here, babe." Brick patted his lap.

As soon as she was settled, straddling his thighs again, he reached behind her and undid the clasp on her bra, letting her breasts fall into his hands.

"Like this, Skye? Is this what you imagined?" he asked as he captured one breast with his lips, sucking her nipple into the heat of his mouth, while his fingers found the nipple on her other breast and tweaked it.

Skye groaned and thrust her chest forward.

Happy to oblige, Brick feasted on first one breast and then the other, making sure he paid attention to the other with his hand. He was so engrossed in the small breathy moans Skye was making that it took him a moment to realize her hands had claimed him and were sliding up and down his length.

When he was close to coming, he pulled back. "Need to be inside you now, babe."

Grabbing the lacy panties, he yanked.

"Did you just … rip those right off me?" Skye asked, amazed.

"I'll buy you another set," he promised.

"That was so hot, but I'll hold you to that," she teased.

Spanning her waist with both his hands, Brick lifted her and lowered her down on his hard length, inch by delicious inch.

"Are you close, babe?" he asked.

"Yes," she panted as she rocked her hips.

"What do you need to come?"

"It's okay if I don't as long as you do. I can … uh … attend to my … needs later."

"Like hell you will." Is that the kind of men she'd been letting touch her? Ones who'd cared only about getting themselves off and not about making sure their girl was taken care of. Keeping one hand on her hip to hold her still, his other found her throbbing little bud and began to work it while his lips claimed one of her breasts again.

Skye gasped, and he could feel her squirming against him as sensations began to build inside her. Her breathing increased till it was coming in uneven pants, and when his name fell from her lips in a strangled cry, and her internal muscles clamped around him, Brick gripped both her hips and began to thrust inside her, allowing himself his own release.

It seemed to go on and on, a never-ending train of pleasure.

By the time the bright white lights of ecstasy had faded, and he could see again, he found Skye snuggled against his chest, her face pressed against his neck.

"My girl always comes," he murmured, stroking a hand along her spine.

"Because you care about me," she murmured back, her fingers petting his pecs.

Brick pressed his lips to her forehead. "More than anything else in the world."

* * * * *

December 5th
8:34 A.M.

Skye was humming as she climbed out of Caleb's SUV.

Sooner or later, she was going to have to do something about getting herself a new vehicle, but for now, she was kind of enjoying being chauffeured around by her hunky ... boyfriend?

Caleb was her boyfriend now she guessed.

They hadn't really talked about labels, or the future in any specific way. She didn't really know why he had suddenly popped back up in her life, although her heart told her it wasn't for any nefarious purpose. Maybe what he'd said was true, he wanted her back and since she never replied to any of his attempts, he'd decided to track her down in person. Everything else must be just a coincidence.

Because the man who had told her he loved her and wanted to be with her would never do anything to put her life in danger.

"Hold on there." Caleb's arm curled around her waist and he pulled her up against him. Keeping her anchored with his arm, he palmed the back of her head and captured her lips in a toe-curling kiss.

They'd started the day with sex in the shower. Skye had never done that before and had thought it might be a little awkward maneuvering around in the small space, but with Caleb it was nothing short of erotically perfect. She wanted to start every day like that but was Caleb intending to stick around? And what about his job?

Skye knew she should ask but she was too afraid of the answer.

"That's better," Caleb said when he pulled back. "I'm only going to be gone an hour, then I'll be here to pick you up. We can go check in with your insurance company, make sure they have everything they need, then I'm taking my girl out for lunch."

"Sounds perfect. I have a little Christmas shopping left to do, maybe we could do lunch at the mall and then some shopping?" While it was true she wanted to pick up a couple more things for Ashleigh's kids, she also had to get something for Caleb. He'd be staying through Christmas at least, right?

"Shopping?" Caleb groaned, scrunching his nose up.

"Hey." She swatted playfully at his shoulder. "You would always go shopping with me when I asked when we were kids."

"Guess I'm a sucker for anything my girl wants to do." He feathered another kiss across her lips. "You going to be okay here on your own for an hour?"

"Of course. It's daytime, the street is busy enough, and the last couple of days have been quiet. Maybe whoever it was has backed off," she said hopefully.

"Maybe."

"But you don't think so."

"Smart move would be to lay low for a while."

Casting a glance up and down the street, Skye ran her hands up and down her arms, no longer feeling quite as safe.

"Hey." Caleb pulled her into his arms again. "I'm not going to let anyone hurt you. Anyone who tries to get to you has to go through me."

"You're not always going to be here though," she reminded him.

"Like hell I won't."

"But your job, Caleb. I assume you took time off to come and see me but sooner or later you'll have to go back."

Something dark flittered through his eyes and she assumed it was the fear of leaving her alone and unprotected. When he spoke his voice was low and soft. "The only way I'd ever leave you, Skye, is if you ordered me to."

Her brow scrunched. "Well, I'm not going to do that, am I? Silly man."

"I love you, Skye, always remember that. And nothing was more important to me than earning your forgiveness and your trust."

"I know, Caleb."

For a long moment he stared into her eyes as though seeking answers to a question he hadn't asked. Eventually he nodded and dropped one more kiss to her lips. "Be safe."

"You too."

As she watched him drive away, Skye realized she would have to get used to the idea of Caleb in danger. While he hadn't talked much about his job or his team, she knew that what he did was dangerous, even if she wasn't sure on all the details.

Even though he hadn't spoken of wanting to join the military when they'd been kids, it was obvious that he loved his job, and like everything else he did she was sure he was good at it.

Which was a good thing because she didn't want him to fight his way back into her life only to lose him all over again.

When Caleb's vehicle disappeared around the corner, Skye turned and headed inside, wondering what the rest of his team were like. He'd told her their names but that was all, and she decided that would be the topic of conversation at lunch today. Since their reconciliation, she'd told him a whole lot more about her life than he'd told her about his. Probably because he was trying to show her that she was the most important thing to him, but she wanted to know what his life was like, and his team would be a big part of it.

She was humming again as she walked through the damaged waiting room. Not even the fact that it should be full of families and their beloved pets right now instead of sitting empty and partially destroyed could dampen her mood.

Of course, she hated the fact that her practice would need to be rebuilt, but the most important thing was that nobody, including any animals, had been hurt. Skye was confident in Caleb's ability to keep her safe. One look at him, all muscle, strength, and fierce determination, and any would be attacker would be crazy to attempt to take him on.

There wasn't much left to do this morning. The insurance company needed a detailed list of everything that had been destroyed and would need to be replaced, most of which she'd done yesterday. Today she just wanted to look through and see if there were any personal things here that could be salvaged.

Sometimes grateful families gave her small gifts for saving their animal family members, and while Skye always told them it wasn't necessary, that the real gift was in saving the life of a pet, she treasured those tokens. Most had no financial value, they were just little animal themed items like the dog shaped bowl she kept treats in, and masks with bunnies on them she wore during surgeries, and she was hoping some of those things might be salvageable.

Skye had been working for a while when the sound of muffled footsteps caught her attention. That must be Caleb back. For such a big guy he moved so silently.

"You're going to have to teach me how you ..." Skye trailed off as she turned around.

It wasn't Caleb stalking through the room toward her.

It was a man dressed in ragged, dirty clothes. His face was smeared with grime as were his hands, and he had a hoodie pulled down low, partially hiding his appearance. But something felt wrong.

Even though he looked like the kind of homeless druggie she'd thought Caleb was that first night he'd made an appearance back in her life, there was something off about this man.

His eyes.

They weren't glazed with whatever drug he'd taken to get his high.

Instead, they were clear and filled with a single minded purpose.

Her.

This man was just pretending to be a druggie searching for a fix in case anyone saw him, but he had been sent by whoever wanted her dead, she was sure of it.

As the man moved toward her, Skye darted sideways, putting the metal exam table between herself and her attacker.

The man growled and lunged for it, trying to shove it up against the wall, pinning her in place. But he didn't know that although the table had wheels it also had brakes. She moved the table sometimes, to get a weak and injured animal to the operating table, or into one of the cages for monitoring, but a panicking animal could send the table flying if she wasn't careful, so the brakes were always on.

Pressing both palms to the table, she readied her weight, then kicked out with one foot, expertly releasing the brake, and shoved with all her might.

Caught off-guard, the man stumbled backward and hit the floor with a groan.

Knowing that all she'd done was buy herself some time, Skye gave the table another shove, this time sending it crashing down on top of her attacker.

Hoping that was enough, Skye skittered around him, careful not to get too close, and headed for the front of the clinic. Even though the back door was closer, if she went out it and the man recovered too quickly she would never make it through the parking lot and down the driveway to the street.

But if she went out the front door there would be people about.

Safety.

Her attacker would be taking a major risk going after her then.

Behind her he was swearing and likely trying to get out from under the table, but she didn't waste time looking over her shoulder.

Skye made it to the door to the waiting room when a hand clamped around her ponytail and yanked her back.

CHAPTER TWELVE

December 5th
9:22 A.M.

The first thing he saw as he walked through the door of Skye's clinic was her eyes, wide and terrified as she was yanked back into her exam room.

"Caleb!"

A man's voice cursed and the next thing he knew Skye was being shoved forward and went stumbling through the room toward him.

Automatically, Brick closed the distance between them and caught her against him before she hit the ground.

The sound of footsteps said that whoever had been there was now leaving in a hurry so he didn't get caught.

"What happened?" he demanded, keeping Skye tucked against him where he knew she was safe. His hand had gone to his weapon, but his choices were leave Skye alone and vulnerable and go after her attacker, take her with him as he went after the assailant and put her back in danger, or let the man get away.

With choices like that all he could do was let the man run.

Skye's safety came first.

"I don't know. One minute I was alone and the next I heard someone. I thought it was you but it wasn't." Skye's voice shook and her entire body trembled as she burrowed deeper into his embrace.

"It's all right, honey. I'm here now. You're safe," he soothed, tightening his hold on her. Brick's gut clenched at the next question he had to ask. "Did he hurt you?"

Against his chest Skye's head shook.

Not convinced, his hands covered her shoulders, and he eased her back enough that he could see her face. "I need words, Skye. Did he hurt you?"

Her face was pale, and although no tears fell her eyes were shimmering. "He tried to shove the exam table into me, but he didn't know it had brakes. I flicked them off and shoved it at him. He fell and I ran. He grabbed my hair as I was coming through the door then you were there. You saved me." The tears that had been threatening to spill free began to tumble down her cheeks.

Skye's shaking intensified until it felt like she was going to shake herself right apart. She was going into shock, and he had to call the cops, report this new attack, then he had to figure out a way to convince her to go with him back to New York. Whoever was after Skye—and he still believed it was her father, even more so now he knew what he'd done to her as a child—wasn't giving up, and he wanted his team as back up before they escalated.

Scooping her up, Brick carried her out to his SUV. Balancing her, he opened the door, set her on the passenger seat, then walked around and climbed into the driver's seat. Turning on the engine, he cranked up the heat and angled the vents in Skye's direction.

Quickly he shot off a text to the detective handling Skye's case, and then to his team updating them and informing them he hoped to be flying in later today and would need a ride from the airport.

Once he was done, he turned his full attention to Skye. She was curled in on herself, shoulders hunched, arms wrapped around her stomach, still trembling.

Muttering a curse, he dragged her over and into his lap, fixing the vents so the hot air was now aimed on his side of the vehicle.

"It's okay now, honey. You're safe," he crooned in her ear as he rubbed his hands up and down her arms, trying to warm her.

"I thought he was going to kill me," her words were muffled against his chest, but he could hear the fear in them.

"But he didn't, because you fought him off." Brick was so very thankful for Skye's determination and strength, she hadn't given up and that was likely the only reason she wasn't dead now. Given the mishap with the first attack he was sure the person orchestrating this would have told the next man he sent after her to get it over and done with quickly so there was no chance of error.

"If you hadn't arrived when you did, he would have gotten me though." The stark fear in her eyes was something he never wanted to see again. "You saved me. Again. Thank you. How could I ever repay you for that?"

"Baby, I don't want you to repay me. I want you safe. I *need* you safe."

Some of the fear faded as her analytical mind took over, wanting to solve this puzzle. "He was dressed like a homeless person, like he was a druggie after the medications we keep there, but he wasn't, Caleb. I've been attacked by a druggie before, I see them sometimes hanging around the clinic. They're always strung out and edgy, they fidget, and their eyes are always glazed. But not this guy. He was calm and his eyes were clear. Whoever wants me dead sent him and was trying to make it look like I was killed by someone high and searching for their next fix."

Muttering a curse at how close he'd come to losing Skye all over again, Brick grabbed her and crushed his mouth to hers in a fiery, passionate kiss. Skye's arms twisted around his neck, and she kissed him back with as much desperation as he felt.

"You are coming back to New York with me," he said as soon as he broke the kiss.

Skye's eyes widened at the order. "I can't go back with you."

"Why?" As far as he was concerned it was a simple ask. She was in danger, he could protect her, and while he knew it was unfair, he couldn't move because of his team, so sooner or later she was going to have to anyway if they were going to be together.

"Why?" she echoed, clearly incredulous. "Because I have to

sort things out with the insurance company and then find builders and start getting this place rebuilt. Because I have a cat and two dogs that I can't just abandon. Because we don't really know each other anymore, and we're just starting to navigate our way around this new relationship."

"What did you think was going to happen?" He had been upfront with her, told her he was in love with her and wanted them to be together. Did she not feel the same way? Was this just a temporary thing in her mind?

"I ... don't know." She dopped her gaze and her shoulders sagged. "You never said anything about the future."

"I told you I wanted to love and protect you forever."

"But we never discussed specifics. My house, and my pets, and my friends, and my clinic, my life is here, and yours isn't."

"So in your mind this isn't ... permanent?"

"I want it to be, Caleb. But I don't know how we'll make it work and you never mentioned it either. Besides ..."

"Besides what?" he prompted when she didn't continue, mollified for now by the fact that she'd outright stated she wanted them to be permanent. He intended to hold her to that.

"You've never told me why you suddenly showed up in my life." There was a tinge of uncertainty in her eyes that struck him deep.

"I told you I came back for you." If he told her the whole truth now there was no way she would agree to go to New York with him. Aware that the longer he let the lie sit between them the deeper hole he was digging for himself, he didn't see a choice right now. Skye's safety had to come first, he couldn't stand the idea of her being out of his sight even for a moment. He'd left her this morning for not even an hour and look what had happened.

"You came *before* I was attacked the first time, like you somehow knew that I was in danger. Did you?"

If there was ever going to be a time to come clean, this was it.

Yet fear of losing Skye rendered him speechless.

Even if she could never forgive him when she learned the truth—and the truth always had a way of coming out—at least she would be alive. If he left her alone and unprotected now, her father could get to her, have her murdered.

Then he'd have her death on his conscience.

Brick was pretty sure that would destroy him.

"Honey, this is one time I need you to trust me. I came because I couldn't stand being apart from you for another second. That is absolutely the truth. I know you have doubts and suspicions, but I would *never* hurt you on purpose. Not ever. Not for anything. If you believe anything at all then believe that. Hurting you would be like hurting myself because you're a part of me, Skye. The best parts. Even if I was too stupid to see it back then, you've always been the other half of my heart. Walking around for fifteen years without your brightness has been like walking around half dead. Back then, I thought it mattered if my father loved me and I would have done anything to earn that love. Now I know I already had all the love I could have needed from you and I threw it away."

Lowering his forehead to hers, he took a deep breath, praying that Skye would remember his words, hold onto them when the doubts he knew would come hit her, and feel his love for her when all logic told her otherwise.

"I wasn't there for you when you needed me, I couldn't protect you from your father, but I'm here now and I am yours. I don't think you realize that you hold the power to destroy me with a single word. I am completely and utterly in love you, Skye Xenos. Please say you'll come with me, let me protect you, we will work everything else out later, but now I need to know that you are safe."

Her hands cupped his cheeks. "I'll go with you, Caleb."

Relief overwhelmed him, but the guilt grew. As much as he wanted to promise Skye he was never going to let her down again, he couldn't.

Because he was going to.

It was a foregone conclusion.

As soon as she learned there had been another reason he'd come back into her life, he would shatter her heart all over again.

* * * * *

December 5th
3:16 P.M.

A hand covered hers.

Stilling the nervous drumming she was doing with her fingernails on the arm of the seat as the private jet they'd flown in began its descent.

"Why are you so nervous?" Caleb asked.

Skye shrugged. Wasn't it obvious?

She was about to meet the most important people in Caleb's life. His family. Not his blood family, he'd told her how his father had all but disowned him when he joined the military, but the people he had chosen to surround himself with. His teammates and their partners and kids with whom he spent all his time. What if they didn't like her?

Where did that leave her fledgling relationship with Caleb?

He worked with these men so it wasn't like he could cut them out of his life, which meant if anyone had to go it would be her.

"You know my team and I will keep you safe."

"It's not that. I'm ... it's ..."

A slow grin curled up Caleb's lips. "Are you worried about meeting my team?"

"Of course I am. They're important to you. What if they don't like me?" It seemed like such a silly childish thing to worry about. After all, there was someone who wanted her dead and had enough money to pay for multiple attempts on her life, but she *was* worried about it.

130

"Oh, baby. First of all, no one is more important to me than you. And second, my team is going to adore you, why wouldn't they?"

"I don't know." Skye fidgeted in her seat. Sometimes she came on a little too strong and came across as quirky. Which of course wasn't a bad thing, she could be a little quirky sometimes, but it just felt like a lot of pressure to make sure these specific people liked her.

"You're so cute." Caleb tweaked her nose, then sobered. "Skye, there's one thing you need to understand. My team and their wives aren't used to seeing me the way I am with you, the way you remember me from our childhoods. You know a guy who loved to have fun and came up with crazy schemes, who was popular in school and friendly to everyone. They know a man who's quiet, doesn't talk much, and built a brick wall around himself because he threw away the love of the only person who ever really cared about him rather than wanting something from him."

Skye took his hand and laced their fingers together. "Is that where you got the nickname Brick?"

"Yep. People always said it was like I had built a brick wall so high around myself that nobody could ever hope to climb it."

"You really regretted hurting me so much you wouldn't let anyone else get close to you?" It seemed like such a small thing in his life that it would make such a big impact. Even when she'd hated Caleb and been destroyed by what he did, she had known that at heart he was a good person and that if he'd known the truth about her homelife he wouldn't have done it. Not that it made what happened her fault, but it certainly helped to know that causing her pain had also caused him pain. It made it that much easier to move forward.

"I love you, Caleb."

Caleb lifted his eyes to meet hers and searched her gaze. The vulnerability she saw there—the same one she had seen each time he had expressed regret—cemented in her mind that Ashleigh was right. It was time to move forward, let the past lay where it belonged, and see where this thing between her and Caleb went.

"You do?" Caleb asked tentatively.

"I always have."

"You still love me now though, even after what I did?"

"I don't think I could stop loving you even if I tried. And I did try, Caleb, but you're so tangled up in my heart that I can't really tell where you end and I begin."

"Skye!" he exclaimed sounding annoyed, not at all the reaction she had anticipated.

"What?"

"Why did you tell me that now? When the plane is landing, and I can't undo your seatbelt and drag you into my lap and kiss you breathless. My team will be waiting, and all I want to do is get you naked and bury myself inside you so deep you'll never be able to survive without me."

Running her fingers through his short, dark beard, Skye then traced them along his lips. "Don't you know I already can't?"

"Baby," he groaned, "you're killing me here."

She laughed when she looked at the bulge in his pants. Some of her tension about meeting his chosen family had melted away when she learned she knew the real Caleb Quinn while his friends knew only Brick.

"You'll manage," she teased.

"Payback, honey, remember payback." Drawing one of her fingers between his lips, he sucked hard then swirled the tip of his tongue around her fingertip, making heat pool between her legs, and she squirmed uncomfortably.

"Caleb," she whispered breathily.

"Payback," he said with a smirk, releasing his hold on her. "You ready to go meet my team?"

"I am." Skye meant it too, no longer worried that they wouldn't like her. Caleb did and that was all that really mattered.

The plane had stopped moving and he unbuckled, shouldered both their bags, then reached for her hand. As he led her out of the small private jet, she saw two big men standing by a black SUV. Side by side as they were they looked intimidating, but they both had smiles on their faces, softening them substantially as she and Caleb approached.

"Thanks for picking us up," Caleb said when they reached the SUV. "Guys, this is Skye. Skye, this is Mouse." He nodded at a man with dark hair a little longer on top. "And Surf." He nodded at a man with dark blond hair. "I'm surprised you left Lila alone."

Surf laughed and shot them both a big grin. "Lila said if she didn't get a break from me soon she was going to start breaking things. Mainly me." From his obvious amusement, it was clear he wasn't upset with his girlfriend for wanting a break from him, just as it was clear how much he loved her.

"Lila hurt her ankle pretty badly a couple of weeks ago when she was abducted. She needs surgery on it, but doctors want to wait till she's a little stronger. Surf has a tendency to hover," Caleb explained.

"Aww, I think that's sweet," she said. She could imagine Caleb fussing around her if she was hurt. When they were younger and her father would break a bone, Caleb was always so sweet, carrying her books for her, and helping her out. Unfortunately, she'd developed a reputation as being a little clumsy, usually because she was always sore from one of her father's beatings, so when her dad broke one of her bones everyone believed the lies she was forced to tell that she'd fallen down the stairs, or tripped.

"I love you already," Surf said, throwing an arm around her shoulders and yanking her in for a hug.

A small grumbling growl emanated from behind her and she turned to find Caleb glaring at his friend.

Gripping her wrist, Caleb tugged her over to his side, making Surf laugh and Mouse roll his eyes. Skye swatted at Caleb's rock-hard abs. Alpha men, they could be so possessive.

"When she heard you were a vet my daughter Lolly was really excited," Mouse said as he ushered everyone into the vehicle. "We got some kittens earlier in the year and ever since she's been obsessed with animals of all kinds."

"Skye has always been great with animals," Caleb said, a note of pride in his voice.

"I'm sure I can answer questions if she has some," Skye offered, sharing her love of animals was always something she enjoyed doing.

"You'll make a friend in Lolly forever," Mouse said.

"The squirt has been bragging that she's going to practice her medical skills on her new brother or sister when the baby arrives in a few months. Then she's going to practice on my baby when its born, Arrow and Piper's too," Surf said with another laugh. "Apparently when you're seven a baby is the equivalent of an animal."

Beside her Caleb went really still and Skye wondered if he was thinking the same thing that she was.

After Caleb had cut her out of his life the idea of marriage and kids had sort of fallen away with it. It's what had ruined the relationships she'd had. Those men had been good men, they would have treated her well enough, but she didn't love them which meant she couldn't give them the pieces of her heart required to have a future with them.

Because those pieces of her heart already belonged to Caleb.

But now he was back and suddenly all her dreams for the future had come alive again.

CHAPTER THIRTEEN

December 5th
9:04 P.M.

"She's out like a light," Brick said softly as he tucked a blanket over Skye, who had fallen asleep on his couch.

"She's been through a lot in a short amount of time," Arrow said, the medic's gaze roaming Skye's slumbering form as though doing a mental examination.

"Yeah, she has, but she's holding it together so well. For now." What Brick was afraid of was what would happen once she learned the truth.

"When are you going to tell her?" Bear asked when Brick rejoined his team at the kitchen table.

After being picked up at the airport, Mouse and Surf drove him and Skye back to his apartment. She'd met the rest of his team, and their partners, and they'd had dinner together. Skye had slotted seamlessly into the group like she had been part of them forever, and he liked the sight of her sitting around with the people he loved.

The women had left about two hours ago, Phoebe had to get Lolly into bed, and Mackenzie had to tuck in her baby boy. Surf had decided Lila needed to get off her feet, and Piper had been having bad morning sickness only at night, so she'd bowed out, and while she was mostly healed Julia still got tired easily, so they'd all headed home as well. His team had stayed because they needed to talk through what they'd learned about the man who had attacked Skye at her clinic this morning.

Even though Brick knew the longer he left things the harder it was going to be to break the news to Skye, he wasn't ready yet.

Wasn't ready to lose this beautiful thing they were building.

Skye was going to feel majorly betrayed, both by him and her father.

Knowing her father was abusive was different from knowing he had hired not one but two people to kill her. Plus had someone burn down the practice she had worked so hard to build. On top of that, she was going to learn he had suspected her father of being involved in a plot to take over the government and tried to use her to get closer to him to find proof.

If she learned the truth now while she was here in New York, away from her home and her friends, she was going to be all alone with no support system.

He couldn't do that to her.

"I want to give it a few days, let her get to know you guys and your wives first. She's going to need people she trusts around her once she learns everything," Brick said.

"She's going to know that we knew as well, she won't trust any of us," Mouse said, waving a hand to indicate the whole team.

"But I'm hoping she'll trust the girls, she won't think they know anything," he said.

"But they know enough to know who she is and why we were there," Arrow reminded him.

It wasn't like they talked to their partners about all the missions they worked for Prey. But this particular case had been a crazy ride and all of their women had been dragged into it in one way or another.

"It might make her feel like all of us are ganging up against her," Surf suggested gently.

Brick dragged in a ragged breath and raked his fingers through his hair, tugging just enough to cause a sharp sting. "I'm prepared for Skye to hate me by the time this is all over. I can deal with that, I'll hate it but I can live with it. I'm not prepared to lose her. Her dying because she's alone and unprotected, that will destroy me."

In all the years he'd known these guys, Brick had never been as forthright with them.

His name had been well earned. He had spent half a lifetime ruthlessly keeping distance between himself and every person he met out of a deep-seated belief that he didn't deserve to have close relationships. After all he'd had everything anyone could ever hope for and thrown it away like it wasn't good enough.

These men knew him better than anyone else on the planet, and yet he hadn't told a single one of them about Skye, about how much she'd meant to him, or about how he had so thoughtlessly discarded her.

He was positive rumors had followed him through the SEALs and to Prey. People trying to figure out what had made him shut down and what it would take to blast through his barriers.

Barriers that couldn't keep out the woman fast asleep on his couch even if he wanted them to.

Skye Xenos possessed the only key to his heart.

If he lost her then that key would disappear along with her.

A hand clapped his shoulder. "We aren't going to lose her. None of us intend to let that happen."

The words were spoken by Domino. Of all the men on Alpha team, he and Domino were the most alike. They had both shut out the rest of the world, and seeing Domino relax and come out of his shell the last few months, ever since Julia had come into his life, had started Brick thinking about Skye even before this case dragged her into this mess.

All his life love had been transactional. His parents' love was conditional on him doing as they ordered, the kids at school their admiration depended on his family's name and money and him being the popular football jock. Mirabella's love was dependent on him becoming a wealthy and successful politician. Skye had been the only one to see him for who he really was and love him because of it.

"She won't understand," Brick said quietly.

"Did you go after her just because Eagle told you to?" Surf asked.

"I've been thinking about her a lot ever since what went down with Julia and Domino," he admitted.

"I'll take that as a no." Surf threw out one of his trademark grins.

"I've thought about her for years and tried reaching out several times to apologize. I would have gone in person earlier, but I was afraid she hated me and wouldn't even give me the time of day. Then I'd have to admit that I really had lost her forever." These admissions were difficult for him to verbalize, but he wanted his team to understand not only his relationship with Skye but also why he'd kept them all at a distance.

"Then that's what you tell her. Knowing her father was involved in this gave you the push you needed to finally face her," Mouse said.

"She'll be angry at first, guaranteed," Arrow added. "But she loves you, anyone who looks at the two of you together can see you're crazy for one another. Eventually she'll understand."

"I wish I hadn't waited so long," he admitted. Fear of putting the final nail in the coffin of his and Skye's relationship had kept him from going to her before his hand was forced, and as a result, they had wasted so many years. Years they could never get back.

"You can't live in the past, man," Surf said, pain evident in his deep green eyes. "Lila taught me that holding onto it robs you of a future."

"Your woman has all of us," Bear said, waving a hand around the room to indicate the whole team. "And she has our families. She's probably going to be hurt and angry when she learns the truth and will likely feel betrayed. Doesn't mean you don't keep fighting for her, for the future that you want."

"None of us are strangers to pain," Domino said. "In our jobs, in our pasts. But it's those pasts that built us into the men we are today, it's what led us to join the military, become the best of the best, and then move on to work at Prey. None of that was easy but we're fighters, it's what we do, who we are, it's a part of us that we can't just turn off."

"If Skye pushes you away when she finds out you weren't completely honest with her then you do what you know how to do. You fight and you don't give up," Arrow said.

"It won't necessarily be easy, the stakes will be higher than in any other battle you've ever fought, but it'll be worth it," Mouse said.

"Guys like us don't know how to give up," Surf added. "Alpha Team never met a battle it couldn't win and we're not about to start now."

Brick smiled at his friends, moved by their unwavering support and encouraging words. These men were more family to him than his own had ever been, they meant everything to him, but he had a new family he wanted to build. One with the woman who would forever own him. Who he could only pray would understand where he was coming from and why he'd made the choices he'd made.

Skye Xenos would forever be his sun, moon, and stars.

* * * * *

December 6th
9:02 A.M.

"You going to be okay without me for a few hours?"

Skye smiled up at Caleb. He was so cute when he was all worried about her and in fierce protector mode. Ashleigh was right, he was kind of like a guard dog. One she doubted anyone would be able to get past to get to her.

An image of her on all fours, naked and panting, with Caleb entering her from behind filled her mind and she knew for sure she was blushing.

What was with that?

She had always been content for sex to be passable, consigned to taking care of her own needs herself, but with Caleb it was different.

With Caleb, she wanted to experience everything.

She wanted her needs to matter too, and she wanted to try new things, things she'd never really thought about before.

"Skye?"

"Hmm?"

"What are you thinking, you just went bright red?"

"Oh … umm … nothing," she lied, hoping Caleb wouldn't call her on the lie. "And, yes, of course, I'll be fine without you for a few hours, I'm not even leaving your apartment. Plus, whoever is after me would have no idea that I'm here with you."

Something passed across his features, but he smoothed it away before she could ask him about it. When he leaned down and kissed her, everything but the taste of his lips fled from her mind.

It was so easy to lose herself in this man.

Maybe too easy, but Skye was done fighting against it.

"It won't always be like this," Caleb said.

"You mean you won't always hesitate to leave my side?" she teased.

"Ha-ha, you've turned into a regular comedian." Dragging her up against him, he lifted her, and Skye automatically wrapped her legs around his waist. Gripping her hips, Caleb held her still as he ground his erection against her center.

A center that was suddenly drenched and needy.

"There will *never* be a day that goes by that I'll like leaving you. Not a single part of you. Not these sweet lips." He dropped a lingering kiss to her mouth. "Not this big, warm heart." His hands on her hips lifted her higher so he could kiss her chest right above where her heart was thundering in her chest. Somehow, he lifted her higher again, supporting her weight as though she were nothing. "Not this stomach which I can't wait to see round with my baby growing inside. And not this sweet center that I am going to bury myself in as soon as I get back." Lowering her, he ground her core against the bulge in his pants again and her whole body sprung alive, wanting more.

Needing more.

Needing everything Caleb had to give.

Hungrily, her lips sought out his, kissing him with a desperation born from fifteen years without him in her life.

"Knock, knock. I hope we're not interrupting," Julia said obviously amused.

Snorts and half-hidden chuckles sounded behind them and Skye felt her cheeks burn all over again.

"You left the door unlocked," Phoebe snickered.

"Yeah, maybe don't do that if you don't really mean it," Mackenzie added, then burst out laughing.

"I think I'm going to die," Skye groaned, dropping her forehead to rest against Caleb's.

He laughed and set her on her feet, dropping one more kiss to her lips. "You guys could have knocked before coming in."

"Hey, we did," Piper said. "It's not our fault you were too preoccupied to notice."

Skye groaned again, completely mortified, but she was a big girl, and she and Caleb hadn't been doing anything wrong. Plus, she could thank her lucky stars that all they were doing was kissing, she'd been ready to have him right there in the kitchen, so his teammates' women could very well have walked in and witnessed that.

Caleb rolled his eyes at the women, but there was affection for all of them written into every nuance of his expression. He cared a great deal for the men on his team and their families, and she was so glad that so far they all seemed to like her just fine.

"Don't leave the apartment on your own," Caleb reminded her.

"I know, you've told me a million times already." Even though Skye felt perfectly safe here in New York away from whoever had been sending men to kill her back in Virginia, she was happy to indulge Caleb's worries.

"Then consider that one million and one," he said.

"Alpha men," Julia muttered under her breath, making everyone but Caleb grin.

Giving them all a reprimanding glower, Caleb said, "You guys know what it's like to have a threat hanging over your heads, so I expect you all to make sure she stays here."

"Aye aye, captain," Mackenzie teased, giving a mock salute and making everyone but Caleb giggle.

Caleb rolled his eyes at them all again then gave her one last kiss. "I don't want anything to happen to you when I just got you back."

Skye felt herself soften at his sweet words. "I don't want anything to happen either. I won't leave here without you, promise."

After another kiss, Caleb grabbed his keys and cell phones. "Be good, ladies."

"Lolly sent an entire list of questions," Phoebe said somewhat apologetically as Caleb headed out the door, setting a sheet of paper filled with childish letters on the table.

"I don't mind, I had fun talking with her yesterday. You might have guessed but talking animals is my favorite topic," she said sheepishly as she set about making coffee. She was missing hers at the moment, but they were safe at Ashleigh's house, and she knew her friend's kids would spoil the dogs and Foggy.

"Domino and I were talking about getting a dog," Julia said. "I've never had a pet before because I grew up unconventionally. Apparently, he thinks it will be good practice for us before we have a baby. Not that I'm ready for kids just yet, I want to enjoy some time just the two of us. Although with baby Mikey, and Phoebe and Mouse's baby due in a few months, and Piper announcing she's pregnant, and Lila and Surf having a baby, I'll admit to feeling a little broody."

"Caleb just said he wants to have babies with me," Skye announced, still a little shell-shocked by his easy revelation. Knowing he wanted a future with her was one thing, but for him to so casually announce that he was already thinking of kids had thrown her.

"Well, duh, the man is crazy in love with you," Julia said.

Skye grabbed the Nutella pastries she'd made early this morning and set them on a plate. "This is all still a little hard for me to accept," she admitted. While she didn't know these women, Ashleigh wasn't here right now and she needed to talk to someone. They had all been so nice and welcoming, and if she was going to have a future with Caleb then these women and their partners were going to be a big part of her life. Part of her family.

"I can understand that," Phoebe said. "When I first started dating Asher, I was fresh out of an abusive relationship, I'd lost who I was, and I was hesitant to believe things were going to work out."

"Ditto," Lila said, dropping into a chair and propping her crutches up against the wall. "After Christian dumped me and I found out I was pregnant, I was so sure I was going to be raising my baby alone. Then when I told him and found out why he'd broken up with me it was hard to accept that everything was going to work out."

"Dom and I had a rocky relationship from the word go," Julia said. "He thought I was spying on his team—"

"Which you were," Mackenzie inserted.

Julia laughed. "Okay, I was, but not for the reasons he thought. My parents taught me to live life to the fullest, enjoy every second, and go after what you wanted, but Dom had learned to live without emotion to survive. He didn't trust anyone, and it took a while for him to accept that I wasn't going to hurt him. I didn't give up though, I doubted him at one point, but after that, nothing could make me give up on him. I think that's how Brick feels about you. I think he's prepared to fight the devil himself for you."

"Antonio fought for me," Piper said softly. "He even had to fight against me, against the fear that held me in a stranglehold. I suspect Brick might have to do the same thing with you."

The sincere care and concern on each of these women's faces helped ease something inside her. Something that had been ingrained in her from a young age, don't trust anyone, don't let them in, if you let them get too close then they'll figure out the truth of her homelife, and that could spell disaster and possibly even death for her.

But she wasn't under her father's thumb anymore.

She'd broken free from his hold and was living her own life.

He couldn't hurt her anymore, Caleb was back and soothing old wounds, and she had a whole group of people ready and willing—wanting even—to welcome her into their little family.

Taking a deep breath, Skye shook off the binds urging her to keep everything to herself, and told her new friends everything.

CHAPTER FOURTEEN

December 6th
1:26 P.M.

"Hmm."

The content sigh coming from Skye's lips lit a fire inside him. A warmth he had only ever experienced when it came to this woman.

Love.

The warmth was love.

For someone who had grown up in a home where love was transactional, based on certain conditions, and withheld as punishment, it had taken Brick a long time to figure out that love was a feeling.

A feeling he was enjoying, recognizing it for the precious gift that it was.

"All good, honey?" he asked, tucking her closer against his side.

"Perfect. Everything is perfect." Skye gave another content sigh and rested her head against his shoulder. "I can't remember the last Christmas I've felt so … Christmassy. Actually I can. It was the last Christmas we were friends."

Even though he knew she didn't say it to make him feel bad, Brick couldn't stop the shaft of pain that cut through him. Yes, he'd made a mistake, thought trying to earn his parents' love was important rather than accepting the love he already had, but it was a mistake he could never completely undo.

It would always be between them, even though Skye had forgiven him.

He knew she wouldn't throw it in his face, that wasn't the kind of woman Skye was, but there would always be that tiny bit of lingering doubt in the back of her mind, making her wonder if she could truly trust him.

"Caleb, do you remember what you gave me that year?"

Tilting his head down to look at her he smiled. "No way I could forget. It was a locket that was engraved with a sun, a moon, and twelve stars, one for each year that I'd known you."

"I still have it," she informed him. "A few months later when you told me we weren't friends anymore I was so hurt and angry I threw it in the pond on our estate. I hated you so much I didn't want anything that would remind me of you. But I couldn't let it go. That same night I snuck out of bed after everyone had gone to sleep and searched until I found it. Took me all night and I was so scared someone would see me and report to my dad, but I needed it. I can't explain it, I just needed that connection to you. It's been tucked away in the back of my dresser all these years. Before we left yesterday, when I was packing clothes, I got it out."

Skye reached beneath her scarf and inside the neck of the red sweater that clung to her figure perfectly accentuating her slim curves and tugged out the locket that hung on a simple gold chain.

Uncaring that they were on a busy Manhattan sidewalk, Brick reached out and gently looped a finger through the delicate chain, staring at the locket. It had cost him a small fortune back as a sixteen-year-old kid, but he'd wanted it engraved especially for his best friend.

Now, as he looked at the twelve tiny stars all he could think about was how many more stars should be on there.

Sixteen.

Sixteen missed years.

Sixteen missed Christmases.

So many times he could have held her, kissed her, and told her how important she was to him.

If he had just bitten the bullet years ago, tracked Skye down, made her listen to his apologies, not left until he'd made her understand how badly he regretted hurting her, then sixteen years might not have passed.

"Don't, Caleb." Skye's hand curled around his, squeezing softly. "Don't be sad, don't have regrets. Not here. Not now. Not when we're together again. We're happy, it's Christmastime and we have our whole lives ahead of us. I didn't tell you about the locket to make you feel bad, I swear I didn't. I told you because I wanted you to know that even when I hated you part of my heart loved you. Couldn't help loving you, couldn't stop, no matter what."

"I don't deserve you, my beautiful sun, moon, and stars." His fingers traced the soft skin of her face as though needing to memorize it in case he lost her.

Even though she didn't know it yet, that was still a very real possibility.

"I'm not perfect, Caleb. I make mistakes too. Don't put me on a pedestal because that's a lot of pressure and one day I'll fail and let you down."

"You could never let me down, honey. Never." Touching his forehead to hers, he let it rest there for a moment before taking her chin between his thumb and forefinger and tilting her face up so he could claim her lips.

"I'm human, Caleb. Just like you. If we're building a future here, then it needs to be on facts. And facts are, I will let you down at some point, just like you'll let me down again. What we have to remember beneath the pain and anger when that happens is that we love each other. I believe that's enough to get us through anything."

Brick hoped it was.

Prayed that it was.

When Skye learned the whole reason he'd shown back up in her life, he hoped and prayed she was strong enough to remember that beneath the new pain he would heap onto her and her anger at being betrayed again, no one would ever love her like he would.

"We need a photo to go in that locket." With determination, Brick grabbed Skye's hand and towed her along with him as he headed for the biggest Christmas tree in the city. He'd get someone to take a picture of them in Rockefeller Center. Standing with the ice skaters and the giant Christmas tree behind them, and snowflakes fluttering through the air, the picture would be magical, and a wonderful reminder of them starting the rest of their lives.

Lives they were going to share.

There was no way Brick intended to give up on Skye, he would fight for her with everything he had. No mission would ever be more important.

"Where are we going?" Skye asked, hurrying to keep up with him with her much shorter legs.

"Rockefeller Center," he replied, dodging around a throng of mothers with little kids.

"Oh, the tree will make a great background for a picture," she agreed.

Hand in hand, they hurried through the throng of people to get to their destination. Once they were there they laughed as they moved about, searching for the absolute perfect point where the tree was centered behind them.

"Right here, this is perfect," Skye said.

"You sure? This photo is going to memorialize the beginning of our relationship as a couple, so I want you to be happy with it."

Slipping her arms around his waist, Skye stood on tiptoe to kiss his cheek. "Caleb, so long as you're in the photo with me I'll be happy with it."

She was right, he had to stop trying to overcompensate for the fact he knew he was going to let Skye down again. It was already a done deal, there was no going back and redoing things, he was just going to have to show her that he was serious about being real with her, which meant doing exactly what she'd said. Mistakes would be made, but their love could weather any storm, he believed that, and he would do everything he could to never let her down again, be someone she could always count on.

"Excuse me, would you mind taking our picture?" he asked an older couple who were walking arm in arm.

"Happy to," the man said, taking the cell phone Brick held out.

Drawing Skye into his arms, he kissed her with what he hoped was enough love to convince her that she was everything to him.

From the happy little moan that trembled through her, and the way she drifted closer as though her body needed to soak up more of him, he assumed she knew.

"Such a beautiful couple," the woman said as he pulled away from Skye and took his phone back. "And he's such a looker," she added with a wink. "You're a lucky girl, dearie."

As the couple wandered off, Skye curled her hands into the lapels of his coat and tugged him down so she could kiss him again.

"She was right, I am a lucky girl. You're everything I always wanted and I'm excited to see what our future looks like. Thank you for not giving up on me, and for giving me time to accept that I was strong enough to forgive and move forward."

"I'm the lucky one. Not only did the most amazing woman in the world fall in love with me, but she forgave me when I probably didn't deserve it and strove to understand why I didn't understand what love was. Our future is whatever we want it to be, and as long as I have my sun, moon, and stars by my side I know it will be a bright one."

* * * * *

December 6th
10:35 P.M.

Who knew it was possible to be this content?

Skye couldn't think of a single place she'd rather be right now or anything that could make things more perfect than they already were.

She and Caleb were curled up on the couch in his apartment. There was some sappy Christmas movie playing on the TV but she wasn't paying it much attention. They'd cooked dinner together in his kitchen, nothing special, just popped a couple of chicken schnitzels in the air fryer then steamed some carrots and green beans to go with them, but working side by side, talking and laughing, it had been way more fun than it sounded.

After they'd eaten, they'd put on a movie, paused it at some point to make ice cream sundaes, and now they were back on the couch. The day had been simple but talking this morning with the wives had been fun. She'd gotten to know them, and they'd echoed the same advice Ashleigh had, that she just take things slow and let them go where they went without trying to worry about everything that could go wrong.

Taking that advice to heart, she'd shared with Caleb about the locket which she'd kept all these years, then felt the need to pack and bring with her when she'd agreed to come to New York.

Skye was glad when she'd dressed for their lunch date she'd put the locket on.

The look in Caleb's eyes when he saw it would stay with her for a long time. Forever. There had been hope in them, and she'd known that was the moment he truly believed they might have a chance at making this thing between them work.

They would.

She was positive of it.

One day she was going to marry this man and have his babies.

Guess there was something that could make this more perfect after all.

With a sly smile, she lifted her hand from where it had been resting on Caleb's powerful thigh as she snuggled against him, and began to stroke her hand along his stomach, her fingers dipping lower with each stroke. Skye wasn't used to feeling so confident in letting her partner know what she wanted, but this wasn't just anyone it was Caleb, and no one knew her better than he did. Especially now there were no more secrets between them, and she'd shared about her father and he'd opened up a little about his family.

"You want something there, honey?" Caleb's low voice rumbled over her like a steamy caress.

Possessed by a boldness she was unaccustomed to, Skye licked her lips and nodded. "There's something I want. You. I want you."

Her fingers trembled, not with nervousness but with anticipation as she unzipped him and shoved his boxers down so his length broke free.

"You're so big," she murmured as she reached out to touch the tip of one finger to the tip of his erection.

Heat was pouring off Caleb as he watched her. Skye wasn't sure if it was real heat or a figment of her imagination. A manifestation of their desire for one another. A deep, heady need she hadn't even known existed.

"I like touching you," she whispered, glancing at him through heavy-lidded eyes.

"What else do you like?" Caleb asked, sucking in a breath when she firmed the pressure of her hand as she stroked him.

Caleb wasn't the first man she'd touched like this, both her previous long-term boyfriends had liked it when she stroked them, but this felt so very different. With them she'd merely tried to get them off as quickly as she could, knowing that was what they wanted.

But here now with Caleb, she watched with interest every minute detail. The way his hips twitched, seeking more of her even as his brain determined to sit back and let her have her fun. The slight ripple of his well-defined abs. His fingers curled into fists, then would slightly uncurl as though subconsciously wanting to reach out and touch her. The rise and fall of his chest became uneven as his breathing began to grow ragged, and Skye knew he was getting closer to finding his release.

Slowing the movement of her hand, Skye leaned down and touched a kiss to the very tip of his length. Caleb's moan of appreciation spurred her on and she trailed a line of kisses down his erection.

When she started back toward his tip again he growled and grabbed her shoulders hauling her over and into his lap.

"Need you, now," he said. With quick, efficient movements he stripped her of her leggings and panties without removing her from his lap. Then with an amazing show of strength shifted her so her knees went over his shoulders, spreading her most intimate area open to him, as he supported her weight with his hands on her bottom.

The first touch of his tongue against her sensitive flesh felt like a brand.

His.

Caleb's.

Forever.

Alternating between smooth strokes along her center, teasing her entrance, and sucking on her throbbing little bud, it didn't take long for pleasure to start building inside her.

It grew and grew, expanding until it felt like her skin was stretched tight with the pressure of holding it inside her.

"Caleb, please," she begged, needing to find the release before she burst.

"Come, babe." His voice seemed to rumble through her, and when he took her little bundle of nerves between his lips again, sucking it into the heat of his mouth, and flicking it with the tip of his tongue, her entire world exploded.

Pleasure was still washing over her in wave after never-ending wave, when he lifted her down and plunged inside her in one smooth movement. The feel of him filling her to complete perfection seemed to give more life to the orgasm still traveling through her every nerve.

With his hand on her hip, holding her still as he thrust inside her with increasing fervor, his other hand found her overly sensitive bud, and worked it, somehow adding a second orgasm to the end of the one just beginning to ebb. The pleasure was so intense, Skye began to sob as she came again.

"You okay, baby?" Caleb asked as both of their releases began to fade, and she sank down to rest against him.

"I'm perfect. I didn't know life could feel like this."

"Feel like what?" His large, warm hand began to rub small circles on her back as tears tumbled down her cheeks.

"Joy. Pure happiness. I didn't know it was possible to be this happy. Did you?"

"No, honey, I didn't. Only you, Skye, only you can make me feel this way."

Nuzzling his neck as the last of her tears fell free, she touched her lips to his skin in a gentle kiss. "Only you, Caleb," she echoed his sentiments.

"I wish this moment could last forever." Caleb's arms tightened around her until his grip was close to crushing. Not that anything in the world could make her ask him to loosen it.

"It will." Pressing her hand above Caleb's heart, Skye held it there. "Because it's just one of many moments like it that we'll share over a lifetime."

Caleb's lips touched her forehead and stayed there for so long she thought he was never going to let her go.

Eventually he pulled back. "Time for bed."

Ignoring the fact they were both disheveled and partially undressed, Caleb scooped her up and started for his bedroom. Once he got her inside, he gently removed her clothes, then stripped out of his own.

Before heading for the bed, he guided her into the bathroom, where he ran a washcloth under warm water, then knelt before her and cleaned her with such tenderness more tears welled in her eyes.

"I love you, Caleb."

"I love you so much, Skye, more than you'll ever know."

Gathering her up once again, he carried her to the bed, pulled back the covers, and laid her down, climbing in beside her.

Immediately Skye curled into him, resting her cheek on the hard planes of his chest. Caleb's arms wrapped around her, holding her tightly against him.

"This is the most perfect way to go to sleep," she said, snuggling closer. No matter how close she was it didn't seem enough, she wanted to fuse their bodies together so Caleb would never be away from her again, not even for a second.

"Can't argue with that." Caleb picked up the locket which still hung between her breasts and ran a finger over it. "I'm so glad you kept this."

"Me too," Skye said through a yawn.

"Sleep now, honey. You are safe here with me, I won't ever let anyone hurt you, there isn't anything I wouldn't do to know you are safe. Not anything."

Feeling like there was some hidden message he was trying to convey, Skye was too tired to figure it out. Instead, she just pressed closer against Caleb's side and allowed the tides of sleep to wash her away.

CHAPTER FIFTEEN

December 7th
2:31 P.M.

"I had to put clothes on and leave my girl in my bed for this, it'd better be good," Brick said as he strode into one of the conference rooms at Prey.

The mood in the room was somber and he immediately tensed.

Leaving Skye early this morning to go to PT with his team was one thing, she'd been warm and sleepy, kissing him goodbye and telling him she'd keep the bed warm. He'd known he'd be back in a couple of hours, and they could have the entire day together.

At least that's what he'd thought.

Until a phone call thirty minutes ago.

Still naked and curled up in his bed, he and Skye had been reminiscing about the past and sharing about their lives over the last fifteen years. Talking about their youth was bittersweet. It was nice to remember the fun times they'd shared, but it hurt to know what Skye had gone home to and some of the punishments she'd suffered because of crazy stunts he'd dragged her into.

It sucked knowing how many times he'd caused her pain, and that he was going to do it all over again.

No matter how many times Brick told himself to tell Skye everything, fear kept holding him back.

As soon as she knew the truth, she'd be out the door.

Alone and unprotected.

Hurting and he wouldn't be able to soothe those pains.

Brick would much rather face down an army of armed militia with nothing but his bare hands to defend himself with than see the look in Skye's eyes when she learned he hadn't been completely honest with her.

"What's going on?" he asked as he pulled out a chair and dropped into it. All Eagle had told him on the phone was that he had news on Skye's case that he needed to hear in person. Skye had wanted to come, but he'd convinced her to wait at home. If this news was bad, he wanted to be the one to break it to her, not have her told in front of a group of men she barely knew.

"We got a hit on a print left at Skye's practice by the man who attacked her," Eagle informed him.

Relaxing into his chair, he studied his boss. "That sounds like good news. Who is he?"

"Another Russian. Maksim Petrov," Bear replied.

"Any connections to Dimitri Kuznetsov, the man Skye killed in her house?" he asked. Two Russians sent to attack Skye was no coincidence.

"We're still looking into it, but I'm going to say yes," Mouse said.

"Seems too big a coincidence otherwise," Arrow added.

"Agree." Brick gave a brisk nod. "What do we have on Maksim?"

"Similar background to Dimitri," Domino replied. "Former Russian special forces, now works as a merc. Unlike Dimitri who has a reputation of liking to play with his victims first, Maksim has a reputation of being brisk and efficient. If you hadn't shown up when you did ..."

His friend let the sentence trail off, but Brick could already imagine in vivid detail what would have happened if he'd been just a minute or two longer at the precinct.

One red light.

One extra car at a give way sign.

That was all it would have taken.

Then he would have lost her forever.

"This guy has a one hundred percent success rate. He's who

you call when you need a job done and you want it done fast and right. He's not going to be happy that he didn't complete the job. She's a blemish on his otherwise stellar reputation," Eagle said, shooting him an apologetic glance.

"He's going to come back for her," Brick said dully. It wasn't like he'd thought bringing her to New York was going to get her out of danger, her father had a lot at stake, and he likely believed Skye was working against him. Hemmingway wasn't going to give up on eliminating Skye as a threat, and it didn't look like Maksim Petrov was likely to either.

It had been two days since Skye had left Virginia. Her father must know she was here by now. Hemmingway knew who he was, and obviously knew that he was working at Prey and handling the Mikhailov plot since Skye wasn't targeted until after he showed up in her life. It was to be anticipated that Skye's father would assume she was staying with him at his place, so he'd know right where to find her.

"We need to keep her safe," he said with a hint of desperation.

"We'll be watching your place around the clock," Bear assured him.

"All we need is to catch Maksim or whoever goes after her next then we'll have the proof we need to go after Hemmingway Xenos with everything we have," Surf said.

Until her father was in custody, Skye was never going to be safe.

Even after Hemmingway was arrested, he still might have the resources to pull off an assassination

One problem at a time.

"We never should have dragged Skye into this. If we'd done a little more research we would have known she hadn't even spoken to her father in years and wouldn't know anything we could use." Dropping his head into his hands, he massaged his temples where a headache was brewing.

This was on him.

He'd hated the idea of lying to Skye but couldn't allow anyone else to do this because deep down he'd known he needed the push as an excuse to try to apologize in person.

If he'd been stronger, not so desperate for any excuse to re-enter her life, she wouldn't be in the middle of this mess.

It wasn't until no one offered any consolations—not that he'd been fishing for them—that Brick realized the atmosphere in the room had grown tenser.

"What else?" he asked, sure there was something they hadn't told him yet.

Nervous glances were exchanged, and he didn't need to have spent the last decade and a half honing his gut instincts to know something was wrong.

"One of the insurance people stopped by Skye's vet clinic this morning to meet with her partner Ashleigh," Eagle began slowly.

"And?" he prompted. Whatever it was he wanted to know, like ripping off a Band-Aid, best to just get it over with.

"And instead of finding Ashleigh waiting for him, he found her body," Eagle said softly. "She'd been beaten to death with a hammer, it was left behind at the scene."

All the blood seemed to drain from his body.

Dead.

Skye's best friend was dead.

This was no coincidence.

Maksim Petrov had gone back to finish what he'd started only Skye was no longer there.

While he'd made sure the woman he loved was safe, he'd left the people she loved vulnerable.

It had never occurred to him that her father would go after anyone else.

He'd been wrong.

And now an innocent woman was dead.

This was going to kill Skye.

She'd blame herself. She was a smart woman, she might not

know everything that was going on and her father's involvement in it, but she knew someone wanted her dead, and she would see her friend's murder at their clinic as being connected.

"How am I going to tell her this?"

No one answered his rhetorical question.

The truth was, there would be no easy way to inform her that her best friend had been horribly murdered and it was because someone wanted to hurt her instead.

"We can do it together," Bear offered.

"Whatever you need from Prey you'll have," Eagle added.

There was sympathy in the gazes of the six other men in the room. Not just sympathy but empathy. They had all been in positions similar to the one he was in now, knowing the women they loved were in danger and hurting and there was no way to stop it from happening.

"I think this is something I need to do alone," he said as he shoved back from the table, feeling like he was about to head off to face a firing squad.

"We have your back, brother, that means we have Skye's back as well," Surf said.

"If she needs someone to talk to she can call Piper," Arrow offered.

"Whatever you guys need make sure you ask," Eagle said.

"Know that while you're taking care of her, we're watching over both of you," Mouse said.

"No one is going to get to either one of you on our watch," Domino added.

Trusting his team to take care of everything else so he could focus solely on Skye and helping her get through this, Brick headed from the building and climbed into his car. There was no way to prepare for heading home to shatter the heart of the woman he loved and strap a pile of guilt to her she would never be able to escape from.

* * * * *

December 7th
3:40 P.M.

The second Caleb walked through the door Skye knew.

Something was wrong.

When he'd got a call earlier from his boss asking him to come in, they'd both known it was about her situation. Reluctantly she had agreed to remain behind when he'd asked because she assumed that whatever information his team had learned he would tell her himself anyway.

But she hadn't been expecting bad news.

She was here, safe, what possible bad news could there be?

Her house maybe?

This man had already taken her clinic away from her, and after all the work she'd put into making her home hers it would be devastating to lose it, but at least it wasn't a person. Her dogs and cat were safe at Ashleigh's house so at least they were safe. If she and Caleb were really going to make this work, she was going to have to move anyway since he was tied to Prey. With her clinic gone it made the thought of moving here easier, it would be hard not to see Ashleigh every day and not being able to watch her kids grow up, but they could still talk all the time, and visit.

Drawing in a deep breath, she stood to face Caleb as he locked the door behind him and set his keys and cell phone on the coffee table.

"Whatever it is just say it," she said.

"Let's sit," Caleb said.

The universal warning of upcoming bad news made her tense further until her body felt tight enough that one wrong move— one wrong word—could make her snap.

"I don't want to sit, Caleb. Just tell me."

"We need to sit." Caleb's voice was too soft, too soothing, it tore across her raw nerves like sandpaper.

When he took her hands and gently maneuvered her onto the couch, Skye wanted to pull away, insist he just spit out whatever was going on, but she wasn't going to waste time arguing over it.

"Okay," she said once they were both seated. "Say it."

Caleb's hands still held hers and his fingers squeezed, giving her the impression he was trying to infuse his strength into her.

This was bad.

Worse than the worst-case scenarios she could come up with.

"I'm so sorry to have to tell you this," Caleb started. When she nodded in acknowledgment he continued. "This morning the insurance agent went to meet with Ashleigh at your clinic. After waiting out the front for a bit and no one showing up, he headed inside. I'm so sorry, Skye, he found Ashleigh's body. She'd been murdered."

She didn't react.

Didn't move.

Barely breathed.

Like a part of her mind believed if she remained completely still Caleb's words might not see her and therefore they wouldn't be true.

That was crazy of course, his words were true whether she wanted to accept them or not.

"Skye?" Caleb reached out to cup her cheek in his palm, but she jerked backward, yanking her hands from his in the process.

"Ashleigh is dead?" She'd only seen her friend a couple of days ago, they'd texted just this morning, confirming that Ashleigh would be able to meet with the insurance agent and handle things. Skye had been guilty that she'd left town leaving handling everything to her best friend and partner, but Ash had assured her that it was no big deal, and she could meet with the agent after dropping her kids at school.

"I'm so sorry."

"Murdered?"

"Yes, honey."

"At the clinic?"

"Yes."

Pieces of the puzzle began to tumble into place inside her mind and the picture she was seeing was horrific.

"Where I was attacked," she said slowly.

"Skye—"

"This was because of me."

"No," Caleb said quickly.

"Yes. Someone wants me dead. They tried twice already and burned down the clinic. Whoever k-killed Ashley d-did it b-because of m-me."

Air sawed in and out of her chest.

Shakes wracked her body.

Tears blurred her vision.

Her pulse pounded in her ears.

This was her fault.

Her very best friend in the entire world was dead because someone hated her enough to want her dead.

Ashleigh was dead.

Sweet Ashleigh who had always been there when she needed a friend.

Who had more than earned Skye's trust even though she found offering trust to anyone terrifying.

Who had the world's sweetest kids, and shared them with Skye, letting her be part of their lives and watching them grow.

Children who had now lost their mom.

Because of her.

Dead.

Killed.

Murdered.

Ashleigh was gone.

All her fault.

All her fault.

All her fault.

The words marched around and around inside her head, refusing to stop, getting louder and louder as reality sunk in.

Her best friend was dead because of her.

Because she'd run to New York to be with Caleb, removing herself from the situation, making sure she was safe, leaving behind the people she loved vulnerable and alone.

And Ashleigh had paid the price for Skye's selfishness.

How was she supposed to live with this?

How was she not going to be crushed by guilt?

Skye would love to believe this was all some great big coincidence, but after she was attacked twice, once at the clinic, and it was burned down, her friend being murdered there a couple of days later couldn't not be connected.

Could it?

Could it all be a coincidence?

Could she have been killed by a random person?

Clawing at Caleb, she grabbed handfuls of his sweater. "Is this my fault? Tell me it's not, Caleb," she begged. "Tell me she didn't die because someone wants me dead."

Even through her tears, Skye could see the pain in his face. "Baby, come here."

When he tried to gather her into his arms, she shoved him away. "Tell me!" she shrieked.

"Honey, this is not your fault, but—"

"No!" Skye beat her fists on his chest. If he wasn't going to tell her that Ashleigh hadn't been killed in her place then she didn't want to hear anything he had to say.

How could this be happening?

Things were supposed to be getting better but everything had fallen apart.

"Come here, baby."

Again, he tried to pull her into an embrace, but she scrambled backward. Black spots began to dance in front of her and Skye realized that she was struggling to suck in enough air. Panic was squeezing her chest until her lungs couldn't possibly attempt to do their job.

"Skye, honey, stay with me."

Caleb's face swam in and out of focus as he obviously leaned in close.

"Can't … breathe …" she forced out.

"You can, baby, you can. I know how awful this is, but I'm here, I'm right here." His large hand picked up hers and he placed it on his chest, her palm pressed against his heart. "Feel this, Skye. Feel each beat, feel each breath I take, try to match your breathing to mine."

He may as well have asked her to grow wings and fly to Mars.

Right now, she couldn't control anything not even something as simple as her own breathing.

Reacting to the lack of adequate oxygen, her head began to get light and her body heavy.

It would be so nice to give into the temptation the darkness pressing down upon her offered.

In the darkness would be peace.

"Come on, Skye. Breathe with me, baby," Caleb's worried voice urged.

Beneath her palm each beat of his heart pulsed through her hand and up into her body, his chest rose and fell evenly, not like her own.

Even as she wanted to let herself hyperventilate into unconsciousness, their bodies were connected by a million invisible threads, and she began to match him breath for breath. As her heart rate slowed and it was easier to draw in air, the heavy weight of guilt crushed her down.

"Caleb," she pleaded, not even sure what it was that she was asking for.

Apparently, he knew exactly what it was she needed. Scooping her up, he settled her on his lap, grabbed a throw blanket from the back of the couch, and tucked it around her. His hands stroked her back, and her hair, his lips touched kisses to her wet cheeks, and she could feel his pain as surely as she could feel her own.

"Oh, baby, you're breaking my heart. I'm so sorry. Listen to me, Skye, please. Don't blame yourself for this. It is not your fault. The blame lies squarely on the person who wants you dead. No one else. You hear me? I will not let you blame yourself for something that isn't your fault."

"Whose fault is it?" she asked. There had to be something she had missed because she had no idea why she was being targeted. There wasn't a single person she could think of who would want her dead.

Caleb had to know something, it was why he'd come back into her life.

Skye knew it, was sure of it, but she still didn't know how it all fitted together.

Maybe if she'd figured it out sooner her best friend wouldn't have been murdered.

Sobs burst free and she wrapped her arms around Caleb's neck, clinging to him as her entire body jerked with the force of her weeping.

This had to end soon because she didn't think she could take any more.

CHAPTER SIXTEEN

December 8th
8:08 A.M.

"How're you doing, honey?" Brick asked as Skye blinked open her eyes.

Her head turned slowly on the pillow as though it were exorbitantly heavy and took enormous effort on her part to move. For a long moment, she didn't say anything, lost once again inside her head, and he started to worry.

When he reached out to brush his fingertips across her pale cheek she blinked, and her gaze cleared a little.

"I'm … better. As good as I can be right now, I guess."

Skye looked better, calmer. Still much too pale, and much too fragile, especially with the bruises from her tangle with the intruder that first night turning a sickly shade of green, but there was a spark in her eyes that hadn't been there yesterday.

Yesterday she'd scared him.

For a while there, he hadn't thought he'd be able to pull her back from the brink.

Even though she'd been mere millimeters away from him it had felt like there was a giant chasm between them that he could never hope to cross.

Her guilt and utter devastation had torn him apart inside, ripped him to shreds as effectively as if she had placed the blame on his shoulders.

There was a part of him that felt like he could have avoided this. Maybe if he hadn't been so focused on Skye, on winning her back, keeping her safe, and the guilt he was dealing with because he hadn't told her everything, he might have seen that her father would lash out. Hemmingway Xenos despised his daughter, and the man believed she was working with Prey to bring him down. He wanted to destroy Skye and what better way to hurt her than to kill her best friend?

Holding Skye in his arms as she was consumed with grief, he'd been so close to calling Arrow to bring something to sedate her so she wasn't suffering.

Her pain gutted him.

Did she know he would do anything to take it from her if he could?

It worried him that she probably didn't know that. Skye was only just learning to trust him again, and after he'd treated her so carelessly, she likely had no idea just how deep his love for her ran.

"Caleb?"

"Yeah, baby?"

"I'm angry."

Anger was so much better than grief-stricken, and Brick found himself breathing a little easier.

"I'm angry that someone thinks it's okay to pay a hitman to kill me. I'm angry that they burned down the clinic I worked so hard to build. I'm angry that they made me run from my home. And I'm angry that they killed my best friend."

Because they were lying side by side in bed, with Skye tucked safely against his side, he could feel her body trembling with rage.

Rage that right now she had no outlet for.

"I want him dead," Skye continued. "I've never wished that someone would die before. Not even my dad on the worst days when he was beating me, and I was in pain and scared he would lose control and kill me. Then I just wished that he would stop. That he'd leave me alone. But now, I want whoever took out a hit on me to die a long, slow, and very painful death."

If Skye wasn't still teetering on the edge of a breakdown, he would tell her the truth about her father here and now. Instead, he leaned over and kissed her forehead. "It's okay to be angry, honey. What's happening to you isn't fair. You are so sweet, so caring, so loving, you deserve only good things. I wish that the evil in the world had never touched you. There is nothing wrong with wanting someone who has caused you so much pain, who took your friend from you, to suffer."

Skye chewed on her bottom lip. "It doesn't make me a bad person?"

"Not even close."

She nodded, looking thoughtful and he wished he knew what was running through that beautiful mind of hers.

"What do you need, honey?" Brushing a lock of hair off her forehead he tucked it behind her ear, then let his knuckles linger on her cheek.

"I ..."

"You can tell me. Whatever it is I'll give it to you."

"I think I need ... someone to ..."

"To what, baby?"

"I feel so empty, so exhausted like my whole body and mind are so heavy I can hardly hold myself up anymore. What I need is someone to ..."

"Hold you up for a little while?"

Her nod was tentative. "I feel like a baby asking for this."

Brick chuckled. "Honey, I *want* to do whatever you need. I'm feeling kind of helpless over here that I can't fix this for you. You giving me something to do will help both of us."

Skye's smile was still tentative. "I need someone to take care of me," she admitted.

"Done." Touching another kiss to her forehead, Brick threw back the covers, scooped a naked Skye out of the bed, and carried her into the bathroom.

Yesterday afternoon she had sobbed in his arms until exhaustion took over and she passed out. Nightmares had plagued her, and every time she woke all she could do was beg him to tell her that her friend's death wasn't her fault. His words had done little to soothe her and she would sob all over again until passing back out. Eventually, he'd just stripped them both naked and tucked them into bed where she'd spent a fitful night.

Setting her on the counter, he got the bath running, then added some of the bubble bath and bath oils Skye had brought with her. Grabbing her shampoo and conditioner he set them on the side of the tub.

Once the bath was full and the room was steamy, he shut off the faucet and picked up his girl. Stepping into the bath, he settled them both down with Skye nestled between his legs. Of course, his body snapped to attention, but this wasn't sexual, this was about taking care of the woman he loved when she was vulnerable and in need of love and attention.

Cupping his hands together, Brick scooped up warm water and let it fall over the top of Skye's head. He repeated the process until her hair was wet, then he squeezed a little of her shampoo into the palm of his hand and began to work it through her long locks.

"Hmm," Skye moaned as his fingers massaged her scalp. "That feels so good. Nobody has ever washed my hair for me before. Well, I guess when I was very small, but I don't remember that. My dad certainly would never lower himself to take care of his own child's needs, and my mom just did whatever her husband told her to do. Nannies were instructed that I was to be as independent as possible. I learned to do things for myself from a very young age."

Skye's quiet admission stirred up his protective instincts. He'd wanted her father to go down the second he learned the man was likely involved in Kristoff Mikhailov's plot. Hemmingway deserved more than a jail cell for the hell his team and their women had gone through. But for the pain the man had caused his own daughter he deserved nothing less than death.

"Tilt your head back," he instructed, moving Skye slightly away from him so he could tip more water over her hair, washing out the shampoo suds and letting them join the bubbles. "I'm so sorry, honey. I hate that you had no one to love you."

"I wasn't alone, Caleb." Skye looked over her shoulder, locking her gaze on his. "I had you."

"Until you didn't." Every time he thought about the life Skye had kept hidden from the rest of the world—from him—he felt a new wave of anger and shame directed squarely at himself.

"Don't," she said softly as she leaned back against his chest. "Don't rehash that. Your friendship was my lifeline and you're here now."

Picking up the bottle of jasmine fragranced conditioner, Brick squirted a little into his palm and began applying it. "No one was around to take care of me when I was a kid either. I didn't have it as bad as you did, no one hit me, but ..."

"But you were hurt by your parents too."

"Everything they gave me depended on me performing some task. If I wanted a new toy then I'd better get an acceptable grade on a paper, or in a class. I wanted a car, my GPA had to be perfect. Even when I was really young it wasn't if you want dessert eat all the food on your plate, it was if you want some ice cream then you better have been the star of football practice, got all your homework done, room tidy, and hour-long piano practice complete. There was no warmth, no love, no comfort offered. Tears and complaining were punished, following orders was rewarded, and the only time I felt even a little affection was when I did what they wanted."

"It must have been so hard to have both your parents treat you like that. At least my mom wasn't mean, she was just scared of my dad and did whatever he told her to."

"Both my parents were so busy with their careers and planning out my entire life. My dad felt like he got into politics too late and didn't have the name or money to climb as high as he could up the ladder. He planned to change that with me. I wasted so many years desperate for any affection they doled out that I would do anything they wanted. I thought if I tried hard enough one day they would just love me because I was their son. I thought they would eventually see me for me, not just as a tool to be used."

"I'm glad you finally realized that, that you found your own path."

"My parents were so angry at first when they learned I had enlisted. They were furious they couldn't go and undo it. But then my dad decided that spending a couple of years serving could actually help my political career, help people see me as someone who was trustworthy and who would fight for them. But I didn't join to pad a political resume," he said, disgusted by the thought, and that his father thought it was okay to dishonor every man and woman who had served by diminishing what they did.

"Of course you didn't," Skye said as she pressed back against him. "You're a protector. It's what you do, who you are. You're *my* protector, Caleb."

"And you're my everything."

* * * * *

December 8th
8:36 A.M.

My everything.

Skye could never get enough of hearing Caleb tell her how much he cared about her. Each time the words soothed a little more of her old hurts. One day they'd be gone completely and she wouldn't just have forgiven him but have forgotten as well.

She didn't need a clean slate, their pasts had shaped them both into the people they had become, and the more time she spent around Caleb the more she liked the man he was. Strong, courageous, brave, and so very sweet and gentle when she needed him to be.

Falling in love with him all over again, wiser and older this time around, almost made the pain of the past worth it.

"This is exactly what I want for our future," she whispered as her head tipped back. Caleb's fingers were like magic as they massaged her scalp. He'd already well and truly worked the conditioner into her hair, but she couldn't make herself tell him because each stroke of his fingers felt like it was easing some of the tightness in her chest.

"What, honey?"

"You and me, together, talking, sharing, taking care of each other. Neither of us had that when we were children, but we can have it now. I want to make it so you never hurt again."

"That's what you do just by being here. I don't deserve you but I'm too selfish to let you go."

Frowning, Skye scrambled around until she was facing him. "Don't say that, Caleb. I already told you not to put me on a pedestal. You do deserve me and I deserve you. We deserve this. We deserve to love and be loved. We deserve to have a real family." Tears rolled down her cheeks and she didn't fight them. Caleb deserved her honesty, and her feelings were real and tumultuous right now. "I'm struggling right now not to blame myself for Ashleigh's d-death, but the logical part of my brain knows it's not my fault, it knows that we've both suffered so much and we're due something good."

Running her wet, bubbly hands along his chest up to his shoulders, she shifted to her knees and moved closer. This man, who literally put his life on the line for strangers, didn't believe he deserved happiness.

Skye was determined to change his mind.

"You're my something good, Caleb. When we get to know each other again and you ask me to marry you I'm going to say yes. And when we have kids, we're going to love them so much they will never doubt for a second that they're wanted. We might not be able to give them all the material advantages we had growing up rich, but I think both of us would have traded all the wealth for people who loved us. That's what we can give our children that our parents could never give us."

Caleb stared at her, his mouth hanging open, his eyes a turbulent mess of emotions.

Then he grabbed her and crushed her against her.

"Gonna have to stand by that one, honey. I don't now and never will deserve you."

"Then we'll have to agree to disagree," she said, melting into his embrace. "For now. Until I convince you otherwise."

Throwing back his head he laughed, loud and free like he used to when he was a boy, and the change in him was immediate and dramatic. Somehow, he managed to look even more deliciously handsome when he was carefree like this.

"Come here, I'm not finished taking care of my girl yet."

Drawing her back between his legs, he hooked an arm around her shoulders and tipped her back as he used his other hand to cover her eyes as he dipped her hair into the bubbly water to rinse out the conditioner.

"You're good at washing hair," Skye said when he helped her sit back up.

"You think I'm good at washing hair you should see how much better I am at washing bodies. Especially bodies that look like this."

While Skye would have sworn till she was blue in the face that she was nothing particularly special to look at, the way heat and desire flared in Caleb's eyes she felt like the most beautiful woman in the world.

Settling her so she was resting back against the side of the bath, this time Caleb settled between her legs as he grabbed some of her jasmine-scented body wash and squeezed some into his palm.

A throbbing started between her legs as she watched him pick up her left arm, washing each finger, then her hand, making his way up her arm. He moved with excruciating slowness, paying great attention to every inch of skin, massaging each muscle, and rubbing over each joint. His fingers were long and nimble, rough with callouses that told the story of how he'd spent the last fifteen years.

When he finally reached her shoulder, her nipples were hardened pebbles practically begging him to do her chest next, but all he did was throw her a sly smile and pick up her other hand.

While he repeated the process, working his way from her fingers up her arm, the tingling in her center grew. Skye knew what Caleb was doing, he was seducing her with each touch, telling her without words that he loved every single part of her, and that when they joined their bodies it wasn't just sex, it was joining their souls as well.

This time when he reached her shoulder his hands swept across her shoulder blades to her neck, kneading the muscles around the nape of her neck.

Skye moaned in delight, and her head fell forward almost of its own accord.

Massages had never appealed to her before, maybe because after being abused as a child there was some instinct ingrained in her psyche that touch caused pain. But what Caleb was doing to her was the opposite of pain, it was a sensual delight.

Letting his hands drop lower they brushed so close to her breasts that she almost cried out.

A soft chuckle rumbled through him as though he was enjoying everything he was doing to her, knowing how much he was affecting her, how much he was turning her on.

If she was honest with herself she was enjoying it too.

Her stomach was fluttering, and her body quivering in anticipation.

Torn between wanting him to hurry up and asking him to slow

down, make this last forever.

For now, they were in a protective little bubble, away from the rest of the world and the horrors waiting for her in it.

A bubble she wished never had to burst.

Kneading her breasts, when his rough palm brushed across her pebbled nipples, Skye couldn't help but cry out this time.

"You've been very patient," Caleb said as his soapy hands smoothed bubbles across her stomach, dropping ever lower. "Do you deserve a reward, baby?"

"Yes, please."

"Please, I like that. Definitely a reward."

Finally, his hand dipped between her legs, dragging a finger through her tingling center, and pausing to circle her throbbing bud before withdrawing again.

"Caleb," she cried out in frustration.

He merely laughed and reached for one of her feet. Forcing her to endure his torturously slow sensual massage all over again as he massaged the ball of her foot, working his way across the arch to her heel. Then up her leg, kneading her calf muscles and then brushing his fingers along the back of her knee before claiming her thigh.

When he was ready to change to her other leg, he once again let his magic fingers tease her center, making her body tremble in anticipation.

This time he worked down her leg from her thigh to the tips of her toes, and when he released her foot and their eyes met electricity seemed to zing between them.

"This where you wanted my hands?" he asked as both of them parted her legs. One finger slipped inside her, another quickly followed, and Skye rocked her hips almost subconsciously.

Caleb's other hand rolled her needy little bud between his thumb and forefinger. Inside her his fingers hooked, teasing the spot that immediately had a mass of sensations bubbling quickly to the surface.

Holding onto his shoulders as the sensations continued to build until they were almost unbearably strong. When Caleb's mouth crushed against hers, claiming it with a kiss that sent tendrils of love unfurling inside her, her world exploded into fireworks of pleasure.

Not wanting the feeling to end, almost blindly, Skye used her grip on Caleb's shoulders as leverage as she hooked her ankles around his hips and pulled herself closer. Lifting herself higher she sunk down slowly, savoring every second as she took him inside her.

When he was buried deep, they began to move together, their hips thrusting in unison like they were two halves of the same whole.

Which Skye believed they were.

Caleb's release burst inside her and set off another wave of pleasure, one that seemed all the more powerful because she was sharing it with the man she loved.

Neither of them spoke for a long time, they just held onto one another, drank in the fact that they had each other. Nothing and no one—not even themselves—was ever going to come between them again. Whatever storms life threw at them, they would weather hand in hand. Losing Caleb was not an experience she intended to endure a second time.

Eventually, Caleb touched a kiss to her temple, then scooped her into his arms and stood, stepping out of the bath and snagging a towel, wrapping it around both of them.

"I've got you all soapy and clean, now it's time to feed you. I seem to remember someone had a slight addiction to pancakes. Pancakes for breakfast, pancakes for lunch, pancakes for dinner, pancakes for snacks, pancakes for dessert."

Skye laughed. They were her favorite food and she loved them with all sorts of toppings. "I would love to make pancakes with you."

"Uh-uh." He shook his head. "Today I'm taking care of you.

That means once we're dressed, you're sitting your cute little backside down in a chair at the table and not lifting a finger."

A warm feeling spread through her, the only person who had ever cared enough to take care of her was Caleb, and now he was here, helping her through the worst thing to ever happen to her. Despite the fact that her life was in danger, and someone wanted her dead, Skye had never felt safer.

CHAPTER SEVENTEEN

December 9th
9:14 A.M.

"We learn anything else?" Brick asked as he took a seat at the table in the conference room.

Leaving Skye this morning was harder than it had been two days ago when he'd come into Prey to be blindsided by the revelation that Skye's best friend had been murdered. Even though Skye was doing the best she could, he knew she was struggling with heavy guilt in addition to her grief.

Each minute was a struggle, and he wanted to be there by her side to help her battle against the devastation that was threatening to pull her under.

But the only way she was ever going to get a chance to fully heal was for the threat to be eliminated, and that meant finding proof that her father was the politician involved in Kristoff Mikhailov's plot. Just because they knew that politician was a presidential candidate and that realistically Hemmingway Xenos was the only one who fit the bill didn't mean they didn't need proof.

This was the real world, not some book or movie, and they were talking about a *presidential candidate*, one who was popular and charismatic at that. They needed real tangible proof before they would be allowed to make a move.

Proof he was determined to find because the life of the woman he loved depended on it.

"Ashleigh Christou fought for her life with everything she had," Eagle replied solemnly but with a hint of pride in his tone.

"There were dozens of defensive wounds, and she managed to scratch her attacker."

"We have DNA?" he asked.

"Yep," Eagle answered.

"We get a hit on it?" Brick was perking up, suddenly okay that he'd come. This time he wanted to be able to take home some good news to Skye.

"Sure did," Eagle said.

"And you like keeping me in suspense because …?"

Eagle laughed. "The DNA matches our Russian hitman Maksim Petrov."

"As soon as we knew there was a DNA sample, we ran it against what was already in the database from a previous murder Maksim committed," Mouse elaborated. "Since we already had his fingerprints from the second attack on Skye and the guy had an otherwise perfect record, we assumed he would want to finish what he started."

"Likely had been staking out the clinic hoping Skye would return," Arrow said. "Skye and Ashleigh both have dark hair, when he saw a woman with brown hair go into the clinic, he likely just assumed it was her. By the time he got in and delivered the first blow he would have realized it wasn't his target, but by then he had to finish the job anyway or leave behind another living witness. That's just conjecture but it's our working theory."

A theory Skye wasn't going to like.

Another thought occurred to him.

"Ashleigh knew that Skye was here and staying with me, at the time we didn't think it was a risk because we didn't think anyone else was in danger. Maksim Petrov could have interrogated her while he was attacking her, gotten Skye's location out of her." Just because her father would have other means of learning Skye's location, and likely had already known the addresses of all of Alpha Team from the moment he realized they were his adversaries, he didn't like thinking the assassin with something to prove knew exactly where Skye was.

"I don't think she's at any greater risk than she already was even if Ashleigh did tell Maksim where Skye was staying," Surf assured him.

"Domino is watching over your woman," Eagle reminded him. "Alpha Team is taking turns watching over your place, you guys are safe and protected. If it will make you feel better you can move her in here to one of the apartments, or we can find another safehouse for her to stay in until this situation is resolved."

"I'll talk to her about it when I get home," Brick said.

"I've been thinking about something," Bear said slowly.

"What?" he asked.

"Was Hemmingway Xenos having us watched or his daughter?" Bear asked. "He knew the second you made contact with her because that same night he sent someone after her. We assumed his motivation for wanting her eliminated is because he believes she has betrayed him and is working with us to stop him, but really, he has to know the same thing we now know. That Skye has had so little contact with her father that there is nothing she could know that would be incriminating."

"So why send not just one mercenary after her but two? Why burn her clinic down, and kill her friend?" Brick asked.

"Punishment for even daring to speak to someone about him? Control, anger? He was abusive, probably didn't like that she'd managed to break free of him, but he had bigger plans than worrying about one errant daughter. Maybe now he sees this as a chance to punish her for everything he believes she's done to betray him and his power over her, rather than a way to keep her quiet," Bear suggested.

"Does it matter?" Arrow asked. "Either way, he wants his daughter dead."

"I don't know, but I don't think we should just make general assumptions. Hemmingway acted rashly when he sent Dimitri Kuznetsov after Skye that night. He rushed, made a snap decision to take Skye out, and it backfired because he didn't stop to think everything through. If he had he would have known that Brick would never leave her alone and unprotected. Then he sends someone to burn down her clinic, stupid move, draws more attention to her and her case. Then again, another hitman sent so soon after the first, he knew Prey was involved, that was asking for us to whisk Skye away and keep her somewhere safe. Hemmingway is letting his anger guide him instead of his logic, that means he's making mistakes. Mistakes we need to take advantage of," Bear said.

"We need to get a clear read on his motivations so we know what his next move is going to be," Eagle agreed.

"What if he doesn't even know his own motives anymore?" Mouse suggested. "He was a pawn being used by Kristoff and Zara, they had plans to use him as a puppet for their own purposes. Now they're out of the picture what does he plan to do if he does end up winning the election?"

"Does it matter?" Brick asked, getting frustrated. Right now, he didn't care about what was motivating Skye's father, he just wanted proof the man had been involved in Kristoff's plot so they could get him arrested.

"If we want proof, everything matters," Eagle said. "We tried to take a shortcut in using Skye, that's on me. I thought she might get us access to her father's house and life so we could find something. I didn't make sure we had all the intel we needed before coming up with the plan to use her. Now she's in danger, I don't take that lightly, and I'll do whatever necessary both to keep her safe and eliminate the threat against her."

Brick knew his boss took his responsibilities for those in his care seriously and would forever hold onto a piece of guilt over putting Skye in the crosshairs of her father.

But this wasn't on his boss.

Yes, if Eagle hadn't suggested using Skye, she wouldn't be in danger now, but his boss hadn't known the whole story when he'd asked Brick to make contact.

"If you'd known I had a history with her beyond that we grew up neighbors and went to the same school, would you have asked me to go to her and use her?" he asked Eagle.

The man hesitated for a moment. "No," he admitted. "I wouldn't have wanted you to compromise yourself that way. I would have found a different route that didn't involve using Skye."

"Right. This is on me and me alone. I should have told you everything when you asked me. I should have been honest with Skye from the beginning. I shouldn't have been a coward all these years and faced my mistakes in person rather than hiding behind a computer. If I could go back and do this all over I would do it differently, but I can't do that. All I can do is what I should have from the beginning and tell Skye everything."

It was time.

Past time.

When he got back to his place, he was going to sit Skye down and admit everything. That all these years he'd wanted to go to her in person, beg for forgiveness. That when he had finally approached her it was with ulterior motives. That her father was so much more evil than she realized and was the one threatening her life.

Everything.

He needed to get this burden off his chest because it was not only getting in the way of the future he wanted with Skye but his ability to keep her safe.

Brick just prayed that she loved him enough to forgive him.

* * * * *

December 8th
9:49 A.M.

Her emotions were all over the place right now.

One moment Skye felt so happy, so full of love and joy about her future and her relationship with Caleb that her heart wanted to burst. The next she was all but in a ball on the floor sobbing over the loss of her best friend and the guilt she carried over Ashleigh's death.

Then there was that little gem of the fact she'd actually killed someone.

Somehow in all the mess of the last few days and everything that had happened, she hadn't even begun to process that.

She was a vet, she saved lives, she didn't end them unless there was no other choice. When it was time to help a beloved family pet leave this world so it was no longer in pain and suffering she did it in a humane way. She didn't stab those animals in the back and watch them bleed out all over the floor.

Shaking her head to dislodge the images of that man dying in her home, Skye instead tried to focus on who he had been talking about. Over the last week, she had replayed his words a million times, wondering if she had imagined the whole thing and he'd never said that someone had sent him to her.

If she hadn't been attacked again, her clinic destroyed, and her friend murdered, she might have believed that her shock-addled mind had conjured up the whole thing.

But the fact those things had happened only confirmed it.

Someone wanted her dead.

They weren't going to stop sending men after her to do it.

Who were they?

Was she crazy for getting the feeling that Caleb knew who it was, or at least had an idea?

Skye felt bad for having doubts about him, but she couldn't shake the fact that all of this had only started once he'd shown up. It was like he knew she was in danger and had come to protect her. If that was true, did it mean he'd told her all that stuff about regretting what he did just so he could stay close to her?

Was he going to break her heart all over again?

No.

She didn't believe that.

He'd been sincere when he'd apologized, she'd seen the pain in his eyes, and heard the guilt in his voice. Skye believed he was truly remorseful, if she didn't she wouldn't have been able to forgive him and give him a second chance.

But if he'd known she was in danger, and that had tipped his hand, made him move from sending emails, texts, and letters to approaching her in person, why didn't he just say that?

Sure, she might be a little hurt that he hadn't been upfront with her, but she could hardly hate him for wanting to protect her.

If he had come because he knew she was in danger why not tell her?

What was she missing?

And why was she so afraid to ask?

It was like there was a part of her that knew whatever he was keeping from her—and she had already reached the decision that he *was* keeping something—she wasn't going to like.

How bad could it be?

Couldn't be worse than him cutting her out of his life when they were teens. Nothing could be worse than that.

She had to stop being such a coward and ask him.

If Ashleigh was here right now, her friend would tell her to face her concerns head on. Stand up for herself and demand an answer. But also to keep an open mind and to trust her heart. At heart Caleb was a good man, Skye believed that, and had to hold onto it no matter what she learned.

After all, she truly believed it couldn't be worse than losing him the way she had fifteen years ago.

If she could survive that she could survive anything.

"Ash, I wish you were here to remind me of that," she whispered to the quiet apartment.

Tears filled her eyes and for a moment she gave into them,

dropping down onto the couch, letting the shirt she'd been folding drop to the floor, she pulled her knees to her chest and rocked as she wept.

"I'm so sorry. This was all because of me, and now your sweet babies have to grow up without their mommy, and I have to go on without you. I'm so sorry, Ash, so sorry. Can you forgive me?"

Skye had no idea how long she rocked and sobbed, and begged for forgiveness, in the end it was the persistent ringing of her phone that pulled her out of the meltdown. The first meltdown she'd weathered without Caleb at her side.

He'd been true to his word the day before, taken care of her, and not let her lift a finger to do anything for herself. He'd cooked for her, carried her around even when she'd reminded him there was nothing wrong with her legs, he'd tried to keep her mind occupied so she didn't dwell. When fits of tears had come, he'd wrapped her in a firm embrace and held her, and when she'd been crushed with guilt, he'd told her over and over again that it wasn't her fault.

When he'd left this morning, he'd told her that one of his team would be watching the apartment so she was safe, and that if she needed anything she could call him, but she'd been determined to make it through this time on her own. She wanted Caleb as a partner not as a crutch to help her through a horrible time in her life.

Assuming it was him calling to check on her, she picked up her cell phone from the coffee table and answered without even checking the caller ID.

"Hi," she said, sniffing, trying to get her crying under control so she didn't worry him.

"Hello, daughter."

The voice caught her completely off-guard and she froze, not sure what to do.

All it took was hearing her father's voice to throw her back in time. Turning her back into the terrified child, cowering in a corner, begging him not to hurt her, apologizing for whatever he claimed she'd done wrong, and promising she would never do it again.

The pain.

The fear.

It all came crashing down upon her and she started shaking so badly that the phone almost tumbled from her hand.

"Not going to greet your father?" he sneered. "Seems like you've lost your manners since you went running off to become a vet."

Her father had never understood why she loved animals and wanted to save them. As a child, he'd always been annoyed when she'd go wandering off to help some bird or squirrel that she saw injured. Hemmingway Xenos wasn't a man that cared about anyone but himself, and that she cared so deeply about animals was a constant source of confusion and irritation for him.

Why had he called her now, out of the blue?

It had been over a decade since she had last spoken to him, since she'd last seen him, why was he suddenly calling her?

"Wh-what do you want?"

"Like you don't know," he scoffed.

She honestly had no idea.

Why would she?

They were father and daughter in genetics only. Other than shared DNA they had nothing in common, and neither one of them had any interest in maintaining a relationship. They had separate lives, and she couldn't see any reason why those lives should intersect now.

"I have no idea," she replied.

"Don't play stupid, it doesn't suit you, Skye," he snapped. Obviously, her answers were annoying him, but then didn't everything she did annoy her father?

If he wanted her to know what he was talking about he was going to have to clue her in. "I'm not playing stupid. I have no idea why you would call me now."

"So you're not at your boyfriend's place right now?"

Her brow furrowed. "Do you mean Caleb?"

"I never liked that boy. Always knew he was bad news."

"Caleb is a hero. He served in the military, he saves lives."

"Is that why you decided to turn against your own father, betray him, for some *hero*?"

"Huh?" What did that even mean? "Betray you? We haven't even talked about you except ..."

"Except for exchanging information," he sneered like he'd won a victory.

Telling her father she'd admitted to Caleb the abuse she'd suffered as a child was only going to make him angrier, and the pit of horror in her stomach told her she didn't want to do that. That whatever he was talking about was bad enough without adding to it.

"I don't know what information you're talking about," she said honestly.

"I'm not in the mood for games, child. I want to know what you told him. I don't think you know anything important, but I need to be sure, he tracked you down for a reason after all."

"Caleb? He tracked me down to apologize," she said, more to herself than her father.

A bark of laughter came through the phone. "Stupid as ever I see. Your boyfriend is using you to get to me. If you haven't figured that out on your own then you're even stupider than I thought you were."

Her head was spinning.

Caleb knew something about her father?

That was why he'd come to her?

Not to apologize, not because he thought she was in danger, but to use her?

No.

That couldn't be true.

It couldn't.

He wouldn't do that to her.

He wouldn't use her so callously.

Would he?

Did she even know who Caleb Quinn really was?

From this conversation, it was painfully clear that she didn't.

She didn't know him at all.

"If you think you can betray me and get away with it you're crazy," her father's voice sounded distant even though she still held the phone to her ear. "You will pay for this, you can't escape me forever, Skye. Sooner or later I will get my hands on you."

"You," she whispered. "You were the one who sent that man to kill me. You had someone burn my clinic down and kill my best friend."

"And you know me well enough to know that once I set my mind to something I always get it. Enjoy your last hours or days of freedom because once I get you, you're going to wish you didn't survive that first attack."

With that her father disconnected the call leaving her alone with an icy ball of betrayal sitting heavily in her stomach.

Her father wanted her dead.

The man she loved had been using her all along.

Skye had never felt so alone as she felt in this moment as she sat frozen on Caleb's couch, unable to process the nightmare her life had just turned into.

CHAPTER EIGHTEEN

December 9th
10:38 A.M.

Something felt wrong.

As he walked toward the vehicle where Domino was sitting watching over his building, Brick rubbed at the back of his neck where the hairs were standing on end.

His gut had never let him down and right now it was screaming at him.

"Hey, man," he said, opening the passenger door and sliding into the seat. "All good?"

"Nothing to report," Domino replied. His friend eyed him shrewdly and the appraising once over Domino gave him made him feel exposed. "What's wrong?"

"Don't know," he replied honestly. "You sure you haven't seen anything?"

"If I'd seen something I would be up in your apartment right now."

Domino didn't sound angry by the implication that he was somehow not doing his job and had allowed danger to slip too close to Skye. Instead, he sounded understanding. There wasn't a man on his team who hadn't gone through something similar to what Brick was dealing with right now.

"Your gut telling you something?" Domino asked.

Brick nodded. "I just don't know what."

"No one has gone in who doesn't live here," Domino said, obviously trying to assuage him. "And Raven has me looped into the security system, no one has even been on your floor since you left. Skye is safe in there."

Sighing, he dropped his head into his hands. "Maybe I'm just projecting my own uneasiness."

"You going to tell her?"

"Yeah. It's time. Past time actually." If he could go back in time, Brick would have told her the whole truth that very first night when she'd spotted him in her parking lot watching over her. Maybe if he had been completely honest it would have taken longer to win Skye's trust and forgiveness, but it would have been better than earning them only to lose them all over again.

"Good luck, man. I know what it's like to rip yourself raw in front of another person, but when it's in front of the person you love it's easier. Just remember that she loves you. She might forget that for a while, but deep down her feelings won't change."

Brick prayed that was true.

The difference between them though was that while Domino might have had doubts about Julia when they first met her, he'd never betrayed her in the way Brick had betrayed Skye. When Julia had learned the truth about who Domino was she'd been able to accept it because it was obvious he was nothing like his family. Domino hadn't hurt Julia like he'd hurt the woman he loved.

Still, he'd made his bed and now he had to lie in it.

"You got this," Domino encouraged as Brick opened the door and climbed out.

As he made his way across the street and into his building, his feet felt like they were weighed down with lead. The temptation to hold off, wait till Skye had come to terms with her loss and the guilt she was dealing with, until he had the proof he needed so she was safe, was strong but Brick fought against it.

This wasn't something he could put off forever.

All he could do was not give into his fear this time and explain things in a way that Skye understood why he'd done what he'd done.

It was asking a lot, and he was relying on the fact that she loved him. Underneath the pain and betrayal he was about to heap onto her already overburdened soul, he hoped their love was strong enough to survive.

At least he hoped that until he reached his place, opened his front door, and stepped inside.

Then that hope died.

Skye was sitting on the couch. She wasn't moving and seemed to be barely breathing. In her hand she clutched a phone, but it wasn't held to her ear like she was speaking with anyone. At her feet laid one of his shirts, a pile of folded laundry on the coffee table beside the basket with the remaining clothes waiting to be folded.

Tears streamed silently down her cheeks.

She gave no indication that she was aware he was there, and his concerns flipped into overdrive.

This was why his gut had been acting up.

Somehow it knew that things weren't right with Skye.

"Honey?" He set down his keys, cell, and wallet, and approached her slowly, hands held up, palms out, trying to convince her he was no threat.

There was no response.

"Baby? Skye? What's wrong?" Brick kept his voice low and soothing, speaking as he would to a spooked animal that was seconds away from flight.

Slowly she blinked and her head turned in his direction.

There was no cognition in her eyes for a long moment and he almost wished that moment had never ended when pain so deep it bled out into the room filled her soulful brown eyes.

"You lied."

Those two whispered words tore through his body and soul like bullets, causing more damage than any real bullet ever could.

"I'm sorry, baby. I'm so sorry."

When he reached out to take her hands in his, she flinched like he was going to strike her and that one little move finished the job her words had started.

She was afraid of him.

Not only did she not trust him again, but she was now convinced all he was going to bring her was more pain.

Brick couldn't even argue with that.

All he'd ever brought her was pain.

Even as kids when she joined him in some silly scheme, he'd sent her home to receive a punishment he'd never known about.

"I'm sorry," he said again, helplessness rendering him almost speechless.

How did he fix this?

Could he fix this?

Like his broken apology had flipped a switch Skye, sprung to her feet. "So it's true?" she screamed.

"What's true?" How much did she know and who the hell had told her? There was no way anyone from Prey would have gotten to Skye first and told her. Even if he hadn't been coming home to do it, none of them would have gotten between him and the woman he loved and told her he'd been lying to her.

"You were using me." There was so much pain in her voice he could barely function.

"No. I never used you."

"You're lying," she shrieked. Holding out her phone she shook it at him. "I know. He told me. You came to Virginia not to apologize but to use me."

"I came because I couldn't stay away any longer." Although she didn't believe him truer words had never been spoken. Fear of rejection had kept him back all these years but when he'd been pushed into acting he had.

"I don't believe you."

"I know."

"You played me for a fool."

"No, baby. Never."

"You wanted to use me because you know my father is mixed

up in something and you thought I would give you an in. Bet you were disappointed when you found out I haven't had anything to do with him in years."

"Is that who called you?"

"I thought it was you, calling to check on me. Imagine my surprise when I heard my father accusing me of betraying him and working with you. I knew there was something weird about how you popped up in my life and then I got attacked. I knew you were involved somehow. I was afraid to ask you because I didn't want to be hurt again."

"I never wanted to hurt you."

Skye scoffed. "Of course you did. You knew it would happen. It's why you didn't tell me the truth. I was struggling to set aside my suspicions, but Ashleigh said I should follow my heart. My heart said it loved you. Said you loved me too. My heart is an idiot."

"Your heart knows the truth," he said fiercely. "It knows that you are everything to me. When we learned your father was involved in a plot to take over the government my boss thought the fact that I had a past with you gave us an in, a way to find proof. He was sending someone to work you for information, I couldn't let it be anyone else, it had to be me. You know I regretted what I did when we were kids, I've tried apologizing dozens of times. I was afraid to face you in person, but this pushed me into it. That's why I came, Skye. Yes, I wanted to see if I could get proof of your father's involvement through you, but more than that I wanted a chance to see you again. I owed you an apology in person and I wanted your forgiveness, your trust, and your love."

"Maybe if you had told me yourself I would believe you."

"I should have. I know that. But I was so afraid of losing you. I knew you would feel betrayed."

"You *did* betray me," Skye corrected.

Brick acknowledged that with a nod. "When I found out just

how dangerous your father was and what he'd done to you, I was afraid if I told you the truth you would run and wind up dead at his hands."

"So you came to me knowing you were putting me in danger?" she demanded.

"No. I didn't think your father was a threat to you. I'd been watching you for a couple of days before you saw me. He must have been having you or me watched. When he found out we'd been talking he obviously thought you were working against him and decided to take you out. I didn't think he would physically hurt you, I didn't think he would have your clinic burned, and I didn't think your friend would wind up murdered."

"But you knew *you* would hurt me. Again. And you didn't care."

"I cared. I hated lying to you. So many times I almost told you the truth but I always backed out. I was a coward. I should have faced you in person to apologize years ago, and I shouldn't have come to you with ulterior motives."

"Why would you do this to me? Haven't you already hurt me enough? Why couldn't you just leave me alone? I was happy. I had a home I loved, a job I adored, and a best friend who was like family. Now I have nothing."

She was breaking his heart.

Ripping it from his body and cutting it into tiny pieces.

"I was selfish, I'm sorry, baby, so sorry I hurt you."

Tears continued to flow down her cheeks, but she didn't appear to notice, making no move to wipe them away.

When he stood and moved toward her, Skye quickly backed up. "Don't," she whispered. "Don't lie to me again. You're not sorry. If you were you wouldn't waltz back into my life just to destroy it all over again. I have to go, I have to get out of here." Her voice and movements became panicked and jerky as she darted past him toward the bedroom.

"Honey, you can't leave," he reminded her somewhat

cautiously. "You know you're in danger. Your dad isn't going to back off. My boss said you can stay in one of Prey's safehouses."

"No. I'm not staying near any of you. They all knew, they all wanted to use me, I don't want to be near any of you."

"Please, honey, give me more time to explain, talk this through with me. Don't leave me, Skye. Please."

* * * * *

December 9th
11:13 A.M.

Don't leave me.

Those words tore at her heart.

They shouldn't. Caleb didn't deserve her forgiveness a second time. He wasn't a stupid teenager anymore, he was a man who had made a conscious decision to come back into her life, knowing he had hurt her in the past, to try to use her.

That was mean.

Cruel.

Skye had thought Caleb was a better man than that but what did she know?

Obviously, her ability to read people was useless.

Completely useless.

She was an idiot.

What was the saying? Fool me once shame on you, fool me twice shame on me. She was the one who had allowed Caleb back into her life, giving him the opportunity to hurt her all over again.

She had to get out of here.

Feeling completely strung out, she grabbed her bag and began to shove clothes into it. Aware of Caleb watching as she frantically raced around the room gathering all her clothes and belongings and tossing them haphazardly into her bags, Skye did her best to ignore him.

This wasn't about him.

He'd made decisions that affected both of them and now he wanted to play the pity card and beg her not to leave.

How dare he.

Anger.

She had to focus on her anger right now. If she allowed herself to think that he had only come back into her life to use her she was going to fall apart.

Once she had everything packed, Skye found her fingers were shaking so badly she could hardly zip up her bags.

"Here, let me help." When Caleb gently nudged her out of the way so he could close her bags for her she lost it.

"Don't!" she screamed. "Don't help me, don't pretend you care, don't … just don't. I can't …"

She couldn't even finish her sentences.

All she knew was that she had to get away from Caleb.

Grabbing the two bags of clothes, she snatched up her purse, left her cell phone on the floor where she'd dropped it earlier when she was trying to comprehend what Caleb was telling her, and ran for the door.

"Please, Skye, don't go. I need to know you're safe. If you hate me, if you're angry with my team, at least let us protect you. Please, it's the least we can do."

"No. I don't want to be near anyone that reminds me of you."

A clean break.

That's what she needed.

"Honey, you're breaking my heart."

If she didn't know better she would believe him, he sounded heartbroken.

But she wasn't going to be stupid for him again.

"Seems only fair, you've crushed mine."

Without a backward glance—Skye didn't quite trust herself to look at Caleb again, if she did she was afraid she would cave and stay, do anything to wipe away his pain—she flew out the door.

She had no clear plan. No idea where she was going or what she was going to do. She was a long way from home and as she burst out onto the street, she remembered that Caleb had one of his teammates watching his house. Had it really been just to keep her safe or had they thought that maybe she would lead them to her father?

Did Caleb think she was involved somehow?

Was that why he thought it was okay to use her like this?

Or did he just really not care about her at all to the point where hurting her on purpose was just nothing as far as he was concerned?

Home.

She wanted to go home.

Even though her place would forever be filled with memories of both the horror of realizing someone had broken into her home and was there to kill her, and the special moments she'd shared with Caleb including the first time they made love.

She was going to have to move.

And how would she face restarting a new vet clinic without her best friend by her side?

Her entire life had fallen apart in just the space of a week.

Still home was better than here, she could hardly wander around the streets of New York indefinitely. Especially with the weather, there were snowflakes in the air, only this time they didn't give her a warm Christmassy feeling, they just made her cold.

Ice cold.

It felt like a block of ice had settled inside her heart and was chilling every part of her body.

Hopefully, it would eventually turn her numb.

Right about now numb sounded perfect.

A cab. She needed a cab. The last thing she wanted to do was hang around the city where she knew Caleb and his team were lurking. That meant a hotel was out so home it was. She had her purse so she had her credit cards, she'd get to the airport and book a flight home.

In a fog of betrayal and broken heartedness, Skye hailed a cab. The drive to the airport was a blur. She barely remembered buying a ticket, checking in, or making her way to the gate.

The flight home felt much longer than it would have been, and by the time they landed, she found herself stumbling through the airport, barely able to remain on her feet.

Soon.

Soon she'd be home. She'd take a long, hot shower, and do her best to scrub off the filth that felt like it coated her skin. Then she'd fall into bed. Even though she hadn't eaten since breakfast she wasn't at all hungry, instead, she felt nauseous.

Sleep was what she wanted.

Sleep meant freedom from her thoughts and feelings, at least for a little while.

Unless nightmares came for her.

Knowing her luck they would. Dreams of Caleb, of his lies and betrayal, of almost being raped and murdered, killing a man, being responsible for her best friend's death, would likely haunt her.

So much pain, so much suffering.

Somehow, she managed to make it outside. The cold air woke her up a little bit and as she headed for a cab, she realized she wasn't quite ready to go home yet.

Maybe she needed to punish herself a little first.

After all, she was the reason Ashleigh had been horribly murdered, surely she had to pay for that.

Was losing Caleb a second time payment enough?

It didn't seem like it.

Joining the line for the cabs, when she finally climbed inside she gave the address for her clinic rather than her home. She'd go there first, spend a little time in the place where her friend had been beaten to death, then when she was ready she could walk the rest of the way home.

By the time the cab pulled up outside her clinic, Skye felt exhausted. She'd thought she knew what exhaustion felt like, there had been plenty of times when she'd felt too scared, in too much pain, to go forward.

But nothing like this.

This felt like every molecule of her being had been thrown into a blender and all that had come out was mush.

"I'm so sorry, Ashleigh," she whispered as she bypassed the crime scene tape and ducked inside. "If I could have changed things so I was the one who died I would have. Do you know that? Do you know you were the very best friend a girl could ever have? You were always there for me. Always. No questions asked. You pushed me, encouraged me, and made me a better vet, a better person. I love you so much and I can't believe you're gone. It doesn't feel real."

Dropping her bags at the door, she walked through, searching for the place where Ashleigh's life had been stolen from her.

Bloodstains.

On the floor of what had been Ashleigh's exam room.

Here.

Right here.

This was the spot where Ashleigh had been beaten to death.

There were several puddles of blood on the charred floor.

That was all that was left of her best friend.

Gone.

Ashleigh was gone.

It hadn't sunk in yet. It was so hard to believe that her friend wouldn't come bouncing into the room babbling away about something. Or call and ask if Skye wanted to come over for dinner.

"I didn't know, Ashleigh. I didn't know you were in danger. I didn't know he was using me, I didn't know he didn't care."

Her fingers found the locket she'd kept all these years. A reminder of happier times with Caleb, of what could have been.

Now it was a horrible reminder of the terrible mistakes she had made.

Mistakes her best friend had paid for with her life.

Tossing the locket across the room, Skye burst into noisy sobs. It wasn't fair. Why did she have to be born to an abusive monster? Why did the only man she would ever love not love her back?

Skye didn't know she wasn't alone until pain blasted through her abdomen.

There had been no loud noise.

Nothing to tell her why she suddenly hurt so badly.

When she looked down, she was surprised to see the front of her pink sweater turning red.

Dizziness had her falling to her knees.

What was happening?

Footsteps caught her attention, and she looked up to see a man grinning down at her. Who was he?

Those eyes.

She'd seen them before.

The man who attacked her here a few days ago. Likely the same man who had killed Ashleigh. Who had been waiting here for a chance to kill her too.

Collapsing onto the floor, Skye's last thought was that it seemed only fitting that her blood mingle with her best friend's as her life drained out of her.

CHAPTER NINETEEN

December 9th
8:22 P.M.

Who knew he actually enjoyed witnessing someone else's pain?

Hemmingway had always known he didn't mind inflicting pain, but it was never about the pain perse. It was more about the control. Doling out fitting punishments to mold his daughter into the person he wanted her to be, not that it had ever worked.

But now, as he watched Skye lying on the floor, blood coating her clothes and her hands, he realized that he was anxious for her to wake up so he could watch as pain filled her eyes.

Impatiently he paced around the basement. "Come on," he urged.

"She has lost a lot of blood," Grigoriy Golubev mentioned as one might state that paint was peeling.

"No sell backs," he said quickly. The nice little bundle he'd made selling his daughter to Grigoriy was enough to help him finish financing his campaign. With Kristoff gone there was no more dirty Russian money to pay for the campaign. He had enough in his personal finances, but he might have had to sell one of his properties, or some of his artwork, maybe even one of his classic cars, to make sure he had enough to get himself elected. Now he didn't have to worry about it.

Grigoriy chuckled. "I have no intentions of reneging on the deal. The girl might be shot but it won't interfere with my plans for her. My son has a Christmas gathering planned and I intend to give her to him as a gift of entertainment for the night. He and his friends can have their fun with her, and if she doesn't survive after that no harm done. There is never a shortage of beautiful women after all."

If he was a better man, hell if he was even a normal man, he would care that his daughter's fate was to be used as the night's sexual entertainment for a group of rowdy, violent, drunk young men, but he didn't.

All he cared about was the fact that she was now out of his hair.

"Your son won't care that she's injured?" Hemmingway confirmed.

"As long as she has enough strength to have a little fight left in her I'm sure they can find a way to use her wounds to their advantage. After all, what good is a willing girl, the fun is in her fight and inevitable loss."

Hemmingway had never thought about it before. He liked sex of course, and he had a willing wife at home who was always happy to do or perform any acts he asked, but he'd never really entertained the idea of finding a less than willing participant. His entire life had been focused on building his political career, there had been little time for anything else, but now that he was so close to living out his dreams perhaps that was an idea he could look into in the future. Might be difficult with his new position as leader of the free world, but he was sure that where there was a will there was a way.

"The girl will have plenty of fight in her," he said. Skye had always been one to fight back against the inevitable. No matter how many times he punished her for playing ridiculous games with the Quinn kid, she always went back for more. Stupid really, why not just do as he ordered and save herself the punishment?

Probably because she knew no matter what she did he would punish her anyway.

Spare the rod and spoil the child.

That was a proverb he had always believed in. His father had beaten him when he was a boy, and he was none the worse for it.

His father's father had beaten him, and his father's father's father had beaten him. It was a family tradition, and one that had worked. Each generation had been wealthier and more prestigious than the one before.

From farmer to store owner.

From store owner to state government.

From state government to President of the United States of America.

Not bad in four generations.

Then along came Skye and took their family backward.

Vet.

What a ridiculous occupation.

Not that he was saying that there wasn't a need for people who could care for animals, but for the daughter of a Senator with presidential goals, playing with animals all day was just as bad as going back to being a farmer.

Disappointment didn't even begin to describe how he felt about his only child. Too bad her mother had had massive complications during childbirth and had needed a lifesaving hysterectomy to survive. Otherwise, he would have kept having children until he had one who could actually follow in his footsteps.

Instead, he was stuck with this stupid girl.

Well, she would be gone soon, and he was sure there would be a way he could use her death to his advantage. Crime had been a big part of his campaign and to have his own daughter stalked and then abducted was something he could spin. Especially if he had Grigoriy's people dump her shot and violated body somewhere. When she was discovered, he would play the role of grieving father to the hilt, gather more sympathy, more votes, and when election time rolled around he was positive he would win in the biggest landslide this country had ever known.

A moan drew his attention back to the floor where Skye was moving weakly as she came around.

"Wake up, daughter dear," he sang.

"Father?" The word was barely a hint of sound falling from her cracked lips and her eyes opened slowly as though her lids were very heavy.

"Unfortunately."

"What ...? Why ...? I don't ..." her stammered sentences were every bit as annoying as everything else to do with the girl.

Really, she couldn't even be shot and keep her ridiculous questions to herself. For as long as he could remember, she had been peppering questions at any adult within a ten-mile radius.

Even as a toddler she was always asking why. Why was the sky blue? Why do birds fly but fish swim? Why do seeds grow in grass but not in sand?

The never-ending drone of questions used to drive him crazy until he had implemented a no-talking at the dinner table rule. Mealtime was usually the only time he spent with his child and he firmly believed children should be seen and not heard. Once she learned that lesson dinner had been a much more enjoyable event.

"Someone shot me," Skye said like she couldn't believe it.

"Well, you had evaded him once already, he wasn't going to let you get away again. No time to make it look like an accident, or just another druggie in search of a fix. Fast and to the point this time, no allowing room for error. Maksim has a reputation to uphold," he said. He probably should have hired Maksim the first time around, but Dimitri had already been in the area and he'd wanted it done quickly. Lesson learned. Next time he would go with quality over ease.

"But I'm ... not dead," Skye mumbled.

"Not yet. And not until the man I've sold you to is finished with you." He gave a nod at Grigoriy, and Skye's gaze bounced between the two of them.

"I don't ... understand."

"I think you do," he corrected. "I made it pretty simple. I need you out of the way, Grigoriy needs a Christmas gift for his son, his son is in need of entertainment for a party he's throwing. Enter you. Once the party is finished then if you're still alive someone will finish you off and dump your body. Let me assure you that they will be doing you a favor. After Grigoriy's son is finished with you, you will wish for death. I understand he is not a very gentle lover." Hemmingway snickered at his own little joke.

"But I'm ... you wouldn't ..."

"What? You're my daughter so I wouldn't sell you to be used and killed? Don't kid yourself, dear, I would absolutely sell you to get you out of my way. Don't you understand what's at stake here?" It was clear from his daughter's dull expression that she did not. "I am in the process of becoming the President. The *President*," he repeated. "I cannot, I will not, allow anything to interfere with that. Not even my daughter. You brought this on yourself, Skye. I didn't ask you to go cavorting around with the enemy. You picked your side and you picked wrong."

"I didn't know," she whispered softly as a single tear trickled down her cheek.

Hemmingway shrugged. "You never were the brightest bulb."

"So, you're just going to send me off with this man?" Skye's gaze darted to Grigoriy and then skittered away again.

"In a couple of days. Until then you'll remain here where I know no one will think to look for you."

Once Skye was out of the way he could focus on the upcoming year. The final run toward recognizing his dreams. By this time next year, it would just be a formality, but the title would be his for the taking.

Then he could decide what the future of this country and the world would look like.

He and he alone was in control of the earth's future.

CHAPTER TWENTY

"Where is she?" Brick roared into the too quiet house.

"Hold it together, man," Bear said.

"Hold it together?" he repeated, beyond incredulous. "How am I supposed to do that?"

"Because she needs you to," Mouse said like it was that simple.

"Does she? Because maybe what she needs is for me to disappear out of her life. All I do is bring her pain." That was the worst part of all of this. No matter what he did, he didn't bring Skye peace. Happiness, joy, a sense of belonging he'd never experienced with anyone else, that's what Skye brought into his life. Why couldn't he do the same for her?

"That's your fear talking," Arrow said.

"Is it? Or is it reality?"

"It's your guilt reminding you that you hurt her, but once we find her you can apologize again," Domino told him.

"She's not going to forgive me. Ever. That ship has sailed. Maybe if I had been the one to tell her but not when she found out like she did. She'll never understand why I didn't tell her."

"You're not giving her enough credit," Surf countered. "She's had a major shock on top of everything else that she's just been through. Of course she freaked out. Give her some time, once the dust settles, I think you'll find she's able to see past the pain and betrayal and realize that you love her."

"You guys are crazy," he muttered. Brick was positive that any chance he had of a future with Skye had been blown out of the water the second she answered her father's call.

"We've been where you are. Mackenzie forgave me for the way I ignored her after Uganda," Bear said.

"And Phoebe forgave me for thinking she was abducting my kid," Mouse added.

"I almost killed Piper," Arrow said.

"I handcuffed Julia to a bed, and she thought I was planning on raping and murdering her," Domino added with a grimace.

"Lila forgave me for dumping her without any warning," Surf said. "Before you offer any protests you need to remember the power of love. If I was Skye, I'd be hurt now too, but I would also remember that I love you. Have a little faith. Love can work miracles, you'll see."

Brick wanted to believe that so badly.

Skye had told him that their love was strong enough to weather any storm. Did she mean it? When the pain and betrayal she was feeling right now dimmed a little would she remember that she was his entire world? That there was absolutely nothing he wouldn't do for her?

"Where is she?" he repeated. Right now, he couldn't think any further ahead than the next few seconds. They'd jumped in one of Prey's private jets when they realized Skye was on her way back to Virginia. They'd arrived at her house before her because they hadn't had to worry about baggage claim and airport busyness.

Only Skye had never shown up.

Her plane had landed and she'd been on it.

But instead of catching a cab to her house, she'd obviously gone somewhere else, but where?

Where would she go?

"You know her better than anyone else," Domino said. "Where do *you* think she would go?"

If he knew he would be there already. Even if she hated him, and even if she didn't want him anywhere near her, he loved her and it was his job to protect her, make sure she was safe.

He'd been so sure she would want to come home, what had changed that?

Had she decided to go to a hotel?

With her friend gone there was nowhere else she would …

"I know where she is." Without waiting for anyone to ask him questions, he ran out the door, heading straight for the rental.

The guys followed him and jumped into the vehicle, and he sped off down the street, wondering why this hadn't occurred to him before. Skye was mired in grief and pain right now, she wasn't ready to feel anything else, he was sure she would go to the last place her friend had been alive.

Their clinic.

When he pulled up in front of the building, he didn't even bother to turn off the engine, just jumped out and ran for the entrance. Slipping under the police tape he threw open the front door.

"Skye?" he called out.

No answer.

Because she wasn't here or just didn't want to talk to him?

"Honey, I know you hate me right now, but I need to know if you're okay," he said as he ran into her exam room, shining the flashlight on his cell phone around the room searching for her.

It was empty, and so was the office area out the back where her desk had been.

The operating room was empty, and the space where they kept animals in cages if they needed to remain under observation.

That only left Ashleigh's exam room. Was she trying to torture herself by hanging out in there imagining what her friend's final moments had been like?

Given the fact she was battling guilt over the death he could see that.

"Skye, you in here?" he asked gently as he stepped into the room.

Empty.

Again.

Damn. He'd been so sure that if she hadn't gone home, she would be here. There was no other place he could think of that she would go to. She wouldn't have gone to her parents even if her father hadn't called her. There was no other family she could seek solace with, and she wasn't going to go to Ashleigh's house and stay with her husband and kids. Her credit card hadn't been used to check into a hotel, Prey was monitoring it, and she hadn't rented a vehicle so she wasn't driving around somewhere.

So where was she?

Frustration and fear warred inside him, and he slammed his fist into the wall, barely feeling the stab of pain spiraling from his knuckles up through his wrist.

His gaze roamed the empty room as though he could conjure Skye out of thin air.

Instead of finding his woman, the beam of his flashlight glinted off something. Absently, he crossed to it and bent down scooping up whatever it was.

When it rested in his palm he almost wished he hadn't.

It was the locket.

The one Skye had kept after he'd ended their friendship. Held onto because part of her still loved him despite the way he'd treated her.

Obviously, that part of her no longer existed.

Curling his fingers around the locket, he sunk down onto his backside, hanging his head between his bent knees and staring at the floor.

No.

Not the floor.

Something on the floor.

Large puddles of something.

His heart stopped beating. He would have sworn it did. Air no longer entered his lungs as they refused to do their job.

Blood.

The puddles were blood.

Skye had been here, he'd been right about that, she'd come here, obviously upset, left the locket behind, and then something had happened.

Maksim Petrov was still out there, it was why he hadn't wanted Skye to run off on her own no matter how upset she was. It was why they had jumped on a plane to follow her here. Whether she liked it or not, she was his and he protected what he loved with everything he had.

"Guys!" he yelled. His team would be close by, giving him the time he needed to process, knowing he would let them know when he needed them.

"What's up?" Surf asked as they all appeared in the room.

"Blood." He angled the flashlight so it picked up the blood. "I was right, Skye was here. She wasn't alone." The sight of her blood, spilled all over the floor, was making him queasy so he quickly moved his cell phone so it no longer picked up the sight of the blood.

"We might have some good news," Bear announced, lowering his cell phone from his ear. "Raven thinks she might have found a connection between Maksim Petrov and Dimitri Kuznetsov. Both are connected to a man named Grigoriy Golubev. He's Russian, he and his family fled when he was a teen to Romania. He's very wealthy and fairly widely known to dabble in all sorts of illegal activities, although he works hard to make sure there is nothing that can tie him to any of it."

Shoving to his feet, he slipped the locket into his pocket. "Let's go talk to him."

"Not that simple. Grigoriy Golubev is a Romanian diplomat, which means he has diplomatic immunity. Eagle is working on it, detailing what we know and making calls to the Romanian President, trying to get them to waive his immunity. He's confident he can get them to do it, but it's going to take a little time," Bear consoled him.

Time.

Time Skye might not have.

From the amount of blood on the floor, the injury Skye had sustained was serious. It wasn't enough to indicate that she had bled out in here, but enough that he knew wherever she was she wasn't in good shape.

Not that anything above a paper cut was acceptable when it came to Skye.

Scratch that, not even a paper cut was acceptable.

He wanted to wrap Skye in bubble wrap so nothing could ever hurt her again. For now, he'd have to settle with getting her back, and then he could worry about earning her forgiveness all over again.

Whatever it took.

The world needed Skye's brightness, and he needed his sun, moon, and stars.

* * * * *

December 10th
2:49 A.M.

Cold.

Her muscles ached from hours of holding herself rigid because shaking caused unbelievable pain.

The stench of death was in the air.

Damp and musty, like being buried in a coffin underground.

Skye was frozen from the outside to a place deep down inside.

She knew it wasn't just because of the chill in the air, it was the amount of blood her body had lost.

It had been a long time since Skye had felt physical pain like this.

Of course, in the years since she'd fled her parents' house to go to college, she'd hurt herself. Stubbed toes, paper cuts, and accidentally touching a frying pan while cooking, all caused temporary pain, but it was nothing like this.

This pain didn't fade a few minutes after the injury was caused.

No, this pain just kept getting worse.

And worse.

And worse.

It consumed her entire body with a white-hot fiery agony that got worse with any movement no matter how small.

Skye did her best to lie completely still, slowing her breathing as much as she could so her chest barely rose and fell with each intake of air, but lying on the cold concrete floor it was impossible not to move at all. The hard, unforgiving floor would be uncomfortable enough to be stuck on even if she was uninjured, but with the lingering bruises from her tumble down the stairs and the gunshot wound in her stomach, it was like lying on a bed of nails.

Nails that poked and needled at her, taunting her.

Tormenting her.

Almost worse than the horrific pain was knowing that nobody was looking for her. Nobody even knew she was in trouble.

Caleb and his team were back in New York. They likely knew she had gone to the airport and had assumed she'd flown back home, but they had no way of knowing she'd never made it to her house.

The man who had shot her must have used a silencer because she never heard the gunshot. Realistically, Skye knew that a silencer didn't completely silence the shot, but there were only businesses on either side of the clinic and they'd already been closed by the time she arrived. There had been no one there to hear anything.

Even if someone had witnessed her unconscious and bleeding body being loaded into a vehicle no one would suspect it was her own father responsible.

Should she be surprised her father was selling her to some man who planned on giving her as a gift for his son and his friends to use for the sexual entertainment at a Christmas party?

No, not after the hell he'd put her through as a child, and yet she was.

Stupid.

How stupid could she be?

Pretty stupid apparently.

Shock that her father would so callously dispose of her was bad enough, but she had to be a complete idiot to keep giving Caleb her trust even though he kept breaking it.

Caleb.

Stupid or not she loved him.

With every fiber of her being.

Had she overreacted by running off?

Her current predicament said that yes she had.

If she'd stayed in New York, listened to what Caleb had to say she wouldn't have been shot and abducted. She didn't even have to stay with him, he'd offered to put her in one of Prey Security's safehouses.

But she'd been upset.

Hurt.

Betrayed.

That betrayal had extended to the rest of his team, his entire company. His boss had deliberately sent him to her to use her, and his team, and likely their wives as well, all knew that she was the stupid girl who was being used. It made her question all her interactions with the women she had been beginning to see as friends. They couldn't have replaced Ashleigh, but they could have been real friends, a support system, maybe one day a family.

Now they'd never be anything but a memory.

A memory she wouldn't have for very long because soon she'd be dead.

Tears tumbled in a near constant stream down her cheeks, but she didn't cry, not properly. Just the tears. They were all she could manage.

Helplessness made her frustrated.

She wasn't a little girl anymore, she should be able to do something to help herself now.

Looking down her body, the bloodstain on her stomach made her queasy.

Normally, Skye wasn't squeamish, couldn't be a vet if you were, but this was different. This was *her* blood. And there was too much of it for her to think she was going to be able to fight her way out of this.

But she couldn't just give up.

Despite the hole in her heart that matched the one in her stomach, her love for Caleb hadn't just disappeared.

It couldn't.

He was part of her.

A part that had caused her a lot of pain but also one that had brought her a lot of happiness.

She'd told him that no matter what happened they would weather it. That their love could stand strong through the storms of life.

Could it?

Right now, it felt impossible, and yet the sound of Caleb's voice echoed in her ears.

Don't leave me.

There had been so much pain in his voice. And he'd sounded so remorseful. Was it possible that he had used his job as an excuse to come and see her in person?

She had ignored all his attempts at reaching out when he'd emailed, and called, and texted. It was possible—likely even—that she would reject him in person too, that was what she *had* done when he'd shown up in her clinic parking lot. If he hadn't been so persistent then she would never have considered forgiving him.

That persistence had pushed her to examine herself, the kind of person she was and the person she wanted to be.

It forced her to acknowledge that she'd never stopped loving Caleb.

Had his new betrayal severed those feelings?

No.

Those feelings would never go away.

So, if she lived she had two options. Number one, she could walk away, move on with her life, or at least try to, and no doubt spend the remainder of her years trying to forget her greatest love and pretend that part of her wasn't missing. Or, number two, she could forgive him, accept that while he should have been honest with her, he hadn't wanted to hurt her.

Did she believe that?

Perhaps it really did make her stupid, but she did believe him.

Mainly because she couldn't think of any other reason why he would have stuck around once he realized she hadn't had any contact with her dad in years. That would have ended his job, she was sure of it, yet he hadn't left. He'd hung around, working to earn her forgiveness and trust.

That meant something.

It had to.

It did.

If she got out of this mess alive, she wasn't sure she could just jump right back into a relationship with Caleb but maybe they could find a way to work through this. Maybe one day she could trust him again.

Because without trust she wasn't sure their love was enough to build a future on.

Not that she'd have a future if she died in this hellhole.

Shoving away the queasiness, Skye gripped the short chain that ran from the metal cuff around her wrist to a hook embedded in the floor, and very carefully lifted her torso.

The resulting tearing pain felt like it was ripping her apart.

Instead of giving in to it and sinking back down, Skye pushed onward, suddenly fueled by rage that her father thought any of this was okay.

Abusing her was awful enough, but to sell her, that was insanity.

And it was her father's fault that Ashleigh had been murdered.

Picturing the sweet little faces of Ashleigh's children, Skye somehow managed to move until her shoulders were propped against the wall. Those kids deserved justice, Ashleigh deserved justice. The only way that was going to happen was if she got out of here and told the world who her father really was.

Skye wasn't going to die in here and she wasn't going to be some plaything for a man with more money than morals.

As carefully as she could, Skye pulled up the hem of her sweater.

A scream fell from her lips as the material which had been embedded in the wound when the bullet tore through her clothes and then her flesh was ripped out. At least she knew the bullet wasn't still inside her. She'd been shot in the back, and the fact that she was drenched in blood on her front told her there was both an entry and an exit wound.

All it took was one glance at her wounds for her anger to deflate.

All the righteous fury in the world couldn't undo an injury.

Her skin was torn and red, enflamed and already showing signs of infection. Unless she made it to a hospital soon, she was unlikely to live long enough to be used and violated by the Russian man's son and friends.

Looked like whether or not she could forgive Caleb and have a future with him had become a moot point.

She wouldn't be living long enough to ever see him again.

CHAPTER TWENTY-ONE

December 10th
3:54 A.M.

The house was quiet.

Quieter than Brick would have anticipated.

Given what Grigoriy Golubev was rumored to be involved in he would have bet anything that the place would be teaming with security.

Instead, the house was surrounded by a simple brick fence, there was no wire on top, no sensor system that they could see. The metal gates weren't locked, and as he and the rest of his team slipped through them there were no guards visible, not even motion sensor lights turned on.

It seemed that Grigoriy wasn't concerned about anyone raiding his property. Either cops or any of his associates in his illegal dealings.

The guy was cocky, Brick had to give him that.

Maybe he truly believed that his diplomatic immunity was going to protect him from everything.

Eagle could be very persuasive, and once the man set his mind to something he always got it. He'd charmed his now wife and mother of his children into giving him a chance after having her thrown in a prison cell. If the man could do that, he could do anything.

And in this case, he had done the seemingly impossible.

With everything that Grigoriy Golubev was suspected of being involved in, and then the fact that two of his associates had been linked to the attempts on the life of the daughter of a presidential candidate, the Romanian President had been persuaded to waive immunity. Nothing was going to protect Grigoriy, not once they found Skye held prisoner on his estate.

She had to be here.

Brick wasn't sure he could survive much longer not having her back in his arms where she belonged.

Once he had her there, he'd do whatever it took to regain her trust.

Quit Prey if that's what she wanted, move to Virginia so she could remain close to her best friend's children, and rebuild the clinic they'd shared. Hell, if she wanted him to, he'd endure a flogging and crawl across burning coals. Nothing was off the table as far as he was concerned, as long as he found a way to make her love him again.

Her love was vital to his survival.

After spending just days with her he knew that down to his soul.

Moving like the well-oiled machine that they were, Alpha Team moved steadily and stealthily toward the house. The property was big but not huge, and although he kept expecting guards to approach as they made their way across the manicured yard none ever did.

The house was dark, and all it took was picking a lock to gain access.

No screech of a security system announced their arrival and Brick started to get concerned.

No matter how confident he was if Grigoriy Golubev was here with a kidnap victim then surely he would be taking measures to make sure he was protected. Since that clearly wasn't the case did it mean that Grigoriy wasn't here?

Had he already left the country with Skye in tow?

If he had, their chances of finding her dropped dramatically.

It wouldn't be impossible, Prey was already working on gathering intel on the man but Skye was injured and they didn't know how badly. There was every chance she wouldn't survive long enough for them to find where she'd been taken.

Or she could already be dead.

Not willing to accept that without conclusive proof, Brick followed Arrow as they made their way down to the basement.

The team was splitting up, he and Arrow would check the basement because that was where Skye was most likely to be. Mouse and Domino were taking the first floor, and Bear and Surf the second.

As much as his protective rage made him want to be the one to find Grigoriy Golubev and beat the man to a bloody pulp until that rage dissipated, more than that, he wanted to be there for Skye. Besides being physically injured, she was emotionally traumatized from everything her father had put her through.

Everything *he* had put her through.

Even if she hated him, he *would* be there for her.

They quickly located a door in the kitchen that took them down to the basement, and watching each other's backs, they descended.

It was as quiet down here as it had been upstairs and outside.

No signs of life.

Panic had him wanting to buck protocol and scream Skye's name, go running wildly into the space, not caring if there were any threats lurking, and search for her until he found her.

But he didn't.

Because her safety was more important than soothing his panic.

As they left the stairs and entered a large, open space, the smell hit him.

Metallic.

Blood.

He'd know that smell anywhere, and the scent of it in a place he knew Skye was—or had been—made his gut churn with nausea.

224

Weapons up, lights shining around the corners of the dark room, they found nothing.

Nothing.

The large space was empty, there were chains embedded in the walls, and cages in two of the corners. It was obvious that the Romanian Diplomat kept people against their will down here.

When the dancing light of his flashlight glinted off a puddle of something he almost lost it.

The room was empty of threats, and he hurried over to kneel beside the puddle of blood beside the chains on the far wall.

Skye's blood.

He knew it was hers even without DNA testing confirming it.

She'd been here but now she was gone.

"Drop the weapon."

Bear's voice echoing through their comms had both him and Arrow snapping to attention. Had they found Grigoriy Golubev?

The only way he was going to get answers as to where his woman was, was if the Diplomat gave them up.

"We got one man in a bedroom on the second floor," Surf's voice said quietly. "It is not Grigoriy Golubev, its Maksim Petrov."

A switch snapped inside him.

Something broke.

A piece of him that would forever be scarred by the hell Skye had been put through.

Ignoring Arrow's calls for him to wait, he took off up the stairs at a blind run. Nothing mattered to him other than getting answers.

That was his job.

What he did.

The skill that made him an asset to his SEAL team and now to Prey and Alpha Team.

There had never been a person he had met that could withstand his interrogation techniques. He had an innate ability to read people, to know what would be the most effective way to gather the intel he needed.

Never before had he prayed for his ability not to fail him like he did as he raced up the stairs.

Skye's life depended on him finding out where she was.

She was counting on him, and he vowed here and now he would never fail her again. He would never put himself, or his own fears before Skye and her needs.

She was his everything and it was time he started treating her as such.

Nobody tried to stop him as he shoved past the rest of his team to face down Maksim Petrov. The man who had tried to kill Skye once already, who had murdered her friend, and who was likely the one who had abducted Skye. He was standing in the middle of a bedroom, beside a bed with mussed covers, a weapon in his hand, aimed at Bear.

"Do you know who I am?" Brick growled.

There was resignation in the dark eyes that stared back at him. No fear, but a sense of acknowledgment and acceptance. "You're the man who was there the day at the clinic. Don't know your name, don't care, but I assume you're Skye Xenos' man."

Rage unlike anything he'd experienced blanketed him, not in a haze of red, but in a cloak of black. It consumed him.

"She's my heart."

Maksim shrugged. "Business, not personal."

Like that explanation was going to do anything to assuage his fury.

"You took her."

Another shrug. "That was the job. I don't fail. I would have preferred to kill her, but my orders were changed."

So at least she was alive.

Brick swayed as relief threatened to knock him to his knees.

"Changed to what?"

"She's been sold to Grigoriy Golubev, the Diplomat is giving her as a gift to his son."

"Sold?" he roared.

"Entertainment for a Christmas party," Maksim said, and from the amusement dancing in his dark eyes he'd shared that bit of information only to annoy him.

"She was here?" he asked.

"She was. After I shot her I brought her here."

Blocking out the shot part so he could function, Brick asked, "Where is she now?"

"Grigoriy left a few hours ago. Told me I could stay here for a while, but that he needed to leave. Took the girl with him."

"Where were they going?" Sounded like Grigoriy Golubev had been tipped off that his immunity had been revoked and left Maksim Petrov behind to take the fall. Right now, Brick cared less about the diplomat than he did about getting to Skye.

"Her father's," Maksim replied.

Finally, they had what they needed.

Proof of a crime to have Hemmingway Xenos arrested. Once they had him in custody, they could search for evidence he was involved in Kristoff's plot.

"We all know what happens next," Maksim stated.

The man fired his gun, five shots fired in unison and Brick heard the sound of a body hitting the floor, but he had already turned away, his focus only on Skye.

* * * * *

December 10th
5:13 A.M.

Back where it all began.

It made sense that this would be where she died.

Even though Skye knew she had only been temporarily dropped off here because the Russian man, Grigoriy Golubev, didn't want to be caught traveling with a dying kidnap victim, she felt like she didn't have long left. She was to be picked up at sunrise and flown out of the country, delivered to Grigoriy's son in preparation for his party.

As Skye tried to breathe through the pain eating her alive, she looked around the attic.

How many hours had she spent locked away up here?

More than she cared to figure out.

The box where her father used to lock her up was still up here, although thankfully he hadn't put her inside it. Probably because she wasn't going to be here for long so he thought it wasn't worth the effort, but she'd seen him look at it and smile when Grigoriy Golubev's goons had dumped her in here.

She hadn't always been locked in the box when she was put up here in the attic. Sometimes he just locked her in here, no food, no water, no bed to sleep on, and left her for days. Then there were times he brought her up here to beat her, or whip her with his belt. Some of the beatings had been so bad she was positive he was going to kill her.

Now more than ever, Skye could feel death hovering close by.

It whispered across her skin with each cold shiver, it ate her up with each wave of pain, it inched ever closer with each harsh breath.

Sweat dotted her brow and she was no longer sure if it was because of the pain, the effort of trying to remain conscious, or if infection was seeping into her bloodstream.

Tired.

Skye wanted to slip away into blissful unconsciousness, but pain prevented it.

Her entire body burned with it. To the point where it was hard to think of anything else, and yet as exhausted as she was, thoughts of Caleb were never far from her mind. He hovered beside her, next to the whisper of death, sharing this journey with her even if he was miles away with no idea that she was in trouble.

When would he learn about her disappearance?

Would he?

Or had he already given up on her?

It wasn't like she would blame him if he did. He knew he'd betrayed her again, and she'd told him she had to leave. If he'd decided to give her the space she wanted that was what he should have done. There was no earthly way for him to know that she'd never made it home.

She should have listened to him and stayed in New York.

She'd let her pain override her common sense and she knew better.

Skye had no one to blame but herself for the fact that she was going to die a painful and lonely death.

A lone tear trickled down her cheek as her mind finally reached a brick wall and crashed.

Movement woke her sometime later.

So she wasn't dead yet.

That didn't bode well for her.

Someone was coming which meant her time was up. She'd been hoping she would already be dead before she made it to Romania or wherever this party of the Russian Diplomat's son was happening.

Of course, she wasn't going to be that lucky.

When in her life had she ever lucked out?

If she had any energy left, she would have lifted herself into a sitting position, at least met her fate head-on.

While Skye might not have lucked out in life, she'd had plenty of wonderful moments. Memories she had to cling to now. She'd known freedom when she went to college and could live her life on her own terms, she'd known the joy of having a job she loved, she'd known true friendship, and she'd known what it was to be loved.

All in all, despite the abuse she'd suffered and the betrayal by the man she loved she'd lived a good life.

A full life.

If this was how it ended, then so be it.

A shadowy figure moved toward her and she braced herself for more pain.

Pain she would endure by focusing on the highs rather than the lows.

An image of Caleb filled her mind. Despite everything, when she thought of the highs in her life he was there. Teasing, laughing, loving, he'd brought her at least as much joy as he had pain.

No.

More joy.

In this moment, as she faced the horrors of the end of her life, knowing exactly what was in store for her, she knew that if given a chance she would have been able to forgive Caleb for not being honest with her and using her.

Grabbing onto the image of Caleb she refused to let go of it.

He'd never know it, but he would be the only thing that got her through the next few days of hell, and when her time came he would be her last thought.

"Skye."

Caleb's voice.

And the image of him in her mind was growing bigger like he was moving closer.

Maybe her strung-out mind was hallucinating now.

She'd take it.

Hallucination or real thing, Caleb would provide the comfort she needed.

"Baby, I'm so sorry I wasn't there when you needed me."

She would have sworn that he knelt beside her and his knuckles swept across her cheek. She could feel their touch on her chilled skin because warmth seeped into her.

But Caleb wasn't here.

Caleb was back in New York.

"Hold on, honey, we're getting you out of here."

This hallucination was perfection. He was soft and sweet, reassuring and comforting, and Skye found she didn't even care that it wasn't the real thing, beggars couldn't be choosers and she'd take what she could get.

"This is going to hurt, baby, but I need to check your wound."

No.

Why was hallucination Caleb suddenly trying to cause her pain?

Instinct had her swatting at the hands that moved toward her gunshot wound. "No."

"I'm sorry, honey."

Hallucination Caleb sounded like he was in almost as much pain as she was.

Could hallucinations feel emotion?

Wasn't he just a figment of her imagination?

When hands probed at her stomach, she screamed, her shoulders jerking off the floor. Okay, that was real. Too real. No hallucination.

"*Hell.* I'm sorry, baby, I hate causing you pain, seems it's all I do."

Oh my gosh.

He was real.

This wasn't a hallucination it was the real Caleb.

How was that possible?

"Caleb?"

His eyes met hers, stormy and full of emotion. Pain and regret stood out starkly, along with a heavy dose of guilt. Lifting his hand he palmed her cheek, his fingertips caressing her skin with a gentleness that brought tears to her eyes. "I'm here, honey."

"How? I don't ..."

"I'll explain everything, but right now I need to get you out of here."

She had no idea how this was possible.

Just when she had been ready to accept that fate had a horrible plan in store for her, all of a sudden, she'd been given a reprieve.

Of course, she was thrilled not to face violation and death, but now that Caleb was here she felt the last of her strength had drained away.

"Tired," she mumbled.

"I know you are, baby, but I need you to hold on a little longer for me, then I promise you can rest for as long as you need."

Even though every molecule of her body screamed for sleep, she forced her eyes to remain open. Caleb's fingers curled around her wrist, she assumed taking her pulse, but his gaze was unfocused, and he was talking to someone else.

His team?

Her ability to focus let alone think was fading. She was just too tired. Everything was huzzy. Huzzy? No fuzzy? Hazy? She wasn't even sure what she meant.

"Okay, baby, I'll be right back, just hold on for me, okay?"

Maybe she nodded in agreement, she honestly didn't know. All she was doing was holding on like Caleb had asked her to do, that was all she could manage right now.

When he rose and moved away from her, Skye almost cried out and reached for him. Why was he leaving? How had he known she was here? Did he know her father had sold her to a Romanian Diplomat who was going to give her to his son?

The questions spun around in her mind making her dizzy.

Gunshots rang out and she flinched.

A shadow moved on the opposite side of the attic to where Caleb had headed.

Her father.

She saw him slinking from the door that led to the hidden passageway.

Skye didn't know what he had planned but he had a gun in his hand.

One he lifted and aimed at Caleb.

When she turned her head she could see Caleb at the main

door to the attic, unaware that there was a threat behind him.

No matter what had happened between them or what the future would have held for them, whether she trusted him or not, she loved Caleb wholly and completely.

As her father moved closer, his weapon still trained on Caleb, Skye somehow found the strength to lunge to her feet and fling herself between her father and the man she loved.

The shot was fired.

White hot agony burned through her chest.

And then blessed darkness descended.

CHAPTER TWENTY-TWO

December 10th
6:00 A.M.

At the sound of the weapon firing, Brick spun around.

And came face to face with his worst nightmare.

Skye was stumbling, falling to the floor. Her father stood behind her with a weapon in his hand. While Hemmingway Xenos was looking at his daughter in shock, there was no remorse on his face, and when he lifted his gaze to Brick, he could see determination there.

They fired at the same time, but Brick always hit what he aimed at.

While Hemmingway's bullet went wide, slamming harmlessly into the ceiling, his struck the man between the eyes, dropping him instantly.

Confident in his ability, Brick didn't bother pausing to confirm that Skye's father was dead, he kicked the weapon out of the way, then threw himself to his knees beside the woman he loved.

A woman who was now drenched in blood.

"No, no, no. Baby, no. Why did you do that?" he murmured as he rolled her slumped body over. He was wearing body armor, Hemmingway's bullet would never have pierced his skin, but his girl didn't know that. All Skye had seen was her father pointing a weapon at him, and the stupidly brave woman had thrown herself in front of it.

After everything he'd done to her, she'd risked her life to save him.

Brick just prayed she hadn't *given* her life to save him.

"Arrow, get up here. Now!" he screamed into his comms. Eagle had worked his magic while Alpha Team had traveled from Grigoriy Golubev's house to Hemmingway Xenos' and gotten warrants for the man's arrest. Even though Hemmingway's men had been told to stand down, the man obviously had his own personal army because despite the fact that cops had come in with Alpha Team they'd all been shot at.

"Coming," Arrow's voice echoed through the comms.

"Caleb?" Skye's weak voice croaked his name and his attention snapped back to her.

"I'm here, honey," he assured her as he ripped at the sweater she was wearing so he could see her wounds.

There was the older wound on her stomach, already red and infected looking, but it was the gushing wound low on her chest on her left side, just below her heart, the had his own heart racing in his chest.

Too much blood.

It poured from the wound, puddling on the floor beneath her, soaking into the knees of his pants as he pressed his hands to the hole, desperately trying to slow the flow of blood. Instead, all that happened was her blood stained his hands.

She was bleeding out.

He had enough medical knowledge to know that her chances of living were slim. Her body was already weakened from the untreated gunshot wound, this second one, hitting her where it had, meant it would take a miracle for him not to lose her.

Even though Skye was the one who had been shot, Brick felt like his life was bleeding out in front of him right along with Skye's.

How was he going to go on without her?

Knowing this was his fault would destroy him. Festering wounds would slowly consume him because he was to blame for Skye running off and being alone and in danger. If he had been completely honest with her from the beginning, she would have had no reason to run. If he'd figured out she'd go to the clinic and not her house he would have been there, prevented her from being shot, or at least rushed her straight to a hospital.

Instead, she'd been abducted and shot again.

Skye's eyes were open, her gaze unfocused, but at least she hadn't left him yet.

"You hold on for me, okay, honey?" he begged. He'd beg, plead, and bargain with anyone—including the devil himself—if it kept the woman he loved alive.

Her head gave the slightest of jerks, which he took to be a promise that she would fight with everything she had not to leave him.

Vaguely he was aware of his team surrounding them.

Arrow dropped to his knees on the other side of Skye, setting up an IV in the back of one of her hands.

Blood.

What she needed now was blood.

"Do we know her blood type?" he asked no one in particular.

"We'll type her at the hospital," Arrow said.

"I'm O neg, she needs blood now, take mine." Brick would gladly give her all of his blood, he just needed her to live.

"Medivac is on its way, but we can get a unit going into her now," Arrow agreed.

Brick never took his gaze off Skye's as Arrow set up a field transfusion. Every second counted right now, the medics might be here soon, but Skye was literally dying right in front of him.

"Stay with me, baby," he said, reaching out to take her hand.

Surf was keeping pressure on the wound on Skye's chest, Mouse was holding the IV bag, Arrow was moving between tending the transfusion kit, and keeping a check on Skye's vitals. Bear and Domino stood guard around them as though they could physically fight off death if it tried to come for Skye.

All of them looked helpless, they were protectors, they were men of action, they did things, took care of things. That there was nothing they could do to save Skye besides try to stop more blood leaking from her wounds and attempt to replace it with more blood was hard on all of them.

"You hold on, Skye, you fight. I need you. I'm not ready to lose you. I'm so sorry that I didn't tell you the truth, but I'm more sorry that I let so many years go by without tracking you down and making you listen to my apology. I wish I had chosen you all those years ago, and I wish I had come to my senses quicker, and I wish I hadn't let fear hold me back. Damn, baby, I have so many regrets, but the biggest is not making sure you knew without a shadow of a doubt how much I love you. You're the sun, moon, and stars of my world, you're my everything. I love you, Skye, I love you so much."

Her hand in his was so cold, and her skin so pale it was virtually translucent, making the blood staining her skin seem that much more vivid.

Tears fell from his eyes in a steady stream, but he made no move to wipe them away. There was no shame in shedding tears when your heart, your soul, your everything was dying and there was nothing you could do to stop it from happening.

Skye's lips moved but he couldn't make out what she was saying.

Leaning down he touched his ear to her lips.

"Sorry … have to … leave you …"

The words were nothing more than a hint of a whispered sound on a breath of air, but they packed more of a punch than any other words ever spoken.

"No, honey! You're not leaving me. I won't let you go, Skye. I won't. I need you!" he screamed.

Still despite his pleas, her eyes fluttered closed, and the hand he still held in his went completely limp.

"No! Skye!"

More people filled the space, they pulled him away from Skye, got between him and his woman, and he lost it.

Brick screamed, begged, threatened, but his team pulled him back, held him when he would have torn anything standing between him and Skye out of his path. Arrow kept his hands clamped around his arm, and it was only when he realized he was still giving Skye blood, likely the only thing standing between her and death that he finally calmed.

"They're doing everything they can," Bear said, his voice quiet, but firm. "Don't make it harder on them. Everyone is fighting for your girl, but right now the way you can fight for her is by calming down and holding it together. She still needs you, don't let her down this time."

With those words echoing in his head, Brick forced himself to calm down, to hold it together.

When one of the EMTs shot him a glance, he nodded to say he had himself back under control, and the man moved to the side letting him have access to Skye. They'd intubated her, wrapped bandages around her wounds, and moved her onto a stretcher.

She was so still.

So quiet.

The bright warmth that always shone from her was no longer visible.

Stooping, he touched his lips to her forehead and held them there for a long moment before finally straightening. "I'm not done fighting for you, my beautiful, bright, sun, moon, and stars, so you better fight alongside me. If you come back to me, Skye, I promise I will never hurt you again, never betray you, never let you down. For the rest of our lives, I will love you with everything that I have. I will find a way to make things up to you, but I can't do that if you leave me, honey. Stay with me, Skye. Don't leave me."

* * * * *

December 10th
6:22 P.M.

Nothing.

How much longer was it going to be?

They'd been in the hospital for twelve hours, Skye had been in surgery all of that time, and not once had anyone come out to give them an update.

Brick had to believe that at least meant she was still alive. If she wasn't, someone would have come and told him.

Him and the huge gathering that was here for Skye.

She thought she was alone in the world, that he'd betrayed her—and he wasn't denying that he had messed up, badly—that the rest of his team had used her, that their wives didn't really care about her.

She couldn't be more wrong.

Everyone was suffering a major case of guilt. His whole team felt bad for making her feel used, as did their wives. Eagle Oswald was doing what he always did and placing the responsibility for the whole thing squarely on his shoulders. He was here as well, along with his wife Olivia and the rest of the Oswald siblings.

Fifteen-year-old Cleo was keeping her two-year-old brother Roman, and cousins—Eagle and Olivia's two-year-old Luna, Falcon and Hope's thirteen-month-old Adelia, Hawk and Maddy's two-year-old Louie, and Sparrow and Ethan's ten-month-old Connor—entertained. Olivia was seven months pregnant with her second child, youngest Oswald Dove was also seven months pregnant with her and Isaac's first. Sparrow and her husband Ethan were just days away from the birth of their second child yet they were here. As were Hawk and Maddy whose second child was due at the end of the month.

Despite what Skye believed, she was already a member of the Prey family, and she had the support of every single one of the more than two dozen people who had dropped everything to

239

come and await word on her surgery.

Other than tending to the kids, no one spoke much, his team hung around close to him and every time he felt like he was about to lose it, one of them would step closer and remind him that if Skye hadn't given up then he couldn't either.

The longer they waited the tenser he became. His entire body felt like it was wound tight, and he was just waiting for the second when he snapped and unraveled.

It was coming.

Brick could feel it inching ever closer.

Then finally the door to the waiting room opened.

An exhausted looking older man stepped inside, his eyes widened slightly in surprise at the packed room. "I'm assuming you're all here for Skye Xenos."

"We are," Brick replied, hurrying over.

"You're all family?" the doctor asked, somewhat suspiciously.

They might not be blood, but this was her family. Her father was dead, her mother had been taken into custody and with her husband gone wasn't hesitating to tell everything. Including admitting that Hemmingway had been involved with Kristoff Mikhailov and Zara Duffy, and that Skye had been sold to Grigoriy Golubev who had planned to give her as a gift to his son.

"I'm her fiancé," he replied, arching a brow and daring the doctor to argue. As soon as he could convince Skye to give him a chance, he'd be putting his ring on her finger, so it was true even if it wasn't completely accurate.

The doctor gave a weary sign and nodded. "We almost lost her a couple of times, but she made it through surgery. There was damage to her heart and lungs, and to a few of her internal organs from the bullet wound to her abdomen. Right now, we're concerned about infection, the effects of the blood loss, and the fact that her body was already weak before sustaining the second wound."

None of that sounded good. "What does that mean?"

"It means that we've done everything we can, the rest is up to her."

"When can I see her?"

"We'll be moving her from recovery to the ICU shortly. Once she's settled, a nurse will come and get you. She's got a long road of recovery ahead of her," the doctor warned.

Brick glanced around the room. "She won't be walking that road alone."

With a nod, the doctor left the room and Brick felt his body sag with relief. He might have hit the floor if Domino and Mouse hadn't grabbed his arms. His mind and body felt completely tapped out, and the simultaneous relief that Skye had made it through surgery was tempered by the fact that she wasn't even close to being out of the woods.

The wait to be taken to see her felt longer than the almost twelve hours they'd spent in the waiting room anxiously awaiting news, but eventually a nurse came and took him to the ICU.

That moment where he first saw her would forever be seared into his brain.

Lying in the hospital bed, surrounded by machines, wires, and tubes seemed to be attached to every part of her body, not breathing on her own, she looked so small and fragile. All he wanted to do was haul her into his arms and hold her, but he had to settle for taking the room's only chair, pulling it up to the side of the bed, and carefully cradling one of her hands in his.

Tears streamed down his cheeks for the first hour he sat there, holding her hand, talking to her, begging her to hold on, to not give up.

The first night was hell. Machines screamed warnings as Skye's blood pressure would drop dangerously low. Then her heart gave out altogether and he was forced to watch as a team of doctors and nurses battled to bring her back.

But things would get better.

They had to.

Because he wasn't losing her.

The second day the infection in her first wound began to spread through her body. Brick was forced to sit helplessly by and watch as her temperature climbed higher and higher.

The third day she was rushed back into surgery to try to deal with the infection that was slowly stealing her away from him.

The fourth day was the first time he felt like he could take a breath without choking on it as her body finally began responding to the antibiotics.

Even though he was alone in Skye's small ICU cubical, he was never alone at the hospital. His teammates came and went, begging him to take a small break, go to the hotel, shower, eat, get some proper rest.

Nothing would make him leave Skye's side.

His vigil passed through days five and six in a blur, she wasn't getting any worse, but she wasn't waking up either.

The doctors dialed back the sedatives, hoping her body and brain had been given enough rest that they would start to wake up.

But she didn't.

By day seven Brick was starting to wonder if she would ever regain consciousness. It wasn't just the physical trauma her body had endured, but the psychological trauma he was worried about. Skye had been almost raped and murdered, killed a man, been attacked, lost her clinic, lost her best friend, found out he'd lied, been shot and kidnapped, and known she was going to be sold. How much could one person take?

She'd given him her trust and her heart only to have him abuse both.

Maybe she didn't want to wake up.

Did she believe him when he'd apologized, told her that he hadn't wanted to hurt her, and had used his job as an excuse to see her?

Or did she think it was more lies meant to manipulate her?

Even if she did survive could he ever make things up to her?

Would she ever trust in him again?

Smoothing a lock of hair off Skye's forehead, he tucked it behind her ear, wanting so desperately to be able to touch his lips to hers, and let her feel his love for her. Impotence was the last thing any man wanted to feel, and his inability to do anything to change this situation, bring his Skye back to him, was slowly draining away his spirit.

"Sweet Skye, you've fought your whole life to survive, to find happiness. If I could fight this battle for you so you didn't have to I would. In a heartbeat. But I can't do that for you, honey. I won't give up, I won't back down, I'm here, and I'm not leaving, not ever, but I need you to meet me halfway. Can you do that for me, baby? Can you come back to me?"

CHAPTER TWENTY-THREE

December 18th
11:35 A.M.

Warmth.

A rush of warmth tugged Skye out of the cold, dark place she'd been stuck in.

She had no memory of where she was or what had happened, all she knew was that she was alone and scared.

But as the warmth seeped into her, she realized she wasn't alone.

Someone was there.

A presence she couldn't attach a name to, just something steady, unbreakable, that didn't move.

It was just there.

The warmth started in her hand, and slowly she felt it spread throughout her body. Up her arm, through her shoulder, down her chest and abdomen, and then through both legs, then it spread up, warming her head, and giving her a little clarity.

Memories returned.

The pain in her stomach as the bullet tore through her flesh. The fear of being abducted and told she was going to be sold for sex. The hallucination of Caleb turning into the real thing. And then the searing pain as the bullet pierced her chest as she threw herself between her father and Caleb.

He'd begged her to hold on, not to leave him, but she'd known it was a foregone conclusion.

She was dying.

Only she hadn't died.

She was alive.

With the realization that she wasn't dead, that somehow she had survived came horrible pain.

It shoved the warmth aside and consumed her body.

A hiss of air into her lung caught her by surprise and she panicked.

What was going on?

"It's okay, baby, calm down."

The voice worked like a switch and her eyes popped open.

Everything was hazy and blurry. She tried blinking her eyes, but it didn't seem to help.

Another hiss of air into her lungs made her upper body jerk off the bed.

"Calm down, honey. Stop fighting it. I need a doctor in here! Now!"

Skye blinked again and this time her vision cleared enough to see Caleb standing beside her. One of his hands was pressed to her shoulder, applying just enough pressure to hold her down, from the warmth still enclosing her hand she assumed he was holding hers.

"It's just the ventilator, Skye. Do you hear me? Don't try to fight it, it's helping you breathe."

Caleb's face was close to hers, close enough that she could see the worry in his eyes. Not just worry, there were dark circles under his eyes, his beard was scrappier than she remembered, and his eyes were red.

He looked haggard.

How long had she been here?

Even though she should have been expecting it the next hiss of the ventilator shoving air into her lungs caught her by surprise.

It was one thing to know that it was helping her, and she should be calm and move with it instead of trying to fight against it, it was another to actually do that.

It felt wrong.

Weird.

And when her body tried to take a breath on its own and found instead the machine was sucking air out of her lungs she panicked again.

Voices babbled around her.

Her vision grew fuzzy again.

Then she was sliding away into the darkness once more.

The next thing she registered was something brushing across her knuckles. The pain was still there but it was a little subdued, distant, and the warmth that had first tugged her out of the cold, black world she'd been trapped in was still there.

Caleb.

He was the first thought she had, and when she opened her eyes, she saw him sitting beside her bed, he was watching her and when he saw her awake a light lit in his eyes.

The warmth she'd been feeling was Caleb.

His presence was the steadiness that she felt beside her.

Had he been here with her the whole time she'd been in the hospital, however long that had been?

"Hey, baby," he whispered, and leaned over so he could touch his lips to hers.

It was only then that she realized there was no longer a tube down her throat. After sedating her the doctors must have decided that she was strong enough to breathe on her own and removed the tube.

There were questions Skye wanted to ask. She wanted to know what had happened. How long she'd been here. The extent of her injuries. Her prognosis.

But she had no energy, not even enough to say his name, or curl her fingers around his.

In books and movies, when people had been shot and intubated then woke up, they just kind of bounced back.

Unfortunately, real life wasn't anything like that.

"It's okay, honey, you close your eyes and go back to sleep. I love you and I'm not going anywhere," Caleb said, his lips touching her forehead this time.

Because she was so weak, she had no choice but to slip back into sleep.

Next time she woke there were voices speaking softly somewhere nearby. This time she knew where she was and when she lifted her heavy eyelids her gaze immediately sought out Caleb.

When she saw him she felt herself settle.

He was still there.

He hadn't left.

As soon as he glanced over and saw she was awake a giant smile lit up his face and he came to her side, bending down to kiss her. "Hi, honey."

A man with dark hair and blue eyes that she hadn't met before came to stand on the other side of the bed. "Hi, Ms. Xenos. I'm Eagle Oswald, Brick's boss. I just wanted you to know that I'm the one who asked Brick to go to you, see if we could use you to get intel on your father. If I had known the history between you two, I never would have asked that of him. Everything that happened is on me, and Prey will make sure that we handle anything you need during your recovery. You have the support of me, my family, and every single person at Prey. You're part of our family now."

Was she?

Was that dependent on what happened next with Caleb?

She had no energy left to worry about it, maybe she gave Eagle a nod, or maybe she didn't, as she slipped into sleep she wasn't sure.

When she woke next the room was dark, Caleb was stretched out in a chair beside her bed, his head tipped back, eyes closed, snoring softly. She was glad he was getting some rest, she got the feeling he hadn't gotten much recently.

Not wanting to go back to sleep right away, Skye lay for a long time and just watched Caleb. He loved her, that she knew deep down inside her, it wasn't in question, what was, was whether or not she could trust him again.

It wasn't really about forgiveness. After coming so close to death she wasn't going to withhold her forgiveness. She believed him when he said it was fear that had kept him from her for the last fifteen years and that when her life intersected with his job, he'd used that as the push he needed. She could understand that, the problem was the fact he hadn't chosen to be honest and tell her on his own. Would he ever have told her if she hadn't learned the truth from her dad first?

Right now, she didn't have the energy to figure out the future. As weak as she felt, she was going to have to take things one moment at a time.

Eventually, she drifted back off and when she woke next it was to the smell of coffee.

As soon as she opened her eyes her gaze fell on the steaming cup in Caleb's hands making him laugh.

"You feeling good enough to crave coffee, huh, honey?"

Skye nodded before she even realized that she'd responded.

There was relief in Caleb's eyes as he set the coffee down on the table and picked up a cup of water. "Doctor said you can have a drink if you want one, see how you go with it. Thirsty?"

Actually, she was.

When she nodded again, he held the straw to her lips, and she took a couple of sips. The cool water flowing down her throat felt delightful.

"Good?" Caleb asked.

She went to nod again, then decided that she may as well see if she was up to using her voice yet. "Yes."

It came out as more a weak rasp than anything else, but she'd spoken and it felt like a monumental victory.

"Honey, you have no idea how good it is to hear your voice. For a while there I thought …" Caleb trailed off and a couple of tears fell down his cheeks.

He was crying?

Her big tough SEAL was shedding tears?

It wasn't until that moment that Skye realized just how terrified of losing her Caleb had been, and how close to death she had come.

Wanting to soothe him, and ease a little of his pain, she summoned her strength and lifted her hand, reaching out for him. "Caleb."

He didn't hesitate to take her hand in his, lifting it and touching a kiss to each one of her knuckles. "I love you, baby. And I will spend the rest of my life proving that to you so you never doubt me again."

What little energy she'd recouped had drained away, but as her eyes fluttered closed, she murmured, "Love you."

* * * * *

December 20th
3:44 P.M.

"Caleb!"

Skye woke in a panic, convinced that Caleb had taken a bullet.

"Baby? What's wrong? I'm right here, honey. You're okay, calm down, Skye."

His voice soothed her a little, but the terror had been so real, her belief that he had been shot so absolute.

"Shh, you're okay," he soothed, holding her hand to his lips and touching kiss after kiss to it.

It wasn't enough.

She needed more of him.

"Hold me," she murmured. Her voice was still weak, but her strength was returning little by little.

"Can't, honey," he reminded her, gesturing to the tubes and

wires attached to her body.

"Need you." She didn't care about anything else, she just needed to be in the arms of the man she loved.

"I don't want to hurt you." Even though he said the words, he lowered the bedrail.

"Don't care."

Ever so carefully, Caleb perched on the edge of the mattress beside her and slipped an arm around her shoulders. There was pain in her chest as her upper body was lifted off the bed, but it was worth it when Caleb settled her against his chest.

He was so gentle with her, and it was obvious he hadn't left her side in the ten days she'd been here in the hospital. He loved her despite the pain he'd caused her, and knowing that made her tear up.

She hadn't cried yet over what had happened, there hadn't been time and since she first woke up two days ago, she hadn't had the energy for anything, but now the tears came.

They rolled down her cheeks, and even though she tried to control her sobbing so she didn't aggravate her chest wound, she still wept enough that it hurt.

Everything hurt.

Her body, her mind, her heart, her soul.

She wanted to go back and redo her whole life, this time telling Caleb that she was in love with him when they were teens rather than being scared and waiting to see if he had feelings beyond friendship for her first.

But in life, there were no do-overs.

You couldn't go back, you could only keep moving forward.

"Don't cry, honey, please," Caleb said, his hold on her firm without being tight enough to hurt her, and his hands roamed everywhere, stroking, patting, soothing.

By the time her tears finally dried up, Skye felt wiped out. She hated this, being so weak, the amount of time she was able to remain awake was increasing but she had enough medical knowledge as a vet to know that she had a very long road ahead of her.

Recovery would be slow, the journey painful and frustrating, and she wondered if she'd be walking that road alone.

"Is it too late?" Caleb asked. "Have I already lost you? I know it's not fair of me to put the onus of saving our relationship on you when I'm the one who keeps messing up, but I'm asking you for another chance."

Carefully, he eased her back so she lay against the pillows, and stood, pulling something from his pocket. When he held it up, she realized it was the locket he'd given her when they were teenagers. The one she hadn't been able to get rid of but had removed at her clinic when she'd run from New York.

He must have found it there and held onto it.

"I had more stars engraved on the back of the locket. Twenty-eight stars. One for each year I've known you, they're in an infinity symbol because no matter what I will never stop loving you."

Picking up her hand he placed the locket in her palm and one by one curled her fingers over it. Then he began to unbutton his shirt. Her brow furrowed, wondering what he was doing. He couldn't want sex, she was in no shape to do much of anything except lie here, so what was he doing?

Once he had it unbuttoned, she saw the answer.

He had a new tattoo.

It was the same image that was on the locket, a sun, moon, and twenty-eight stars in the shape of an infinity symbol. All done on the left side of his chest above his heart.

More tears burned her eyes.

"I found a tattoo artist who would agree to come to the hospital and do the tattoo here because I wasn't leaving your side. *You* are my heart, Skye. You're my sun, moon, and stars. My life is darkness without you in it. I already talked to Eagle, if you want to go back to Virginia and rebuild your clinic there then I'll move, we'll find a way to make Alpha Team work with me living in a different state, and New York isn't that far away. If you decide you want to move to New York I made some calls, there's a clinic run by an older woman looking to retire in the next couple of years who would be prepared to sell to you. And I called some real estate agents asking for listings for any fixer uppers in the neighborhoods where some of my teammates live."

Wow he'd thought of everything.

While he had been waiting for her to wake up, he had been thinking about their future and how to make things work.

"Fixer uppers?"

"I know how much fun you had doing up your house, and that if we were to find a place together, you'd want to put your stamp on it. It would be something to do together." He shot her a smile, but she saw the uncertainty behind it. "It'll be fun painting, and laying tiles, and floorboards with you."

"How did you know that's what I'd want?"

"Because I know you, it's knowing myself that's the problem." Sitting beside her again, he took both of her hands in his. "I let desperation for my father's love and approval rule my life when I was younger, then I let fear of losing the only good thing I've ever had keep me away from you. I'm done letting anything get in the way of what I want. I want you, Skye. I want a future. I want marriage and commitment and partnership. I want it all. But only with you. I don't care how long it takes, I'll find a way to show you how much I love you and prove I'm worthy of your trust."

He looked and sounded so serious, and she wanted to say yes.

Yes to everything.

To sharing their lives, to loving him, to trusting him.

"I know these are just gestures, that they don't convince you that I won't ever hurt you again, and I know I have no right to ask for a third chance, but I have to ask, Skye. I know what it's like to live without you in my life, and I know what it's like to worry that I'm going to lose your bright light forever. I sat beside your bed for days, praying you would live, wondering what I was going to say to you when—if—you woke up. I've grappled with my own insecurities and fears and there was only one conclusion that I could come to. I don't deserve you, but I love you with everything I have. That's all I can offer you, Skye. My love. I just don't know if it's enough."

"No, Caleb," she said softly, hating the devastation that blanketed him when he thought she was telling him she didn't want his love. Digging her fingers into his hands, she willed herself to have enough energy to say what she needed to say. "You hurt me worse than anyone else ever has, but that's because I love you like I haven't ever loved another person. You've brought me joy, and fun, freedom. Because of you I know what it's like to belong somewhere. I know what it's like to be loved. You have more to offer me than just your love. It might take time for me to trust you again, but I want to try. I want to work things out between us. I want a future with you. I want … you."

The smile he beamed at her was everything, his relief palpable.

Skye felt the relief echoed inside herself.

A weight felt like it had been lifted from her shoulders, and the crushing loneliness she'd felt when she was locked in Grigoriy Golubev's basement, and then her father's attic was gone.

As long as she had Caleb in her life she would never truly be alone again.

"I love you, Caleb."

"Oh, baby, I love you too. So much."

His hands framed her face, and when his lips found hers it didn't matter that the kiss was soft and sweet rather than the fiery, passionate one she wanted. There would be time for fire and passion when she was stronger, just like there would always be moments of soft and sweet.

Caleb gave her everything a person could ever need.

The road to happiness might be a bumpy one, with ups and downs, and moments where you thought you had hit a dead end, but in the end love found a way, and the journey was more than worth it.

CHAPTER TWENTY-FOUR

January 10th
11:52 A.M.

Brick couldn't believe this was happening.

Just one month ago today he'd been standing around a hospital waiting room, praying that Skye survived her life-threatening injuries. Now he was standing in a church, about to make the woman he loved his wife.

After three weeks in the hospital, Skye had finally been released on New Year's Eve. She had been surprised—shocked really—when everyone from Prey had shown up on Christmas Day to visit her in the hospital and drop off gifts. It wasn't until she met Eagle and his family, all of his siblings, and their families, as well as the members of Bravo, Charlie, Delta, Artemis, and Athena teams that he thought Skye finally got it.

These people were her family now.

They had all been sweet and welcoming to her, even some of the gruffest of the men. And they'd all dropped off little gifts, chocolates, and Christmas decorations to make her hospital room pretty since she was stuck there over the holidays. Despite the fact she was easily tired, she'd managed to connect with every single person who came to visit, and by the time they left all of them had told him how lucky he was to have her.

While she was healing as well as anyone could have hoped for, she was still weak, still in pain, still needing a lot of help to do even the most basic of things, but she was alive and that was all he cared about.

When he had proposed on New Year's Eve before she was

discharged, and they met up with everyone from Prey who wasn't off on a mission for an impromptu party in a local hotel, he hadn't expected she'd want to get married right away. He had thought she'd want a big wedding with a gorgeous dress, the perfect location, and a big reception afterward. Instead, she'd shocked him when she'd said she wanted to get married as soon as they could make it happen because all she cared about was becoming his wife.

So here they were a mere ten days later, ready to tie the knot.

Again, Prey had pulled together to make this wedding happen on short notice. Without the help of the Oswald family and their money, he wasn't sure they would have been able to pull this together. They'd organized a church, prepared the reception, taken care of flowers, and Eagle and Olivia had gifted Skye a gorgeous wedding dress.

Everything was perfect, and he couldn't wait for his bride to walk down the aisle.

His team were standing beside him, the church was full of family, not blood family but people who loved and cared about him and Skye. With her mom in prison there was no biological family for Skye, and he hadn't bothered inviting his parents, he didn't want them here ruining his day. The scandal over the traitorous presidential candidate who'd tried to have his own daughter killed was running wild, and he could just imagine what his parents would think of him marrying Skye in the midst of the media circus.

But Brick didn't care about any of that.

Neither he nor Skye had been cut out for the lives their parents had wanted for them. The lives they had built were honest and real, they were what they wanted, and even though it had taken them longer to get here he was glad they'd reached this place.

"You ready to do this?" Bear asked, his six-month-old son Mikey in his arms.

"More than ready."

The music changed, and the doors at the back of the church opened.

Lolly entered first, a huge grin on her face. The little girl had been thrilled to be asked to be the flower girl, and she looked adorable as she walked down the aisle tossing petals as she went.

Next came Mackenzie, who's eyes lit up as they landed on Bear and Mikey. Phoebe followed, a hand resting on her huge baby bump, in just two more months there would be another Alpha Team baby entering the world. Piper was next, and the beginnings of her baby bump were showing beneath her royal blue bridesmaid dress. Julia seemed to breathe energy into the room as she burst through the doors like the bubble of energy she was, and her megawatt smile was aimed mostly at Domino. Lila wasn't showing yet, but she still rested a hand on her stomach as she walked down the aisle.

Everything was changing, three of his teammates were married, two engaged, two had kids, there were three more babies on the way, nothing was as it had been just a couple of short years ago, and yet he wouldn't change a thing.

Out of the darkness that was their jobs, each of the men he considered a brother had found happiness.

Love.

When his bride took her first step into the church all the air seemed to leave Brick's chest in a rush.

She was breathtaking.

Absolutely stunning.

He had literally never seen anything more beautiful.

The gown she was wearing flowed around her like she was a princess. At first, she'd been hesitant to wear anything that would show the bandages still covering her wounds, or her thin atrophied muscles, but he'd told her she would be gorgeous no matter what she wore.

In the end, she'd settled for a dress with a halter neck bodice with intricate lacework, and a full flowing skirt. Bandages peeked through, but nobody was looking at them when the woman in the dress was so captivating.

Her hair was piled on her head, a couple of loose curls hanging around her face, a tiara snuggled in amongst the long dark strands. Between her two wounds and her lack of strength she hadn't been able to manage heels, even without them she was a little unsteady on her feet, and Brick got the feeling every man in the room was ready to spring to his feet to catch her should she fall.

His girl would never fall again.

No matter what happened, no matter what life threw at them, his arms would always be her safe place, a place that would shelter her from any storm.

By the time she reached the front of the church there were beads of sweat dotted on her forehead, and he knew she had already pushed herself beyond what she could bear.

Stepping forward, Brick scooped her into his arms and went to stand before the minister.

"Caleb," Skye rebuked. "You can't hold me while we get married."

"Why not?"

"Because … I … you … you just can't," she huffed, but he could see she was fighting a smile.

"I can, and I will." He nodded to the minister to get him started. While he wanted Skye to enjoy her day, he didn't want her completely overdoing things and setting her recovery back.

The minister had been briefed on keeping things short, and jumped straight into the main event.

"We're all gathered here today to join these two wonderful people together in marriage. Skye Xenos, do you take this man to be your lawfully wedded husband, in sickness and in health, in good times and bad, as long as you both shall live?"

Skye's heart was in her eyes as she looked at him. "I do."

"Caleb Quinn, do you take this woman to be your lawfully wedded wife, in sickness and in health, in good times and bad, as long as you both shall live?"

"You bet I do."

"I believe you've both written your own vows to say as well," the minister said.

"I didn't know love existed until I met you," Skye began. "I didn't even know what it was, and then a boy came running over to help me put a baby bird back in a nest. As I watched you climb that tree when I couldn't make it, I knew. You cared that I was crying, you wanted to make my world better, you wanted to take care of me. I might have been four years old, but I knew then that I loved you, that you were mine. I don't care how long it took us to get to this point, I only care that we're here now. I promise here and now that I will always find a way to forgive you, and that no matter what happens my love for you will never fade. Just don't do anything else stupid and make me have to forgive you," she teased, making everyone laugh.

"Before I met the cute little girl with pigtails, crying over a baby bird that had fallen from a nest, I didn't know that love could come without conditions. You've put up with more from me than any woman ever should, and that you're here today, willing to pledge your life to me, proves how strong you are. My job as your man is to make sure you never want for anything. Not for peace, not for stability, not for security, not for joy, and certainly not for love. I promise here and now that I will perform that job to the best of my ability, because you're the sun, moon, and stars of my world, and I don't want to live without your bright, shiny presence. I'm yours. Forever."

"I now pronounce you husband and wife. You may kiss your bride."

At the minister's words, Brick captured Skye's lips and kissed her, infusing every drop of love he felt for her into that kiss. Around them everyone clapped, cheered, and set off party poppers sending confetti raining down throughout the church, but Brick had eyes only for his wife.

His heart.
His life.
His everything.

Jane Blythe is a *USA Today* bestselling author of romantic suspense and military romance full of sexy heroes and strong heroines! When she's not weaving hard to unravel mysteries she loves to read, bake, go to the beach, build snowmen, and watch Disney movies. She has two adorable Dalmatians, is obsessed with Christmas, owns 200+ teddy bears, and loves to travel!

To connect and keep up to date please visit any of the following

Amazon – http://www.amazon.com/author/janeblythe
BookBub – https://www.bookbub.com/authors/jane-blythe
Email – mailto:janeblytheauthor@gmail.com
Facebook – http://www.facebook.com/janeblytheauthor
Goodreads – http://www.goodreads.com/author/show/6574160.Jane_Blythe
Instagram – http://www.instagram.com/jane_blythe_author
Reader Group – http://www.facebook.com/groups/janeskillersweethearts
Twitter – http://www.twitter.com/jblytheauthor
Website – http://www.janeblythe.com.au

Faith is being sure of what we hope for and certain of what we do not see.

Hebrews 11:1

Printed in the USA
CPSIA information can be obtained
at www.ICGtesting.com
LVHW050236110823
754927LV00006B/113